Wild With You
(The Connor Family, Book 2)

LAYLA HAGEN

Dear Reader,

If you want to receive news about my upcoming books and sales, you can sign up for my newsletter HERE: http://laylahagen.com/mailing-list-sign-up/

Cover: Uplifting Designs
Photography: Nicole Ashley Photography

Chapter One
Graham

"Graham, you're sure?" Amber asked.

"Yes, I am." I motioned to Matt. "Can you remind your future wife that I never say yes to anything unless I'm sure?"

"He's right," Matt said.

"You're my best friends. Of course I want to be your best man." I grinned at Amber.

We were at a restaurant in West Hollywood. It was the opening night, and I'd invited Amber and Matt to try it out with me. The chef prided himself on having turned fried chicken into gourmet food. He'd kept his promise. The fried chicken was worth every penny, as were the fries and the coleslaw. Matt and Amber had broken the news that she was pregnant when we arrived. They'd also informed me that they wanted to get married as soon as possible.

"We'll have to keep the costs low," Amber continued. "I looked at prices for wedding venues and already have a headache. We're thinking about renting an outdoor space and putting up a wedding tent."

"You don't have to rent anything. You can use my yard. It's big enough, and you like it," I offered.

Amber sighed. "I love it. But that's a lot of headache for you."

I motioned to Matt again. "Remind her that I don't offer anything unless I mean it."

"You two will forever be a pain in my ass. Thank you, Graham. We'll take you up on the offer. And we're buying you dinner tonight," Amber declared.

"That sounds like a fair trade-off." I winked, eating a fry. I planned to help out with some other wedding costs too, but I'd bring it up another time. It would be my wedding gift to my best friends.

"Yeah, so fair. Keep teasing me, and I'll find some best man duties to torment you with."

"Torment me? Here I am, being *the* best man anyone could wish for, and you want to torment me? I still have time to change my mind," I threatened. Amber cut her eyes to me. *If looks could kill.*

When they'd asked me, I'd barely stopped myself from suggesting they ask someone else. Best man duties went beyond organizing the bachelor party and giving a speech. He was supposed to be a voice of reason when the couple needed it, counsel them. My own marriage had failed. How could my advice be helpful? But the three of us had been friends since middle school. I couldn't say no. Besides, Matt and Amber had been together since our senior year of high school. They hadn't needed my wisdom for the past twelve years, so I was confident they wouldn't need it from now on either.

"You're still teasing me. I can make you pay, you know. With or without my future husband's help."

Matt put up his hands in defense. "Hey, I didn't say anything."

"I could feel you siding with Graham."

"Man, you'd better not piss her off. She's even more frightening since she found out she's pregnant."

I laughed. "You know what? Since you're buying dinner, I'm going to order seconds."

Amber rubbed her belly as Matt flagged a waiter. "Make it a second round for us too. I have an excuse to eat for two now, right?"

The second round tasted even better than the first one. As more patrons filtered in, the place was getting too crowded for my taste. It was my own fault for requesting a reservation on opening night, but trying out new eateries was a hobby of mine. While we ate, Amber laid out her plans. "I want to have the wedding before I start showing, but don't have time to organize it. I need a planner." She was heading the PR and marketing department of my soccer club very efficiently, so I knew she'd find a planner in no time. "Why do you keep checking your watch?"

"I have a phone call about a potential player swap in one hour, and I want to be in my car when I take it."

"It's six o'clock," Amber remarked.

"It's with Beijing. Different time zone. But I don't expect it to take long. We can move this party somewhere else after the call."

She scrunched her nose. "We can't, sorry. We have plans later. Still avoiding going home, huh? Do you even spend any time at that swanky villa of yours?"

"Of course. I sleep there." But I didn't do much else there. The house was too big, too empty. I'd bought it after the divorce, and it was halfway between Santa Monica and Malibu. We'd lived in a condo in the city previously, but I'd always wanted to be by the ocean, to hear waves lapping against the shore instead of traffic sounds when I opened my windows. I'd wanted some peace and quiet. Now, I had too much of both and it was unnerving. "It's too big for one person."

"You'll get used to it," Matt reassured me. "Unless you want to sell it and buy something smaller?"

"They don't build anything small in that neighborhood, and I like it."

We went back and forth over several ideas, and as soon as we finished the chicken, I bid Amber and Matt goodbye.

The phone call about the swap was a waste of time, so I scrolled through my e-mails during the conversation. One from Amber popped up in my inbox, titled Best Man's Duties.

The list was mercilessly long, but she'd inserted a wicked grin at the very end, along with the comment, **Don't worry. I think you'll get away with doing just about half of those.**

I had a feeling this wedding was going to bring me trouble.

Chapter Two
Lori

On most days, I *loved* my job. Today, I had a case of triple zillas on my hands: the bridezilla, her mother, and mother-in-law. The three women had been in my office for more than an hour, shouting, crying, and shouting some more.

"Ladies, why don't we take a small break? I can make us some coffee, and I have an excellent cheesecake in the fridge."

"I'd love some coffee and cake," the bride said. I dashed out of the meeting room as soon as the other women nodded in agreement. I hoped the sweet treat would soften my zillas, or this wedding would end up with three color schemes. By the time I returned with the coffees and the cake, they'd calmed down somewhat.

There was still tension in the air, and the break went by in a loaded silence, but after the plates and cups were emptied, the conversation was more civil. I was pretty sure cheesecake could bring about world peace. Still, half an hour later, it became clear we wouldn't decide on the color scheme today.

"I made notes of all the wishes expressed today. I will e-mail the three of you a list of suggestions taking everything into account, and we can go from there."

In my experience, seeing their options laid out for them helped people decide quicker. Plus, if the three zillas didn't leave soon, I'd be late for my next appointment. My brother Jace had asked me to squeeze in a meeting with his boss and two friends of his who were about to get married, and I didn't want to make Jace look bad by showing up late.

"That sounds like a plan," the bride said. The two other women rose from their seats first, thanking me for the cake and coffee, then making a beeline for the door.

"Thank you for being on my side," she said once we were alone. "I know they want the best for me, but they're driving me nuts."

"It will all work out," I promised.

After they left, I drafted the e-mail, summarizing our discussion and making suggestions. Even though I was cutting it close for the next meeting, I wanted to write this while everything was still fresh in my mind.

Before leaving, I checked my appearance. My shoulder-length blonde hair was as unruly as ever, despite the product I'd smeared in it this morning. I tried to tame it some more, but neither my fingers nor the comb did much. With a sigh, I quickly maneuvered it into a thick braid. It was the only style that kept it under control. My outfit was as professional as could be: knee-length dark blue dress with a conservative, round neckline. I'd paired it with nude pumps.

Our meeting point was a coffee shop near Griffith Park. Despite having an office, most clients preferred to meet on location or in coffee shops close to their workplace. My office served more as storage for the wedding and party supplies. Even I got together with my three assistants mostly somewhere in the city.

Luckily, traffic was on my side, so I had time to stop by one of my favorite food trucks, which was three blocks away from the park. Despite the cheesecake, I was starving. I hadn't eaten anything else today, and I wanted some sustenance before the meeting. As a rule, I never ate when I met with clients, even if they did. Since it was early afternoon, there was no line.

"Hi! I'll have a hummus sandwich with falafel, please."

The vendor, Declan had only started working here last week, as a stand-in for the owner, who was on vacation.

"Hey, I remember you. You were here last week too."

"It's one of my favorite food trucks. I stop by any time I'm in the neighborhood."

He prepared my order in no time, and when he handed it to me, he said, "I hope this isn't too forward, but I'd love to take you out."

Okay. I hadn't been expecting that.

"Wow, Declan. I'm flattered… but I can't."

He nodded curtly. "Right, of course. Had to

try though. Hope it won't stop you from returning."

"Are you kidding? These sandwiches are to die for."

I was so hungry I finished my sandwich within minutes. Declan had seemed like a nice guy, and he was attractive enough, but I already had someone I liked to call *the most important man in my life*: my seven-year-old boy.

I looked Matt and Amber up on Facebook on my way to the coffee shop, so I could put faces to the names. Then I ignored some friend requests from random men. I had no idea if it was a single woman issue, or a single mom issue, but they were getting out of control. I hadn't even posted my relationship status.

When I stepped inside the coffee shop, I swept my gaze across the room. It was full of customers, some with laptops propped open on the table, typing away, some just chatting over a drink. My party hadn't arrived yet. I located a single empty table in a corner. The guy who'd entered after me was also eying it. *Forget it, buddy. That table is mine.*

I dashed through the room, muttering excuses when I bumped a few chairs, until I reached the table. I set my tote on it and sat down, mentally reviewing the topics that usually came up during the first meeting.

I kept my attention trained on the door, and when my couple came in, I waved at them. Amber waved right back. Her fiery red bob bounced with every step. As she and her fiancé made their way toward me, I took in the third person. He looked vaguely familiar. It took a few seconds for the connections to click in my brain. With a jolt, I realized he was the owner of Jace's team, the LA Lords. I tried to remember if Jace told me anything about Graham Frazier, but other that he was thirty-two and a great leader, nothing came to mind.

I was certain I'd seen him in photos with the team before, but either all pictures had been black-and-white or I'd mentally blocked how striking his blue eyes were. In fact, he was a striking man all around. On a scale of one to ten, that face earned a twenty.

"Hi! I'm Lori Connor."

"Hi, Lori. I'm Amber. This is my fiancé, Matt, and this is Graham, our best man."

I shook hands with all three, and once we all sat down, I straightened my shoulders, lifting the corners of my lips in my go-getter smile.

"So, what can I do for you? I'm afraid my brother didn't know many details. The most important things to know are the date and the approximate number of guests. Let's start with the date."

"As soon as possible. I'm pregnant, and I'd like to wear my white gown before the bump shows. We thought a Valentine's Day wedding. Is that even possible?"

"Everything is possible. I can work with that; don't you worry. And congratulations."

Valentine's Day was in four weeks. It required

even more hassle than usual, and some suppliers overcharged for speedy services. It wasn't much time, but I'd pulled it off before.

"Thank you. We're thinking about eighty guests."

I nodded. "I have a list of locations that can fit that number."

Amber turned to Graham. "Graham has agreed to host the wedding. He has a beautiful house outside Santa Monica, and the outdoor space is gorgeous. We could install a tent there."

"Perfect. If we've got the location, half the wedding is practically in the bag." I turned to Graham. "But I do have to warn you that hosting a wedding involves a lot of hassle. We'll have a crew milling around your property."

"I can handle it."

I bet he could. He seemed the kind of man who could handle anything. He smiled, and I returned it but then averted my gaze. I was trying really hard not to find him attractive, and I was failing. His face looked sculpted, and I briefly wondered if the rest of him did too. I couldn't tell because his blue shirt was tailored but not stretched. Still, I thought it hinted at steely, defined muscles. Or maybe that was just my overactive imagination.

"Since we're on a tight schedule, you might want to send a save-the-date e-mail to your guests. I have some beautifully formatted wedding templates to show you."

"But we'd be sending regular invitations too?"

Amber asked.

"Some of our guests are more traditional," Matt added.

"Of course. But choosing invitations and having them printed and mailed can take up to a week, even if we hurry. The save-the-date e-mail is so people already know to keep that day free, make traveling plans if necessary."

"Great thinking. I like you, Lori," Amber said. "So what are the next steps?"

"Do you have any preferences regarding color scheme, or even a theme?"

"Not really," Amber said. Matt looked mildly panicked. Graham merely leaned back in his chair. This was business as usual. The bride getting all excited, the man—or in this case, men—checking out at the mention of color schemes.

"I have my laptop with me, and I'll be showing you a few things, so you can have an idea of what's possible."

I extricated my laptop from my tote and positioned it on the table so the four of us could see the screen. Most of the time, the first meeting was about getting to know each other, seeing if we clicked, but Amber and Matt were on a tight deadline. I clicked open the folder titled Themes, and started the slideshow. I had a mix of everything, from classic elegance to shabby chic to more extravagant options.

"Tell me if you like anything. And if you don't, that's okay too. I promise we'll find exactly what you need for your special day."

I trained my gaze on the bride and groom, trying to read their expressions, but out of the corner of my eye, I caught Graham smirking when I said “special day.” Was he a marriage skeptic? I hoped not, because they ruined the buzz. I encountered one in the close circle of the couple every now and then. When said person happened to be the best man, it could become very unpleasant. I'd witnessed one too many awkward speeches.

Maybe Graham's smirk was simply a knee-jerk reaction to the overload of glitter on my screen. Over-the-top wedding arrangements brought out the cynic in everyone, occasionally even in brides. But I wanted to show them the possibilities.

I flipped the image on the screen to a wedding with a vintage theme, then to one with no theme at all, just classic, timeless elegance. I had a hunch Amber would go for that one. When she pointed at the screen, and exclaimed, "This. I want something like this!" I couldn't help the pride surging inside me. "What do you think?" she asked her fiancé.

"This looks about right."

"I thought you might go for classic elegance! Now, for catering, photographers, florists, and everything in between, I work with a network of professionals. It'll be fastest if you trust me to pick the right team to work for your wedding."

"It means less hassle for us, so I say go for it," Matt said. "We should also talk about your fee."

I'd hoped the question would come later, but

I couldn't skirt around it. When I uttered my fee, Amber nodded.

"How much do you think the menus would be?" she asked.

Graham talked before I could answer. "Amber, leave that to me. I told you it's my wedding gift to you."

I was surprised at that. So not only was he putting his property at their service, he was also paying for the wedding menus? That went above and beyond best man duty. He slid a business card over the table, and said, "Ms. Connor, send all invoices regarding the menus to me."

"I will. Call me Lori, please."

"Cost is not an issue, Lori."

Amber nudged him with her elbow. "Hey! Just because you're paying doesn't mean I can't watch the menu costs."

"That's exactly what it means," Graham said.

"Amber, I promise I'll get you the best deals. Your wedding will be perfect. You'll cherish those memories for the rest of your life."

A hint of a sarcastic smile played on Graham's lips. I caught his eye and cocked a brow. He kept my gaze until I looked away squirming. So my instincts had been right. He wasn't big on marriage… yet he was footing the bill for the wedding menus. Intriguing combination.

"I have some layouts for the save-the-date e-mail that I think you'll like. I have to see the location as soon as possible so I know what type of tent will fit best, where to locate it, things like that. Next, we'll be talking about the menu. Once you choose a few options, I'll arrange for a tasting. At the tasting, I'll also have my florist make a few arrangements you can choose from."

"Wow!" Amber blinked. "I feel like half the wedding is in the bag. I'm starting to feel like I'm de-stressing."

"Leave the stress to me, Amber. That's what I'm here for. I'll show you save-the-date templates right now. I also have pictures of invitations."

"Sounds great. But can we get some drinks first?" Amber suggested.

Graham rose to his feet. "I'll go buy some. What do you want?"

Everyone agreed on coffee, and I ended up walking to the counter with Graham. He couldn't carry four cups by himself.

"Thanks for taking on the wedding on such short notice," he said as we waited for the barista to prepare the drinks.

"My pleasure. I'll be sending you the menu budget as soon as I put it together. Do you need a list of best man duties?"

"Amber already took care of that."

"All set to be best man, then?"

"I'd say I am." His tone was challenging, as if he was daring me to disagree. He smiled, and the left corner of his lips caught my attention. Was that a… a dimple? Moving on. I debated bringing up the best man speech, but I wanted to have a plan first, what with him being Jace's boss and all. He fixed those baby blue eyes on me. They looked hypnotic. His light brown hair was messy in a sexy way. I wondered if that was how he looked when he woke up in the morning. I wasn't just squirming now; I felt my body temperature go up.

We spent the next two hours combing through the materials on my laptop, deciding on the save-the-date text, the type of printed invitations, as well as crosschecking our calendars for the next appointments.

"Want to have dinner with us?" Amber asked after I closed my laptop.

"Thank you, but I already have plans. I'll keep in touch."

We chitchatted for a while longer, but then I had to excuse myself. I didn't want to be late to pick up Milo from school.

As soon as I was alone with Amber, I was going to pepper her with questions. I liked to get the scoop: When did he propose? How had he proposed? Had he dropped on one knee? Did they have an audience? I'd barely refrained from asking all those things today. I lived vicariously through my brides. I'd been twenty-three when I discovered I was unexpectedly pregnant. My announcement was certainly not met with a marriage proposal, or hell, even a hug.

I arrived at Milo's school in time for pick-up, and once we were both inside the car, I asked "How was your day, baby boy?"

"Mom! I told you, I'm not a baby anymore. I'm a grown-up boy."

"Okay, okay. How was your day, grown-up boy?"

"We have a new soccer coach. He's cool. I'm starving."

"We'll be at Aunt Val's house in no time."

My siblings and I got together every Friday to have dinner at my sister Valentina's house. It was hands down the best way to kick off the weekend and catch up. There were six of us, so there was never a shortage of news. Everyone was already there and gathered around the table when Milo and I arrived.

My oldest brother, Landon, was fussing over Maddie—his pregnant wife. Next to him, Jace was trying to convince our brother Will to be his wingman when they went out later tonight.

"Afraid you can't get a date without my help?" Will was sporting a shit-eating grin.

"I'm wounded!" Jace exclaimed.

"*Detective William Connor.* My, oh my. Being a wingman is a bit like cheating on a test. Isn't coloring outside the lines a little beneath you?" Val teased.

"Hey, once the badge comes off, I'm officially not on duty. I break the rules in my free time, for a change of pace."

My other sister, Hailey, pulled Milo into a hug then kissed my cheek.

"Do you think we should remind Will that Jace is a sports celebrity? If anything, Jace is probably getting *him* dates. I mean, Will knows how to work the hot cop angle, but hanging out with a professional athlete sure doesn't hurt the prospects," Hailey fake-whispered, chuckling. Will gave us the evil eye.

"Nah, let's wait until after he eats to be mean to him," I said.

My mouth watered as I took in the goodies: sweet potatoes with chili sauce and a mix of garbanzo beans, diced avocado, and chicken. Next to it was a small bowl with lime and coriander dressing. Val was the best cook I knew.

Our parents passed away in an accident when Jace, Hailey, Will, and I were still kids. Valentina and Landon were the only legal adults, and they practically raised us. Mama's cooking had been delicious, but Val's was even better.

As soon as I sat between my sisters, Hailey showed me pictures of a fiery red mane; she was considering changing her hair color. Hailey's hair was a beautiful hue of brown, a rich chocolate. I was the only blonde in the family. My siblings' hair ranged from dark brown—Landon and Valentina—to light brown—Jace and Will.

Milo wedged himself between Will and Jace. My boy worshipped my brothers. His dad took off before he was born, so my brothers were the closest things he'd ever had to father figures.

"Lori, how did it go with Amber?" Jace asked.

"It went well. The wedding is in four weeks, which will mean a lot of hassle, but Amber seems easy to work with."

My agency was fully booked for the next two months, so my assistants already had their hands full. I was going to work on this wedding solo.

"She is. Best head of marketing and PR we've had."

As I savored the sweet potatoes and bean mix, I questioned my brother about Amber. The more I knew, the easier it would be to work with her. Then I couldn't help myself, and also got the scoop on the best man.

Chapter Three
Graham

I couldn't make it in time for our appointment with Lori the next Thursday. Amber and Matt were showing her my property so she could advise where to set up the tent and the ceremony aisle. A last-minute phone call with a potential sponsor took well over an hour. By the time I was halfway home, Amber called to let me know they were nearly done and would be heading out.

Damn shame because I'd wanted to catch them. The meeting last week had been surprising in more ways than one. I hadn't expected it to be so efficient… or for Lori to be that stunning. I had no doubt she'd aimed to look professional wearing that dress. It revealed absolutely nothing. In fact, it covered far too much of her, and yet my imagination ran wild the second she sat in front of me.

When I arrived in front of the villa, I was pleasantly surprised to see Lori pacing in front of a red Honda, talking on her phone. Her voice reached me through the open window.

"I respect that you are my client and I liked working with you in the past, but I will not put up with excuses. If you can no longer afford my services, just say so, and we will part ways."

Her back was to me, and since she hadn't seen me arrive, I could observe her in her element. Her tone was firm, her back straight. Lori Connor didn't take anyone's bullshit. I liked that she had a backbone. I liked the back of her too; she was wearing a pencil skirt, tight at the waist and molding perfectly over the curve of her hips and ass.

"Okay. We have a deal. I appreciate the honesty. Give me a call when you get back on your feet," she said. After hanging up, she spun around.

"Mr. Frazier, hi! I didn't hear you come up."

"Just Graham. Is everything okay?"

She pointed to her car. "Engine won't start. Tow service is on their way, but they said it would take at least an hour and a half. Know any coffee shops or restaurants in walking distance?"

I knew a few good restaurants, but I had a better idea. "Come inside with me. I'll make us dinner."

She blinked, then shook her head. "Thanks, but I'll grab something nearby."

She'd hesitated long enough for me to know she was tempted, so I pushed. Dinner in Lori's company would be a great way to spend the evening.

"Lori, I'll cook. You'll relax and tell me about the progress you made today with Matt and Amber. What's not to like about my offer?"

The corners of her mouth lifted in the most beautiful smile. She crossed her arms over her chest, but her smile was even wider when she answered.

"Well, when you put it like that, it *is* quite irresistible."

Lori brought me up to date on the wedding arrangements within minutes. They'd already decided on the type of tent. Menu tasting was next on the to-do list.

"The tent will be in the backyard, of course. The beach is too narrow to have the ceremony there. We can have it in the backyard as well, or on your deck, to overlook the water. Certainly large enough for eighty. But you'd have everyone traipsing through your house."

"I don't mind."

"I love your house. And the view is to die for."

"Thanks. That's what sold me on it."

I wanted to be near the ocean, and this property was the first to come up. It was far too big for one person, but I hadn't wanted to wait longer. The kitchen opened up to a formal dining area, and a tall breakfast bar separated the two spaces. I pointed to one of the two tall chairs under the counter, and said, "You can sit there while I cook."

"What's on the menu, chef?" Lori climbed on the stool and drummed her palms on the counter, eyeing the double oven on the other side. I leaned with an elbow against the surface, placing my other hand on the short backrest of Lori's chair.

"I have chicken legs. Could whip up a tomato sauce and boil brown rice. I also have pasta. Like gorgonzola sauce? I know an excellent recipe with cream and a mix of gorgonzola cheese and parmesan."

She wrinkled her nose. "Chicken with tomato sauce sounds good."

"You really want to go for the pasta, though."

"How could you tell?"

"Body language. So, why say no to something you want?"

"Oh my God, you can't corrupt me like that. Of course I'll go for the pasta."

She laughed, and seeing her plump lips open up like that for me made me wonder what else I could corrupt her to do. I came closer, moving my hand from the backrest to her back. Lori straightened but didn't pull away.

"I'm very good at corrupting."

She laughed again and tilted her head to one side. "And you had me all convinced you like to follow the straight and narrow path."

"What gave you that impression?"

"Not sure." She licked her lower lip, and I nearly closed the distance and kissed her. Then she averted her gaze, so I backed off. What the hell was I doing, anyway? I moved through the kitchen and took out all the ingredients, starting to prepare our dinner.

"Wow, you *really* cook!" Lori exclaimed while I was chopping onion.

"Yeah. It relaxes me. You thought I'd invite you in for frozen pizza?"

"That possibility crossed my mind." I heard

the smile in her voice and looked at her over my shoulder.

"Your bar is pretty low, isn't it? Let's see if I can impress you."

"Game on, chef."

From where I was standing, I had a direct view of her long legs under the counter. Her skirt reached just over her knees, and my fingertips itched with the impulse to touch her and push the fabric all the way up her thighs. How smooth would her skin be? How delicious would she taste?

"How long have you known Matt and Amber?" she asked, effectively cutting through my thoughts. I set the sauce to simmer and turned to face her.

"Since middle school. They're my best friends."

"It's very sweet of you to pay for their wedding menus."

"I have another surprise up my sleeve, but I'm keeping mum on that."

"Tell me," she beckoned, but I shook my head. "You're doing this on purpose."

"Of course I am. Payback for doubting my cooking skills."

She broke out into a full-on belly laughter that filled the whole kitchen. I couldn't look away from those full lips, those long legs.

Once the food was cooked, we took everything outside on the deck. It was immense. She was right; the ceremony could easily take place here. I had a rattan couch on one side, and a table for six next to it. We ate at the table.

"You should go on those cooking competitions. You'd win everything. Did you take cooking classes or something?"

"All Nana's doing. My grandmother. She's better than any chef."

"Well, this is amazing. Even better than my sister's recipe, but"—she made a gesture to zip her lips—"I'll be in trouble if she gets wind I said that."

"Your secret is safe with me. I didn't know Jace had another sister." I was friendly with all the guys on the team, but we kept a professional distance.

"We're six siblings. Three brothers, three sisters. How about you?"

"I have two half siblings, but I'm not in contact with them. Though I've known Amber and Matt for so long that I think of them as family."

I didn't want to get into more detail. My mother had left when I was two years old, because of my father's cheating. Philandering seemed to run in the blood of Frazier men. My father and grandfather hadn't had any respect for their wives and families. I'd wanted the opposite. But my divorce proved that marriage wasn't easy, even when you give it your best shot. I focused the conversation on Lori. "Which one's the sister with the amazing kitchen skills?"

"That would be Valentina."

"What does she do for work?"

"She owns a perfume and cosmetics

company."

"And the others?"

"Landon recently sold his software company in San Jose and moved here. He's in the process of opening an investment fund. Will is a detective, and Hailey's a business consultant. She travels a lot, and is in the city mostly on weekends."

"And by that sad note in your voice, I'm guessing you wish she'd be around more?"

"Yep." She didn't elaborate, because she focused on her pasta and didn't stop until she'd cleaned her plate. I had a feeling that under Lori's pencil skirts and tucked in blouse was a wild nature waiting to be unleashed. I loved the gusto with which she ate, the passion in her laughter. After our plates were empty, we moved to the rattan couch.

"And? Is the lady impressed?"

"Oh, yeah. Top marks, Chef Frazier. If you ever quit the club, you'd make a killing with an Italian restaurant. The club's been in your family for three generations, right?"

"Yes. My grandfather inherited a fortune and then invested it all in his two great passions: booze and soccer. The booze company went belly up within five years, but the soccer club survived for generations."

It had always felt like my second home. Lately, it felt like my only home. The arena and the offices were next to each other. As a kid, I'd experienced the fondest memories at the club, be it on the neatly trimmed grass, kicking balls with the greatest soccer names of the day, or on the floor of my grandfather's office, listening to him running the place. Soccer had been about the only thing we bonded over.

"That's a legacy to be proud of." She checked her phone and sighed. "I should head out soon."

I disagreed. I couldn't remember the last time I'd had so much fun, and I wasn't ready for our evening to end.

Chapter Four
Lori

"Why don't you call and ask them if they'll be here on time? No point going out before they arrive," Graham suggested.

"Good thinking."

I dialed their number, and they informed me they'd arrive in fifteen minutes, so I could enjoy all this a while longer. I had a major crush on his deck. The dark blue pillows on the rattan couch were so comfy I didn't want to leave. The glass panels at the edge of the deck offered a clear view of the ocean.

"So, how many fires do you predict I'll have to put out on the wedding day?" he asked once I hung up.

"I'll put out any fires, don't worry. That's why I'm here. You just focus on your best man duties." I sank lower on the couch, breathing in the salty air, enjoying the breeze and the sound of the ocean. Graham was watching me. My entire body clenched—again. My God, was he sexy. Pure male, pure testosterone. Every time he looked at me with those blue eyes, he made me aware of parts of my body I'd forgotten existed… or functioned. I wanted to bring up the speech, but I still hadn't worked on a polite way of explaining to him that bad jokes weren't appropriate. Usually, I wasn't one to mince words, but he *was* my brother's boss. I couldn't forget that.

"Say it."

"What?"

"You're fidgeting. What is it? If Amber tried to talk budgets with you again—"

"No, no. It's not that. I was thinking about the best man speech. Have you ever given one before?"

"No, but I've done plenty of speeches, so I'm sure I'll come up with something good. Some fun stories, some jokes."

This was my opening. Here went nothing. "About that… not all jokes are good ones. I've been at plenty of weddings where the best man mentioned divorce stats, jokingly adding that he's sure the couple will make it, and so on. It leaves a sour taste."

"What makes you think I'd do that?"

"Back at the coffee shop, you seemed like you're not a big fan of weddings."

"That obvious?"

"To me, yes. I'm a wedding planner. I pick up on these things." I also found out from Jace that he'd been divorced for two years, which made me think my gut had been right.

"I won't let that spoil Amber and Matt's day. Promise. Can I tempt you with some wine?"

"No, I'll head out in a few minutes."

"You can come back after you give them your car keys. We'll enjoy a glass or two of wine, and then

I can drive you into the city."

"No can do. I promised my son we'll make it in time for his evening TV show."

Graham went very still. I realized it was the first time I'd mentioned Milo. I braced myself for the flicker of interest in his eyes to disappear. I hadn't planned to act on it, but it had been very flattering.

"I didn't know you had a son," he said eventually in a cool, calm tone. He looked down at my hands then back up. His jaw ticked. What was going on? "Is he with your boyfriend now?"

"No boyfriend," I clarified. "Just the two of us."

"His dad isn't in the picture at all?"

I shrugged. "We're better off without him."

"Still, I can imagine it's not easy."

I shrugged again. "The worthwhile things never are."

"How old is he?"

"Seven. And I promised him I'd watch his favorite show with him tonight, so I have to go."

"There is plenty of pasta left. Want me to pack some for him?"

Something funny happened to my insides. They seemed to melt altogether.

"Thanks, but he's at Valentina's house, and he ate there." Since I didn't know how late I'd be staying out with Amber and Matt, I'd asked Will to pick up my son from school, and they'd joined Val for dinner.

"Ah, I see. The second best chef."

I pointed a finger at him. "Hey! I said your pasta was better than hers. That's it. Don't go drawing hasty conclusions."

The corners of his lips twitched, then gave way to a grin. "I'll walk you out."

"Thank you for dinner."

"Thank you for keeping me company."

We walked to my car side by side. A sizzle rushed through me, tightening my nipples. My body hadn't felt so alive in years, and he wasn't even *touching* me. I dealt with the tow service quickly, then hopped into an Uber. This evening had been fun. A little intense too, but a whole lot of fun.

I wondered if Graham cooked for women often. I bet there was no shortage of candidates banging at his door.

***

When I arrived at Val's house, Will was still there. He and Milo were throwing darts at a target my sister had set up in one corner of her living room.

"Mommy, please, can Uncle Will and I finish this round?" Milo asked.

"What about your show?" I countered, ruffling his hair. It was on Netflix, so we could stream it anytime.

"We can watch tomorrow."

"Okay, finish your game."

I left the boys to their dart game and sat on the couch next to my sister.

“Why did you come with an Uber?” Val asked.

“My car wouldn’t start, so I had it towed away.”

"Wine?" She pointed to the glass she was nursing.

"Yes, please. I'll get myself a glass." I wasn't driving, so why not? I took a glass out of her cabinet and sank on the couch again once Val had poured some wine.

"Will looks a bit down," she said.

"My thoughts exactly."

As a little girl, I'd dreamed my brother would become an actor. He certainly was handsome enough, but then again, all my brothers could pass as movie stars without a problem, and I wasn't saying this because I was related to them. No, sir. I had photos with the family everywhere in my office, and more than a fair share of bridesmaids—and even the occasional bride—had sighed at the sight of my brothers.

But Will had never had Hollywood dreams. Still, he hadn't seemed like the type to join the force. In fact, he'd had a few run-ins with the police as a teenager, after our parents passed away. Despite his adventures, he'd also been a responsible older brother. He'd fit the devastatingly handsome but troubled bad boy profile. Now, the devastatingly handsome part still held true, but he'd grown from a bad boy into a badass man with a dangerous job.

We'd learned not to ask, because he wasn't

allowed to speak about his work, but we'd also learned to read clues into his body language. A frown was easy to erase. We could count on a little old-fashioned sibling teasing to do the trick. A scowl required a bit more creativity. Hunched shoulders meant shit had hit the fan. We hadn't yet discovered how to take his mind off that, but we weren't giving up.

Currently, Will's expression was somewhere between a scowl and a frown.

"What do you think? Teasing will be enough?" I asked, sipping wine.

Val nodded excitedly. "If we team up? Of course."

We waited for the boys to finish their dart game. When Milo went to the bathroom, Will joined us on the couch, sitting between the two of us. Val and I exchanged a glance.

"I know that look," Will said.

Damn. My brother could smell a *Connor Secret Intervention* from a mile away.

"What look?" I asked innocently.

"You know I can't talk about work, so don't ask."

Val shook her head mockingly. "After all these years, he still hopes the badge might start working on us. You can't boss us around, brother."

"Watch me try," Will said. He was trying to sound firm, but I could hear the tinge of humor.

"I think he likes to fail," I teased.

"Girls, it's been a shitty day; that's all. No

need for an ambush."

Val brought her hands to her chest theatrically. "Ouch. This is an intervention. I'm wounded that you can't tell the difference."

"Yeah. An ambush requires Hailey's presence too," I informed him.

Our brother burst out laughing. Mission accomplished.

"Mommy, I'm ready to go," Milo said, returning to the living room.

"I'll drive you," Will offered.

"Thanks."

Milo fell asleep on the way home.

"Milo said Father/Son sports day is coming up at school. He asked me to go with him," Will whispered. My heart gave a little squeeze. He hadn't told me about it. "You okay with that?"

"Sure… if it's not inconvenient for you."

"Not at all. Besides, it's good for people to know he's got the handsome part from the Connor bloodline," he said with a straight face. My brother, always so humble.

"Thanks, Will. I appreciate it."

Will often participated at school events. Jace had been on a few occasions, but the presence of a soccer star caused such mayhem that the teachers pulled me to the side and asked if it was possible for Will to come instead. Most of the time, I thought Milo and I were doing okay on our own, but school events were rough. Sometimes he'd tell me about "manly stuff" his friends were doing with their fathers, and guilt flooded me. My brothers were quick to fill those shoes, but I wasn't sure it was enough. It ate away at me to know I couldn't give Milo more, but I didn't know how to do better.

Later that evening, after putting Milo to bed, I dashed across the bamboo flooring, closing the plantation shutters at the windows. It was a particularly windy evening. I owned a two-bedroom house complete with a white picket fence and an orange tree in the backyard. I'd snapped the property up when it was in foreclosure, so I paid a decent price. The area was safe but almost on the outskirt of LA. Still, it had good schools. The entire house had been rundown, but renovating it proved worthwhile.

The coved ceiling and wainscoting gave it an old-school vibe I loved. It was cozy. At the moment, it was also rather dusty, but I hated cleaning with a passion. A cleaning company came in once a week, but dust gathered in between. I'd gotten really good at ignoring it.

I had to wake up early tomorrow. Three times a week, I woke up at five to work out one hour on the elliptical. Twice a week, I ran with four other mothers from the neighborhood, whom I'd come to consider close friends. Now, *running* was something I loved. Filled me with energy. Hailey had once jokingly suggested I think about cleaning as working out, but the trick hadn't worked.

Instead of going to bed, I poured myself a glass of wine and pulled up the website of the bridal shop Amber and I were going to visit. Their dresses were beautiful. I loved them all, no matter the shape or length. I'd dreamed about my own wedding dress since I'd tried on Mom's when I was six. I was *still* dreaming about it, but right now, the boy sleeping in the next room was my priority. I played one of my favorite romantic comedies in the background. I liked listening to music or hearing the dialogue from some of my beloved movies while working.

I was up so late I got hungry… which made me think about Graham. *Again.* My body felt like a livewire just remembering our evening. Despite the fact that my stomach rumbled, I resisted the urge to make a beeline for the kitchen. No more delicious goodies for me. I'd indulged enough tonight… with the pasta *and* the man cooking it.

I marked the designs they had in store in Amber's size and sent them to her. With the tight timeline, we couldn't order one for her. She had to make do with what the store had in their inventory, but I'd chosen this one because they had a large selection. I'd never had a disappointed bride, and I didn't plan to start now.

Chapter Five
Lori

On Tuesday, I arrived a full half hour before Amber at the bridal store. I'd scheduled the menu tasting and florist meeting right after the store visit, so every minute counted. Since I brought customers here regularly, I had something of a VIP status. I asked them to bring out the gowns Amber had indicated, and two she hadn't: a mermaid gown and a classic princess style. Some brides had a clear idea of the type of dress they wanted, only to discover it didn't suit them. I'd also had brides who claimed they didn't even want to try on a certain type of dress, only to end up buying exactly that one. That's why I insisted my brides at least look at all styles.

While the vendors steamed a couple of the dresses, I checked my e-mails on my iPad. One in particular caught my attention.

From: Jeff Finn
To: Lori Connor
Hey! I'm going to be in town in a couple of weeks. Let's go out for a drink.

I closed my eyes, drawing in a deep breath,

then another one. It didn't help. *The nerve of this jackass.*

We'd both been in med school when I unexpectedly got pregnant. I'd dropped out and started the event-planning agency. Jeff was a doctor in Denver now, but he came to LA about once a year for conferences. He'd never, not once, expressed any interest in his son. Yet every time he was in town, he hit me up. He contacted me the first time around when Milo turned one. I'd hoped that meant he'd changed his mind, that he wanted to get to know his son. Turned out it was a booty call. I told him exactly where he could shove his call. Usually he was more *explicit* in his e-mails, as if I was at his beck and call. I knew my worth, damn it. His e-mails made me want to hurl every insult I knew at him, but I took the high road and ignored him.

I didn't use the address I had when we were together anymore, but my work e-mail was listed on my website. I deleted the message right away, but I was in a foul mood.

When Amber arrived, I tried my best to push the matter out of my mind. She was a dream client. She tried on every single dress, and I couldn't help *ooooh*-ing and *awww*-ing.

"They're all so pretty. How will I make up my mind?" Amber twirled in the mermaid gown. "Thanks for having them bring me this one too. I would never have asked for this style, and look how beautiful it is."

Honestly, accompanying my brides to buy

their dresses was a mutually beneficial thing. I made sure everything ran smoothly and efficiently, but being among these beautiful dresses was a feast for my eyes.

"Why don't you put the ones you want in the narrower selection and then try them on again?" the sales clerk suggested.

As Amber pondered this, a buzzing sound came from her purse. She took out her phone.

"Graham's here early," she said. "Lori, can you bring him here in the back? He's outside the store."

"Okay. I'll go get him." He and Matt were supposed to meet us directly at the restaurant where we were having the tasting.

Graham was already inside the store when I reached the entrance. I searched for Matt out on the street through the glass front, but couldn't spot him.

"Hey, Graham. Is Matt early too? He can't come inside. He can't see Amber."

"Don't tell me you believe in those things," Graham challenged. The fire in his bright blue eyes riled me up. Why did he have to be infuriating while also looking sexier than anyone had the right to? Not checking him out took a concerted effort.

"What if I do?" I asked, chin held high.

"If a wedding falls apart, it's because one of them realizes they're making a mistake. Better before than after."

Had he known his was a mistake before?

"Doesn't hurt to stick to the rules," I

countered. As a kid, I'd laugh at my father, an Irishman who'd emigrated to the US, when he recounted some of his grandmother's superstitions. I'd disregarded them as folklore and foolishness, but as an adult, I thought there might be deep-rooted psychological explanations for at least some of them. Maybe seeing the future bride in her dress caused the groom to have cold feet. I had no time to dig that deep, but I planned to err on the side of caution.

Graham shook his head, smiling. The fire in his gaze wasn't dimming, though, and my heart rate was intensifying. It had to be because I was excited to see Amber's narrowed dress selection. Right?

"Matt's not here. I left the club early because it's on the other side of the city and I didn't want to risk a traffic jam. But he works four blocks away from the restaurant where we're having the tasting."

"Okay. Amber is in the back. She's already tried on quite a few dresses. Now she's narrowing down her selection and trying those on again."

Graham nodded, his face softening when Amber came into view, twirling in a brocade, princess-style dress. "You're beautiful, Amber."

"I don't know if I can dance with this one, though. It's so big."

Graham pulled Amber close, and they moved in tandem to the rhythm of an imaginary slow song. The man had *moves*. I wasn't much of a dancer myself, but I could appreciate the way he twirled Amber, the confident manner in which he led the dance.

During the impromptu dance performance, I couldn't resist the temptation of admiring him. Yep, the man was built like a Greek god, no questions asked. I had no idea if it was genetics, or long hours spent at the gym, but I suspected it was a mix of the two.

"It's not as bad as I thought," Amber said as they stopped dancing.

"If we take a few inches off the hem, it'll be even easier," I said.

"I'll try on the other ones too. It won't be easy to decide."

When Amber disappeared inside the changing room with the clerk who helped her in and out of the dresses, I sat on the ottoman that was placed strategically between the changing rooms.

I pulled out my iPad and e-mailed my cousin, Pippa Bennett-Callahan. The Bennetts were cousins from my mother's side, living in San Francisco. Out of the nine siblings, Pippa and four others were running Bennett Enterprises, a company designing and producing high-end jewelry, including wedding rings. While one could find their products everywhere, I often e-mailed Pippa directly. She was the designer and always had something special up her sleeve. When Amber had asked for wedding ring recommendations, I immediately pointed her to Bennett Enterprises.

I looked up briefly from my iPad and found Graham studying me. Energy coursed through me, hot and sizzling like a fireball. Even though sales clerks were running around and Amber was behind a curtain, I suddenly felt alone with him.

When he sat on the ottoman next to me, I thought I might combust from nothing more than his proximity. I could feel the heat radiating off him… and a healthy dose of masculinity too. We were so close that my breasts nearly touched his arm. Thankfully, Amber came out the next second wearing an ivory A-line dress with the skirt modified to fit closer to the body.

***

Graham

"I love it even more than the first time you tried it," Lori said, circling Amber.

"I love, love, love this one," Amber said. "Graham, what do you say?"

I held up my hands. "Don't make me vote on fashion choices. You promised."

"Can you at least tell me if you like it?"

"You're beautiful. But you were beautiful in the other dress too."

"Are you going to say I'm beautiful no matter what dress I try on?"

"You bet."

"Well, okay. That's not much help. Lori, I'm counting on you."

Lori was clapping, her eyes crinkled at the corners from her gigantic smile. Her enthusiasm lit her up from inside, and she was magnificent to watch.

She sounded a little breathless when she said, "I think this is the one, Amber."

Amber twirled some more, and they talked about trimming and shoes. I tuned out after that, but I couldn't make myself look away from Lori. When Amber decided she was buying this dress, Lori hugged her. As she pulled back, she observed the dress longingly, and it hit me that Lori wanted that for herself.

Her son's deadbeat father had taken off, but she still believed in all... this. I knew many in LA who sold dreams they didn't believe in, but my gut feeling told me Lori wasn't one of them. She was honest; she was real. Of course, my gut feeling had been wrong before, but I was almost sure I was right about Lori.

Fuck, I should stop fantasizing about those full lips, about how perfect she'd feel underneath me. Or on top. What was it with me? The better question was, what was it about her that pulled me in? I felt caught up in her spell, and I didn't know how to break it.

Chapter Six
Graham

Amber and Lori talked about the dress right until we arrived at the restaurant where we were having the tasting. When Amber had e-mailed me to ask if I had time for the menu tasting, my first instinct was to reply that they should have it without me. I'd had enough trouble putting Lori out of my mind after our dinner. But eventually I said yes. I didn't want to be a jerk. If I was attracted to Lori that was my problem, not Amber's.

We were led to the back of the restaurant, in a small room with no patrons. Matt was waiting inside already, talking to a woman who introduced herself as Gigi, the florist. Flower arrangements covered every square inch of two tables. A third table was filled with plates. There were six tables total crammed in the small room. It struck me as odd that they were all different, until Lori said, "Let me know if you like any tablecloths we have here. If not, I have more in my car. I can bring them out and change them."

Amber ran her fingers over each table and inspected the various flower arrangements, nodding and chatting with Lori.

"Graham, Matt, which ones are your favorite flower arrangements?" Amber asked.

The arrangements all looked the same to me, but I knew better than to voice *that* opinion. "They're all great."

"Oh, I see. You're going to be just as helpful as you were with the dress. Matt?"

Matt slid me a glance that clearly said *Help*. I could use some help myself at this very moment. I didn't know a thing about flowers. I'd signed up for tasting food, something I *was* good at. I didn't even know what kind of flowers these were. I recognized roses, and what I thought might be orchids, and that was it.

"Amber, I suggest we go with your gut feeling. In my experience, the first choice is always the best one," Lori said, saving my bacon.

Amber tilted her head, glancing between two arrangements for a few seconds, before saying, "Okay, let's go with the orchids. And I'll take the light green and gold tablecloths."

Lori tapped her iPad, making notes. "Excellent. If it's okay with everyone, I'll ask for the appetizers."

There was a general hum of agreement, and Amber, Matt, and I sat down.

"I'll be in the main room of the restaurant," Gigi said. "In case you change your mind about the flowers during the tasting."

After she left, the servers brought the appetizers. Lori stood between Amber and Matt, pointing to the plates. "We have a selection of salmon and dill sauce on a bed of asparagus. Next to it is tuna with black pepper crust. For the guests who don't like fish, they can opt for the roast beef with béarnaise sauce. And of course, we have a vegan option."

Even though I was starving, I forced myself to take small bites, so I could actually taste the food and give my opinion on it, not just scarf it all down. It was no surprise that it all tasted like it cost a million bucks, even though it hadn't. I'd already seen the prices. Lori had kept her word of delivering the best quality at the best rates.

"Lori, I can't possibly eat all of this on my own," Amber said, "or we'll have to go back to the store and have my dress fitted again. Come on. Share my plate."

Lori hesitated, but she'd talked with so much gusto about the food that I was sure she'd love to try it. I stood and brought a chair from the next table, wedging it between Amber's and mine, not giving her the chance to sit between Matt and Amber. The waiter who was in charge of our group immediately brought an empty plate and cutlery, and Lori caved.

Amber forked some food onto the plate. When Lori dipped the asparagus in the béarnaise sauce, she scooted to the edge of her chair, and her skirt rode up her legs high enough to reveal toned thighs. They were mouth-watering. I clasped the fork tighter to keep myself from touching her. Lori caught the hem of her skirt, tugging it down.

Only the flowers and the chairs for the ceremony will be delivered on the wedding day, but I want the rest to be ready the day before. Is that okay for you? It means you'll have people milling around for two days before the wedding. I can squeeze everything in one day if it's too much trouble."

"I don't mind. I'm at the house only in the evening, anyway."

She nodded, absently rubbing the side of her neck with one hand. Was the neck a sweet spot for her? If I placed open-mouthed kisses there, would she moan? If I bit lightly, would she arch for me, beg for more? The wild desire to discover all her sweet spots slammed into me. I looked away from her neck and met her eyes. Her pupils had dilated a notch. Her breath was coming out faster. She clasped her iPad with both hands.

"Right, so the tent will be dismantled and shipped off the day after the wedding. I'll be there to supervise everything."

She pointed on the screen at the schedule for the wedding and the day after. The night of the wedding was marked red until four o'clock in the morning, and then red again from seven to eleven on Sunday.

"You don't have to come back so early on Sunday," I said. "You can have everything shipped back on Monday; I don't care."

"Oh, but the tent company does. They want that tent back before lunch."

"Can't you have someone else oversee it?

You're working the night before."

"My assistants work every other Sunday. My turn this time."

She wanted to drive forty minutes, in the dark, after a twenty-hour workday. It wasn't safe. It was madness, and I wasn't going to allow it. Not in a million years.

"I'll make you a deal. Sleep at my house after the wedding. It's not safe for you to drive back that late. You'll be tired."

She set the iPad on the table and shook her head. "I've done this before."

"When the wedding was in the city, I assume."

"Well, yes. I've had two out of town and spent the night at a local hotel, but your house is just outside Santa Monica."

"How long does it take to reach your place without traffic?"

"Forty minutes."

"You'll get about two hours of sleep."

"More like one and a half," she admitted. "But I'm used to it."

"Driving when you're tired isn't smart."

She rolled her shoulders, crossing her arms over her chest. "Graham, it's fine."

"It's not fine," I countered, moving my chair until I was so close to her that I could smell her perfume. Sweet and spicy. Why was she so stubborn? I had an inkling about what might change her mind. I was figuring her out.

"What if something happened to you? What

about your son?"

"Oh, you're good. I'll give you that."

"I'm guessing he'll have a sitter for the night anyway?"

"He'll be at my sister's."

"Good. And you'll sleep at my house."

She parked her hands on her hips. "I did not agree. We're discussing the idea."

"Tell me the downsides."

"It's not how things are done."

"I don't give a fuck about how things are done."

"It's not professional. I don't want to be in Matt and Amber's way."

I didn't understand what she meant about Matt and Amber, but I wanted to set one thing straight.

"*I* am extending you the invitation, and I won't back down until I get a yes."

"Are we really fighting on this?"

"We're *negotiating.*"

I leveled her with my stare, perching a hand on the headrest of her seat. When she moved her hands from her hips into her lap, her bare upper arm grazed against my forearm. A current of awareness passed between us. It went straight below my belt. The chemistry between us was crazy. Maybe having her under my roof wasn't the best idea.

Her voice was a little uneven when she said, "Thank you for the invitation. I'll take you up on it."

"Perfect."

I was backing up my chair when Amber and Matt came back in.

"I'm ready for the cake," Amber announced.

As we tasted the different options, I paid more attention to Lori than the cake. She was pulling me deeper under her spell. I felt like I didn't even have a choice. She took notes while we voiced our opinions, and then we all got up to leave since we'd covered everything.

"We're also going to need transportation after the party," Matt said as we were about to exit the room.

"I already arranged that. All the guests are going to be taken care of."

"For ourselves," Matt continued. "We're going to sleep at an airport hotel. Our flight leaves at 6:00 a.m., and crossing the city in the morning is a bad idea."

"Oh, I'd been under the impression you'd be staying with— never mind. I'll arrange transportation, of course."

Now I understood her comment about being in the way. She'd thought Amber and Matt were sleeping at my house after the wedding. She slung her bag over her shoulder and only gave me a smile before leaving. A very small, very quick smile. I'd have given anything to know what went through her mind when she realized we'd be alone that night.

Chapter Seven
Lori

Amber turned out to be one of my favorite brides. She was quick to decide and stuck to her decisions. Once we'd pegged down the invitations, the menu, the flowers, and the general decoration scheme, she relaxed.

I'd been terrified she'd come up with outlandish requests. Honestly, I was still daunted by the possibility. We had one week left until the wedding. Plenty of time for her to hop on Pinterest and discover that some brides wanted rose petal canons for their weddings and whatnot. However, either Amber didn't know about Pinterest, or she was better at resisting temptation than the rest of us mortals. But four days before the wedding, she did pull a number on me.

"Can we still whip up a rehearsal dinner?"

"Oh? What made you change your mind?"

"My parents insist. My best friends are also arriving that day, and it would give me a chance to catch up with them. Can you take care of it? Is it too much work?"

"I'll do it. Don't you worry about a thing." Most brides arranged their own rehearsal dinner, but with the commission I was getting, I couldn't say no.

The only issue was that I had to ask Val to keep Milo at her house for that night too, in addition to the wedding night. I knew my sister wouldn't mind, but I still felt guilty for having to ask her. I called Val as I approached my florist's shop. I had an appointment to discuss arrangements for another wedding. Val picked up right away, so I lingered in front of the shop to talk to her.

"Hi, sis. What's up?" she asked.

"Hi, Val. Listen, I'll make this quick. This weekend's bride decided that she wants a rehearsal dinner after all."

"That means I get my lovely nephew for an extra night?"

"Is that okay?"

"Sure."

"Thanks, Val. You're the best. And I'll have to skip Friday dinner. But I promise I'll make up for it."

"Why don't you drop Milo off earlier? I'm trying to work shorter hours on Fridays, and knowing you will drop by will be a great incentive."

Val was a great preacher about work-life balance, about taking time for yourself. In reality, the only time Val had taken an extended vacation had been when she'd been forced to, because she'd been in an accident that left her with a concussion, broken ribs, and a broken leg. However, she was trying to cut back on her hours, and I was happy to help.

"That sounds great."

"I'll ask Hailey to come early too. We can do

girly stuff. Paint our nails, make you pretty for the rehearsal dinner."

"I'm the planner, not a guest."

"You can still look pretty."

"Are you implying I'm not pretty unless you and Hailey work your magic on me?" I teased.

"I did not say that."

"You're not denying it either."

"Where would the fun be in that?"

"Should I be afraid of what you have in store for me?"

"Always."

After hanging up, I added the rehearsal dinner to my calendar. I loved the spike of adrenaline that came with pulling off the perfect wedding on such short notice, even though I was so busy I could barely tell my ass from my elbow. I'd also had two corporate events this week.

When I first went into this business, corporate events were my bread and butter. It was easy money, but it was boring work and I needed a new challenge. I'd always loved weddings, and after attending a bunch of them, courtesy of all our Bennett cousins marrying in the span of a few years, I took the plunge.

Now, I still did a few corporate events per month, but weddings made up most of my business. They were more work than corporate events, but I loved them. Plus, they brought in more revenue, which meant I could offer more to Milo. His college fund was growing nicely.

Later that day, while I was waiting for my next client to show up, I received an e-mail from Graham. I was sitting on a bench, slurping a cherry smoothie with too much agave syrup, watching the gigantic palm trees sway in the wind. Despite having lived in LA my entire life, the sight of the palm trees instantly brought on a vacation mood. From the bush to my right, a whiff of lavender reached me. It was a particularly relaxing moment, but the second I saw Graham's name pop up in my inbox, my heart rate went off the charts. This happened so often over the past few days that I was starting to feel silly. He'd e-mailed me the tickets to the concert. I could either print them out or show them directly on the screen of my smartphone. I immediately replied to thank him.

From: Graham Frazier
To: Lori Connor
My assistant had an electronic version of the tickets. They're attached. Have fun.

From: Lori Connor
To: Graham Frazier
Thank you so much! If you change your mind about payment, let me know. I'd be happy to buy them off you.

From: Graham Frazier
To: Lori Connor
I do want payment.

I scrolled farther, but that was all his e-mail said. I opened the attachment with the tickets to see if the price was on them, but it wasn't. When I closed the attachment, I saw that Graham had sent another e-mail.

From: Graham Frazier
To: Lori Connor
Not monetary. I'd like to cook for you and your son one evening :)

I reread twice, didn't understand, then shot him an e-mail for clarification.

From: Lori Connor
To: Graham Frazier
How is that payment? Means more work for you.

From: Graham Frazier
To: Lori Connor
Told you cooking relaxes me. Especially when I'm in great company. Think about it.

From: Lori Connor
To: Graham Frazier
I will.

From: Graham Frazier
To: Lori Connor

You can't say no, though. It's payment for the tickets, remember?

I laughed but didn't reply. When my client arrived, I had to make an extra effort to concentrate on our discussion. She wanted a vintage wedding, and I couldn't recall all the themes off the top of my mind. My thoughts kept drifting to Graham and his invitation. What was happening here exactly?

Chapter Eight
Graham

"Just a few more. We'll be done quickly, I promise," the photographer said. The team's annual calendar shoot was about to wrap up. Usually I didn't attend, but this year Amber, as our PR and social media manager, had talked me into *being* in the calendar.

"You did well for your first photo shoot," Jennifer said, joining me on the couch where I'd sat for the past ten minutes.

She was Amber's assistant. Since Amber was at my house with Lori, putting up decorations in the tent, Jennifer was in charge. I'd wanted to head out the second my portion was over, but the photographer insisted I stayed until the end, in case she needed to reshoot something.

"I can't believe Amber talked me into this."

"Polls don't lie. Our Facebook fans voted for you to be in the calendar," she said. Amber had told me that before. What she'd failed to tell me was that they'd voted for the *shirtless Graham* option. I'd only found out when the photographer said, "Shirt off please."

"Some heads-up about the shirt would have

been good."

"But then you would have said no."

Smartass. Like I didn't have better things to do than take my shirt off for the camera. As the owner of the club, I was a jack-of-all-trades. I was informed about all the activities, the future directions, and I chaired most meetings. One of my main tasks was setting up the annual planning and overseeing the execution. I was also in charge of player transfers.

"We're done," the photographer announced to the room. We'd booked the entire studio for the day.

"Okay, everyone. Let's head back to the club for the strategy meeting," Coach Dennings announced.

"I'm sitting this one out," I told him. He frowned but nodded. It was the first time I was ditching a strategy meeting after a defeat, but I had a legitimate reason. Lori was at my house. Since we were having a rehearsal dinner, the schedule had moved forward by one day. They'd set up the tent structure yesterday, but the entire crew and Lori had already left by the time I came home. I didn't want to miss her today too.

As I headed out, my own assistant called me, asking to confirm my father's allowance before it went through.

"Yes, wire the money," I confirmed as I climbed in my car, then ended the call. My relationship with him was rocky, but we had an agreement: as long as he didn't bother Nana, he received a nice sum every month. He'd never been interested in running the club, or working in general. My grandfather had run the club until he passed away. I was twenty-six at the time, working as the PR and Marketing Manager. My father, who'd finished off his trust fund by that point, took over the reins, despite not having worked a day in his life. Two and a half years later, the club was nearly bankrupt. He'd used it as his own personal ATM. When shit hit the fan, he resigned. I stepped in as president of the club. Then I found out he'd convinced Nana to sign off her restaurant as collateral to settle one of his debts. He'd defaulted on it.

The restaurant was all Nana had. After ditching my grandfather, she moved to Tampa and bought the restaurant with the divorce settlement. Losing it would have crushed her, so I paid off the debt. But I knew he'd turn to her again if he got into trouble. Sending him a monthly allowance for doing nothing was a safer bet. Nana had dealt with enough crap from my grandfather. She didn't need a son leeching off her too.

When I approached my entrance gate, I spotted Lori's car farther down the street. I found her inside the tent, perched on a stool, securing the end of a piece of linen in a corner. Everyone else seemed to have left already. Yesterday, the tent had been bare. Now, it was adorned with decorations of all kinds. The tables and chairs had also been arranged in wedding formation.

Lori didn't give any signs of hearing me approach, even though my steps were echoing across the floor. When I was close enough, I realized she was tapping her foot against the edge of the chair. She had earbuds plugged in. After stepping down from the chair, she clapped her hands twice, shimmying her hips, then slowly turned around. Her grin was so wide it lit up the space. Then she glimpsed me.

"Oh my God." She took out her earbuds, laying them on her shoulder. "I didn't hear you."

"You're the last one here?"

"Yes. Amber and my assistant just left. How come you're home so early?"

Because I needed to see you.

"We had the calendar photo shoot today. Didn't feel like heading to the club once it was over."

"Oooh, that calendar is my guilty pleasure. And this year, you're in it too, right?"

I cocked a brow. "How do you know?"

"Amber. And Facebook. I voted for the shirtless option, obviously. Please tell me you didn't chicken out and went through with it. It had the most votes."

Finding out that Lori had a feisty side was a *very* pleasant surprise. I felt like keeping her on her toes a while longer.

"You'll have to wait and see. So, what were you celebrating when I interrupted?" I asked, moving closer.

"Nothing in particular. I like listening to

music when I'm alone. It's been a productive day. I finished putting up the decorations, and I'm taking my boy to a concert tonight. A fine gentleman got us tickets. Thanks again."

"No problem." I was close enough to hear a faint sound coming from the earbuds, but I stepped closer still. I wanted to share this moment with her, so I put in one earbud. Johnny Cash was singing a classic.

"That's a great song."

"I know," she said a little smugly. I suspected that if I weren't here, she'd still be clapping and moving her hips. I wanted in on her happy moment, to celebrate it with her. She was grinning again. Her joy was contagious. I couldn't remember the last time I'd felt that way. When I put the earbud back on her shoulder, I couldn't help myself and touched her collarbone. Her eyes widened, but instead of stopping me, she sighed softly. That little sound was my undoing. I knew that touching her wouldn't be enough. I needed to taste her. So I dragged my knuckles down her cheek, framing her jaw with my thumb and forefinger. She licked her lips.

I claimed her mouth the next second. I took my time, lavishing her lips with attention before coaxing her tongue with mine, savoring her like the prize she was.

Her hair was pulled in a braid, but I buried my hands in it anyway. Her warm body pressed against mine, and feeling her full breasts was torture. Touching her hair wasn't enough anymore. I moved my hands down her body, stopping briefly to cup the sides of her breasts, flicking my thumbs over the peaks. Lori ran a hand through my hair, tugging until it was erring on the side of painful, but I liked it. I loved that I could unleash her passion just with a kiss. I continued my exploration, moving my hands downward. When I palmed her ass, she moaned against my mouth and pressed her thighs together. She was wet for me; I was sure of it. It took all my self-restraint not to spread her out before me and confirm it with my fingers, or my tongue. I nearly yanked her top and jeans away. I needed everything separating me from her skin out of the way, but we weren't there yet. So I held her and kissed her until we were both out of breath.

"You taste amazing," I said. The skin around her mouth was red, and her eyelids were slightly hooded. "Stay here this evening. I'll make you dinner. We can pick up Milo and come back here."

"The concert is tonight."

"And if it weren't?" I pressed. I'd forgotten about it.

"Are you… are you asking me out?" she whispered.

"Fuck yes, I'm asking you out. Or in. I promise I'm great company either way." I rubbed the back of my hand along her jaw and she shuddered, pulling at her lower lip with her teeth.

"Pretty full of yourself, huh?"

"I want us to get to know each other better." I'd avoided emotional connections since my divorce, and I didn't know if I was ready for one anyway, or if I'd ever be. But I felt a pull toward Lori, and I'd be a fool not to act on it, especially when the feeling was mutual. "Fuck, you don't want to know what's on my mind right now."

"I'm going to go out on a limb and say you're not thinking about the wedding."

"Close. The night after. If I have it my way, it'll involve a lot less clothing and a lot more skin-on-skin contact."

"Maybe I shouldn't spend that night here."

"You have that little self-restraint? I'd be able to control myself, but if you think you won't—"

She stepped back, interrupting me. "I didn't say that."

"Don't worry. I won't mind if you take advantage of me."

"You've… I… I don't even know what to say to that."

The sound of a phone vibrating again filled the air. She lowered her gaze to her pocket.

"That was my phone. My reminder that I have to pick Milo up from school. I should leave. I want to feed him before the concert, and I'm done for the day here."

She moved away, picking her bag up from one of the tables and slinging it over her shoulder. "I'll see you at the wedding."

"You mean tomorrow at the rehearsal dinner," I corrected.

"Yes, of course. That's what I meant. I mixed

things up." She nodded a little too enthusiastically.

"You never mix things up. I make you feel off-balance."

"No, you don't."

"That's okay, sweetheart. You do the same to me."

I watched with satisfaction as her lips parted slightly and she gripped the sling of her bag tighter. Then she turned around and walked toward the front gate at a brisk pace.

Off-balance was one way to describe it. Currently, I felt like my world had shifted off its axis.

***

Lori

Pulse racing? Yep.

Legs wobbling? Like it was their job.

Butterflies in my stomach? *Oh la la.*

I couldn't wrap my mind around the kiss, mostly because I was still busy reliving it. As I picked Milo up from school, I fought to pull myself together... and failed. That kiss deserved to be relived anyway. When we arrived home, I prepared Milo's favorite snack, peanut butter sandwiches. Our excitement was palpable in the air. Milo was excited about the concert; I was still reeling from the kiss. Graham Frazier had brought a lot of joy to the Connor household.

"Milo, let's get you ready." I'd printed the tickets earlier in the day and flaunted them in front of him. His eyes lit up. He hopped over from his chair and climbed straight into my arms. I held him as best I could, hoping I wouldn't throw my back out in the process. He was too heavy for me now, but I'd never say that to him. He rarely wanted to be in my arms now anyway, mostly only when he was sick, so I was gobbling up these opportunities whenever I could.

We were out the door within minutes and hopped into an Uber. The area around the arena was closed to traffic though, so we walked on foot for about fifteen minutes after we climbed out of the car. We were surrounded by other concertgoers. Laughter filled the warm evening air, and Milo tried to wiggle his hand out of mine repeatedly, excited to inspect the booths selling memorabilia.

I hadn't looked closely at our tickets, but when security at the entrance checked them, he said, "Ma'am, you're sitting in the VIP section. There's a separate entrance."

Milo formed an adorable O with his mouth. He might be seven, but he understood VIP. A few short minutes later, we arrived in the VIP area. Milo squealed with joy.

"Mommy, these seats are so nice."

"They are, aren't they?" The seats in our section were covered with a velvet-like fabric, while the rest were plastic.

As I led us to our seats, I found myself hoping, foolishly, that Graham would be here too, that he'd actually had three tickets. But when we arrived at numbers 9 and 10, I took in our neighbors.

An elderly lady and her nephew occupied numbers 11 and 12, and a young couple and their daughter, who seemed to be Milo's age, sat in numbers 6, 7, and 8.

No Graham. Of course, this band was popular with kids, hence all the parents and grandparents. But I couldn't shake off the twinge of disappointment in my stomach. What was up with that?

Milo and I sat down, but as the band appeared on stage and kicked off the performance with a fan favorite, we jumped to our feet, singing and dancing. We didn't sit for the rest of the concert. I was pretty sure we'd both lose our voices tonight. I snapped pictures of the band, and selfies of Milo and me throughout the evening.

When we returned home, Milo went out like a light the moment I tucked him in. As I slipped into my own bed, I thumbed through the pictures I'd taken at the concert. On a whim, I sent Graham a picture of Milo with the stage in the background.

Lori: The concert was amazing.

I hadn't expected Graham to answer tonight, but I received a text message a few minutes later.

Graham: Very cute boy. What's his name? Does he like *The Hurls* too? I received tickets for it last month.

Lori: His name is Milo and he LOVES them. That would be great. You made this little boy very happy tonight.

Graham: Did I make his mother happy

too?

Lori: Definitely.

Graham: I request photographic evidence.

I sent him a selfie of the two of us.

Graham: You have a beautiful smile, Lori.

I wasn't just smiling in the picture. I was sporting a grin that took up my entire face—the kind of photo dentists might display in their waiting room.

Lori: Thanks. And I will pay you for the next tickets.

Graham: Of course you will. In spades. But not with money.

A sizzle coursed through me, energizing me from the tip of my toes through my sternum.

Lori: That's right… dinner.

Graham: I've upped my price in the meantime.

Lori: Oh? And what does the new price entail?

Graham: I'll tell you in person.

Oh, boy. That sizzle turned into a full-on inferno. Graham had made my body come alive in ways no one had before him. Even though hours had passed, it sure hadn't dimmed the adrenaline spike from his kiss.

Chapter Nine
Lori

On Friday, I arrived with Milo at four o'clock at Val's house. My sisters were in the kitchen, and I was surprised to find that Jace had arrived earlier too. He was leaning against the counter. Milo shot right toward him.

"Uncle Jace, can you show me that dribble you did in your last game?"

"That was the result of two months' work, buddy. If you tried it now, you'd break a leg and your momma would hang me from my… feet."

I chuckled, knowing he'd been about to say balls. I'd instated an ironclad no-swearing rule since Milo started repeating everything he heard. Five years later, my brothers still had trouble adhering to it. Sometimes, so did I. When shit hit the fan, *eff* just didn't give me the satisfaction saying *fuck* did.

At Milo's disappointed expression, Jace added, "But we can work up to it. I'll show you the basics today."

That put the smile right back on my boy's face. I kissed both my sisters' cheeks, and then Jace's.

"You've got some new plants on the porch. They're beautiful."

Val nodded. "All Maddie's work."

Maddie was a very talented landscaper. A few months back, she'd redone Val's entire yard. I couldn't wait for the jacaranda trees to be in full bloom.

"You're here early," I remarked.

"Practice ended earlier. Thought I'd show Milo some tricks before dinner."

I gave my brother a second kiss on his cheek, just because. Milo skidded to the backyard without waiting to be told.

"You should go after him," Hailey told Jace.

"Are you shooing me out?" he inquired.

"It's for your own good," Hailey insisted.

"Or you might unwillingly partake in girl talk," Val explained.

"I'm outta here."

As soon as he was out the door, Val asked, "Should we take the party upstairs? I don't want my kitchen smelling like nail polish."

"Sure. I'd love to raid your closet for a scarf."

Even when she didn't have the budget for a fancy selection, my sister's closet had been a treat. But over the years, her wardrobe expanded. It was a treasure island.

I already had a dress for the wedding tomorrow, and I was wearing my usual attire for the rehearsal dinner: a navy dress with a sweetheart neckline and a wide silver belt around the center. But I wanted to accessorize it with one of Val's scarves. Since it got chilly in the evening, I was also wearing a black velvet jacket.

"So… trying to make an impression, huh?" Val asked when we entered her room. Hailey didn't quite manage to disguise her smug smile, which meant they'd talked about me before I arrived. It was my own fault for giving them gossip fodder and telling them about the kiss yesterday.

"Is she blushing? Oh my God, she is!" Hailey exclaimed. "And she hasn't even had red wine."

Red wine did not agree with me. I always looked like I was developing an allergy after one glass.

"It's just a scarf," I said.

"I have a few that go with your dress," Val said, as Hailey and I sat cross-legged on her bed, uncapping the bottles of nail polish. Val took out a gorgeous red silk scarf, and another one, ivory with beautiful lace details in the center.

"If you want to knock someone off his ass, I'd go with this one." Val pointed to the red one.

"Got my vote too," Hailey piped up. I was drooling at the sight of it, but I knew I couldn't wear it. It stood out too much to qualify as work attire. The ivory one, on the other hand, was perfect.

"I'll take the ivory one. The red one stands out too much. And who said anything about knocking anyone on his ass?"

Hailey was hiding her face as she applied a coat of red polish on the nails of my right hand.

"Graham seems like a great guy," Val said, now plugging in the curling iron.

"How would you know?" I inquired.

Hailey was the one who answered. "We scooped every detail out of Jace, of course."

I groaned. "Girls…."

"What?" Val asked innocently. "You almost melted into a puddle when you told us about the kiss. Thought that warranted some detective work, to make sure he's not a total shit."

She didn't say it out loud, but I knew she'd meant to add "like Jeff."

I'd told them about his e-mail, and they had both suggested a more aggressive approach—such as replying with all the expletives in the world. They argued it was a better way to get things off my chest. I had the tendency of playing out ugly conversations in my mind until I got myself in a funk. But I still thought ignoring him was better than engaging.

When Val went to the bathroom to get the hairspray, I whispered to Hailey, "I dreamed about sexy fun with Graham. Repeatedly."

Talking to Val about these things had always felt a little weird. Maybe because, for so many years, she hadn't just been our older sister, but more of a mother, and I still saw her like that. Hailey was my confidant for all things sexy. Well, had been, back in the days I'd actually had anything to confide other than X-rated dreams.

"Completely normal, considering how hot he is," Hailey reassured me.

"But that doesn't mean anything."

"Would it be so bad to have some fun?" Val

asked, returning with the hairspray. Clearly, she'd overheard me.

"Yeah, it would. For the next few years, I'm sticking to daydreaming."

Even as I said it, I felt a pang of emptiness. After that kiss, I'd wanted to jump him right there, then pop open every button of his shirt and roam my hands over his bare torso. His muscles had felt exquisite even through the fabric, but I'd been greedy to touch and lick his skin. I tried to push that hot memory away.

"Why don't you shake things up a bit? Be wild for a little while," Val suggested.

"When is the last time you've been wild, sis?" I challenged. I often thought my oldest siblings never got the chance to live a little and be wild, let loose. Val had jumped from juggling the pub and our family to building her business. Sometimes I wondered if Val would even know how to let loose and be wild.

"Ufff… I think navel piercings were in style. But we're not talking about me, are we?" Val asked.

"Girls, I'm a single mom, remember? I don't just have myself to think about."

"Single parents do date, you know," Val said.

Deep down, I knew that, but I wasn't sure how to go about changing things without shaking the precarious balance Milo and I had reached.

"Sometimes I wonder if you're single to protect Milo, or yourself," Hailey said.

"What do you mean?"

"You're still afraid to put yourself out there.

You're afraid to let a man in your life," Val explained.

"Of course I am." Was I not supposed to be?

"Dating doesn't always lead to something permanent, obviously," Val said, pointing to both her and Hailey, "but you've been alone for a long time. You deserve some fun."

"You girls are filling my head with crazy ideas."

"Mission accomplished. Val, pass me the Quick-Dry," Hailey said triumphantly.

While Val used the curling iron on my hair, I did Hailey's nails. We'd perfected the art of getting each other ready at the same time during our teenage years.

An hour later, all three of us had our nails painted. Mine were bright red. My hair was styled in a high ponytail with curls cascading down on my back. I'd done my own makeup, trying on a subtle smoky eyes look. I was rocking it. Val handed me a small, unlabeled bottle of perfume.

"What's this?" I asked.

"An exclusive sample."

I sprayed the air and immediately fell in love with it. I detected notes of lilac, vanilla, and something spicy.

"It smells amazing."

She winked. "I know."

Hailey inspected me from head to toe then gave me a thumbs-up. "You're gorgeous."

I *felt* gorgeous as I put on my shoes. I'd brought my trusted nude pumps, because they looked sophisticated but were comfortable. I found Milo and Jace downstairs, gulping water and breathing heavily.

"Wanna kiss me goodbye?" I asked my son.

"Mommy, you're so pretty," Milo said, kissing my cheek.

"You're working?" Jace asked slowly. I nodded.

His brother-senses were picking up on the *trying-too-hard* vibes I had going on. In those years when Will had been part-time bad boy, Jace had watched over me and Hailey like a hawk. At thirteen, he'd seemed more like sixteen. Not only had he been tall, but his strong build had intimidated anyone who wanted to pick a bone with us. He'd gotten excellent at sniffing out "bad intentions." Luckily for me, those instincts had dulled over the years. Jace didn't ask any more question. Will would have. His instincts had only gotten sharper; I blamed it on him being a cop.

He wouldn't have anything to sniff out, though. Yes, I was a little too put together for a working event, but a girl could indulge once in a while, couldn't she? For her own pleasure?

Chapter Ten
Lori

The rehearsal dinner was taking place in the wedding tent. Amber agreed that it made sense to host it there.

"I'm so happy I listened to you about the flooring. I'd have fallen on my ass five times already otherwise," Amber said, tapping her right foot lightly over the faux-oak flooring inside the tent. She'd initially protested, saying it was too expensive and we could just have a thick carpet instead.

I'd explained that a carpet was a good option when laid on concrete, but Graham's yard was au naturel. Green grass as far as the eye could see. Looked beautiful, but could be a death trap when wearing heels.

We did lay a carpet inside the house, to protect the whitewashed oak floors from more than eighty pairs of shoes moving to the ceremony aisle on the deck and then back out to the tent.

For the rehearsal, Amber wore an elegant, pink beach dress. She had her wedding shoes on, white Jimmy Choos with five-inch heels.

"Let's get this thing going." Matt rubbed his hands together, looking at Amber like she was walking on water. Earlier, I'd caught him asking her if those shoes were safe for a pregnant woman. What would happen to the baby if she fell? Amber replied that he'd better catch her. They were adorable.

Not all couples were that way. I always watched with a heavy heart when they'd fight at every planning meeting, snapped at each other even on their wedding day.

As Amber and Matt practiced walking down the aisle, I made note of the wedding party. Six bridesmaids and six groomsmen. I swooped my gaze over every one of them, trying to memorize their faces. I tried to linger the same amount of time on each person, but when I reached Graham—I'd saved the best for last—I couldn't help indulging for a beat longer. God, the man was a work of art. Those lips, those cheekbones. Since he was talking to one of the groomsmen, I decided it was safe to indulge some more and took in the rest of him.

I knew he'd seen me checking him out before I lifted my gaze. My body reacted to him. When I finally did look up, he was smiling at me, and he took my breath away. He gave me the onceover, lighting up every inch of me he studied.

For the rest of the evening, I was aware of Graham no matter what I was doing, as if we were connected by an invisible line. He wasn't making things easy either. Whenever he was by my side, he touched my lower back, my arm, or my shoulder. They were all innocent touches, but damn, did they make my skin tingle. Maybe because he lingered a little too long, leaned in a little too close.

We were not alone, but in a rare moment when I was by myself in a corner of the tent, studying the schedule for tomorrow, he came next to me, and whispered, "You’re stunning tonight, Lori." His voice was thick and sexy, and I thought inexplicably of a lava cake. All that warm, flowing chocolate. Delicious. I felt his presence deep inside me, like a hook pulling right behind my navel.

"Thank you."

I tried to make sense of this crazy pull I felt toward him. Was it because he was handsome? Because I hadn't been with a man in seven years? But I'd met handsome men before him, and I hadn't had the urge to climb them like I did with Graham.

"Did you sleep well last night?" he asked.

"I've always been a troubled sleeper, so like usual."

"I'm not a troubled sleeper, but last night I couldn't stop thinking about you."

I made a small sound at the back of my throat. It sounded a little like a moan.

"If you make that sound again, I'll kiss you right here," Graham said.

I put some distance between us, pursing my lips. "Maybe I don't want you to kiss me."

"Pupils dilated." He touched my wrist. "Pulse quickened. I like my chances."

He pinned me with that molten gaze of his, and I felt my skin heat up all over. If the chemistry between us would be any hotter, we'd set this place on fire. Our moment was interrupted by one of the bridesmaids asking if I had a hairpin. Afterward, I handed out tomorrow's schedule to everyone in the wedding party. Since the ceremony took place on the same premises, it required much less coordinating, but I still wanted everyone to know what was happening when. The maid of honor, Jackie, looked at me funny when I handed her the printout.

"This seems like overkill," she commented. "I know all this."

"You can throw it away if you want. But the wedding day can be hectic and emotional. Doesn't hurt to have it as a backup. You can fold it and make it very small. Won't take up much space in your purse. Up to you."

She cocked a brow. "Isn't this your job? Reminding us what to do?"

"Of course I'll do that. The printout is a bonus."

Both brows lifted now, she turned on her heels and walked to the buffet. I'd ordered some simple canapés for food and had set them up on a buffet table in one corner of the tent. Tomorrow, there would be a five-course menu brought by servers, but they wanted something simple tonight. I brought out the groom's cake toward the end of the evening, after Amber and Matt had given out the gifts for the bridal party and their parents. All that was left were the speeches. I'd told the couple it was a good idea to get some of the speeches out of the way today, so we wouldn't have a dozen of them tomorrow. Too many speeches tended to set a sleepy mood, and animating everyone for the party afterward was no walk in the park.

Toward the end of the evening, I stepped out of the tent to call Milo and tell him goodnight. The smell of lavender and sage surrounded me, instantly pushing me into a Zen state of mind. This yard was something. I'd spied apple and lime trees and even guava. After I finished talking to my boy, I saw Graham come up to me.

"Those were quite some speeches," he remarked. We'd heard four, two from friends of Amber's, two of Matt's.

One was okay. The other one….

"I especially liked the one who'd wondered if there would still be a wedding if Matt hadn't knocked up Amber," I said sourly.

He'd said it jokingly, but the laughter he received sounded fake. Amber had been shooting daggers with her eyes at him.

"I understand what you mean about bad jokes now," Graham said. "Guy was always a bit of an idiot. They wanted to get married for years, but kept postponing it because they didn't have time to plan. Then Amber found out she was pregnant. Matt proposed the same day."

"That's a lovely reaction," I replied. My mind automatically flew to the day I'd found out I was pregnant.

Something in my expression must have given away my trail of thought, because Graham asked,

"Brings up ugly memories about Milo's dad?"

"I don't think of him as his dad. He said we'll try to make it work... then changed his mind and bolted."

"I'm sorry. You and Milo deserve better."

"What can you do? Things don't always work out. But I have a great support system." Feeling the urge to lighten things up, I changed the subject. "I forgot to tell you—Milo sends extra thanks for the tickets."

"He's welcome. Both of you are. But do me a favor?"

"You kind of have me there. Ask me anything."

"Anything? You're sure? That might end up being the most dangerous thing you've said."

If the tingling in my center was anything to go by, it was already the most dangerous thing I'd done.

"So what's the favor?"

He tilted his head playfully, as if considering this. "I'm reserving the right to cash in on it later."

"Decided on a price for the new tickets?"

"I'm still adding up to that tally. Getting more ideas by the hour."

"I sense they'll end up being expensive."

"Very."

"You know I could change my mind and not accept them, right?"

He came a little bit closer. "But you don't want to, do you?"

A gust of wind ruffled my hair, entangling my

ponytail in my left earring. I fumbled with my fingers to disentangle it, but I couldn't see what I was doing, and I suspected I was making it worse.

"Let me," Graham said.

"I think I caught a strand from the back, somehow."

He walked behind me, and I stilled when his thumb touched my earlobe. He was so close that I could feel his hot breath on the back of my neck.

"I like your hair up," he murmured. "I had a perfect view of your neck all evening."

He freed the strand and then traced the pad of his thumb up and down the back of my neck, from my hairline to the neckline of the dress. And then he placed an open-mouthed kiss in the middle.

Feeling his wet lips sent a wave of shock to my body. Feeling the tip of his tongue on the skin he'd warmed with his thumb wired the next wave of shock straight to my center.

He spun me around, and our gazes locked. The pull he had on me was so powerful I couldn't look away even if I wanted to. I stopped hearing the waves, the voices filtering out from the tent. I felt alone with him in our bubble. He pulled me in for a kiss, and I lost all sense of time and space. His lips felt exquisite. I opened up for him, and when our tongues touched, I felt the connection straight between my thighs. I felt him slide one hand at the back of my neck, tilting my head at the angle he needed to explore me better, deeper. When he slid a hand down to my hip, his fingers digging into my flesh possessively, I whimpered at the realization I'd drenched my panties.

Almost as if someone had poked our bubble, I became aware of our surroundings: the sea, the voices.

With a start, I jerked my head back. Everyone was still in the tent, thank God. Lust was dancing in Graham's eyes. It was intoxicating to realize he wanted me. I felt my nipples turn to pebbles in my bra. How could one look affect me so much? Or maybe that was the lingering effect of the kiss.

"Why do you have to be such a great kisser? I'd hoped I imagined it," I whispered.

"You didn't imagine it. You changed your perfume?"

"What? Oh, yes. My sister Val brought me a tester from the new collection."

"I like it. Liked the other one too."

"No one's immune to her perfumes," I agreed.

"Nah, it's just you. I'm not immune to you."

"I'm still working," I murmured.

"So proper." He locked those gorgeous eyes on my mouth, and I felt myself starting to fall under his spell again. But I shook myself out of it. I needed to clear the air.

"Graham, I don't know what this is, but… I'm not sure that I'm who you need. My life revolves around my son."

"I like that about you. It's part of what attracts me to you. You're a fascinating woman, Lori."

Wow. I hadn't expected that. I didn't have the chance to dwell on his words, because as I shifted my feet on the cobblestone pathway, I slipped and fell so hard on my ass that the breath was knocked out of me. I thought I heard a *riiip* too. I felt Graham's arms around my waist, lifting me up onto my feet.

"Did you hurt yourself?" he asked, voice laced with worry. I shook my head, even though my tailbone still hurt like hell. I had bigger issues. When a gust of wind chilled my privates, I groaned. I'd ripped open my dress. The slit had been on the right thigh, but now it went all the way up. I was wearing sheer tights, because it was too chilly in the evening for bare legs, but still. I held the loose parts together with one hand, but I couldn't go back inside the tent this way.

"Lori, are you okay? Did you twist your ankle going down?"

"No, ankle's fine. My pride, on the other hand…."

Amber walked to us. "What happened? I heard a cry."

"That was me," I confirmed. "I fell. The cobblestone is wet from the sprinklers. Take care where you step. We'll have to disable them tomorrow, so no one else falls."

Amber took in the sight of my dress. "You poor thing. Why don't you go home? We're done here."

Normally, I stayed until everyone was gone to check that everything was set for tomorrow, but my dress wasn't decent anymore.

"Yes, I'll do that. Sorry to take off earlier."

Amber waved her hand, smiling.

"Ladies," Graham said, offering Amber and me each an arm. "Allow me to escort you off this death trap."

Amber laughed as she snaked her arm around Graham's. I did the same, because I didn't want to risk landing on my ass again. I warmed all over when Graham tucked me close.

Once we were on steady ground, he let go of us, and I instantly felt cold where he'd touched me.

"I need my tote. Can either of you bring it from inside?"

"I'll bring it," Amber replied. Graham remained by my side while she headed inside the tent.

"Are you sure you can drive?" he asked.

"Of course. My tailbone still hurts, but I'll manage."

A playful twinkle appeared in his eyes. "Massage?"

The thought of his hands on me was doing naughty things to my body *despite* the pain. "No, thanks." Almost unconsciously, I touched the sore spot and winced.

"I'd feel better if you'd let me drive you. You could lie in the back," Graham said. Worry replaced the playful twinkle. I felt as if someone had wrapped a warm blanket around me.

"Graham, I'm a big girl. It's nothing. But thanks for the offer. I'll see you tomorrow morning."

Amber returned with my tote, and I asked them to excuse me from the rest of the party. I couldn't say goodbye myself, given the state of my dress. When I climbed in my car, pain seared the base of my spine the second my ass touched the seat. Maybe taking Graham up on his offer would have been smarter. Lying down instead of sitting sure sounded like a better plan. And it would have earned me more time with the handsome and charming man. But I powered through and started the engine. Despite the throbbing pain in my ass, I smiled a big, goofy smile. I caught my reflection in the rearview mirror. I looked a little loony.

Then I buried my face in my hands, even though no one could see me. My smile stretched into a grin against my palms. Val and Hailey were right—they typically were. All these years, I hadn't just wanted to protect Milo, but myself too. Before Graham, no man had made me want to dip my toe in the dating pool. Would this be a good idea? The man was disenchanted with marriage; he'd admitted it himself. But did it really matter? As my sisters realistically put it, dating led nowhere most of the time. It was a fun thing to do, and I hadn't had fun in a long time. Was it time for changes in my life? Could I handle them? I had no answers. But my loony grin remained in place the entire drive.

Chapter Eleven
Lori

The next morning, I arrived at Graham's house at the same time as the florist, Gigi.

"You can start setting everything up in the tent. I'll be with you in a few minutes. Need to get my stuff inside first," I informed her.

I was already wearing my wedding suit, but I had a spare blouse and shoes, so I'd be covered in case I had another mishap like yesterday. I wanted to bring them to the room Graham had told me I'd be staying in. I realized Graham's car wasn't in his driveway. Even though he had a detached two-car garage next to the guesthouse, he never used it. Did he have errands to run? If he did, they couldn't be wedding related, because I had all those on my schedule.

As I deposited my things in the gorgeous room, I started wondering if my staying here was really a good idea. Wouldn't it be wiser and safer to drive home after the wedding ended and return the next morning? It probably was the smartest thing to do, but the reality was, I'd only sleep a wink if I did that. I'd be a zombie when I'd take my boy to Universal Studios tomorrow afternoon, and he deserved my full attention. Four hours of sleep were better than one.

I was staying. *For my boy,* I told myself. Not because I was hoping to get glimpses of Graham during the night. *Does he sleep in shorts? Naked?* Nor was I hoping to accidentally bump into him after he showered. I chastised myself for giving so much thought to scenarios I didn't want to occur. But just like last night, the more I tried *not* to think about Graham, the more I did.

Before heading out, I checked my phone for any calls or e-mails from vendors. To my dismay, I discovered an e-mail from Jeff.

From: Jeff Finn

To: Lori Connor

I've tried your old number, but it's disconnected, and your assistants won't give me your new one. Don't play games. I just want to catch up.

I snorted, shaking my head. I had no intention of calling him. My phone number wasn't listed on my website, only a number that connected to my assistants' phones. I was thankful my girls hadn't given him my number. I wasn't interested in his booty calls. I'd long since given up on the idea that he'd want to be involved in Milo's life. He'd tossed us aside, because Milo's existence wasn't *convenient* for him. An unexpected child was too much to handle while training to become a doctor.

As usual, his e-mail soured my mood, but I

tried my best to lose myself in the day's tasks. Gigi and I put up the flower arrangements in the tent in no time at all, then focused on setting up an orchid arch at the main entrance. The delicate flowers looked even more beautiful against the limestone exterior of the house.

We moved onto the deck next, arranging garlands of roses and orchids on the ceremony aisle and officiating table. We left the glass railing unadorned so everyone had a clear view of the ocean. The chairs still had to be delivered, and I was eyeing the time on my phone almost compulsively. The delivery should arrive in ten minutes, and I hoped they wouldn't be late. Managing weddings was a lot like building a puzzle. One had to coordinate all the moving parts. I'd built in buffer time in case one of the vendors was late, but I'd rather not have to rely on that.

When I walked Gigi to her car, I spotted Graham's Range Rover. He was back. Energy zipped through me, and the man wasn't even in sight.

"I counted the personal flowers twice," Gigi said.

"Don't worry; I counted them once too. All there." It was my responsibility to distribute the personal flowers before the ceremony. "Thanks, Gigi. Your arrangements are lovely, as usual."

The chairs arrived as Gigi left. They were simple white chairs, a sturdy but festive-looking plastic. I planned to purchase similar ones soon. Wedding planning was a profitable business. I wouldn't have gone into it otherwise, no matter how much it spoke to my romantic soul. But owning decorative sets was the way to make the big bucks in this business: linens, tablecloths, decorations of all kinds. Maintaining an inventory was tricky. One had to always be on top of the trends, and sell existing stock before it went out of style. Typically, the items that were hottest this wedding season were already out of style the next one.

I currently owned a large assortment of decorations and tablecloths, but I was always looking to expand, and I'd had quite a few couples who'd wanted the ceremony in locations where one had to bring everything from seats to officiating table.

The driver and I arranged the chairs in straight rows on both sides of the aisle on the deck. While I maneuvered the seats, my body hummed in a way it hadn't before. Was Graham inside the house on the upper floors? Was he watching?

There was a smaller deck directly above this one, but I suspected one could see the outer edges of the lower deck from that window. I risked a glance over my shoulder once. The sun reflected against the glass front on the upper floor, but I thought I could make out Graham's shape anyway. The humming in my body intensified. My pulse was erratic. I felt it in my throat, my chest. Between my thighs.

After the driver left, I had a window of about thirty minutes until the next vendor was slated to arrive with the special brand of champagne that Matt ordered. I resolved to head to my room and freshen up a bit in the meantime. Perspiration had gathered under my armpits during all that chair maneuvering. I also wanted to use my curling iron on a few strands. I'd slept without taking down the ponytail, and carefully splaying the curls on my pillow, but they still needed retouching.

It was a beautiful day for a wedding. The sun was shining; the gentle breeze from the sea was refreshing. I headed straight upstairs without passing through the living room. When I stepped in my bedroom, I ran into an unpleasant surprise.

A beautiful dress was laid out on my bed. Turquoise silk with a white band around the middle. Had I brought my things to the wrong room? It looked like it, though the rightful occupant didn't seem to have left any other possessions around.

I was relieved that I wouldn't be spending the night alone with Graham, but I was also... jealous. Who was she? Couldn't be one of the bridesmaids because they were wearing lilac. It had to be someone who'd traveled from another city. Perhaps that's where Graham went this morning, to pick her up. They had to be close if he offered for her to spend the night here. In any case, the woman had excellent taste in clothing.

A knock at the door startled me. I whirled around to find Graham in the doorway.

"What do you think?" he asked at the same time I said, "Sorry, I mixed up rooms."

He frowned. "You didn't mix up rooms. This is where you're sleeping."

I pointed to the dress. He smiled, and I felt even more irrational jealously toward the owner of the dress.

"That's for you."

Oh boy. That humming from earlier? It was now a full-blown buzz. It electrified me.

"I don't understand."

"You tore your dress on my property. I owe you a new one."

I stared at him. "I slipped. That wasn't your fault."

He wiggled his eyebrows. "My sprinklers. My fault." I didn't know why, but the words sounded dirty. "You could sue for damages."

"I wouldn't do that." I laughed, looking at the dress with a fresh perspective. It seemed even more beautiful than before. It wasn't too flashy, which meant I could wear it even if I was the planner and not part of the wedding. I pulled on every ounce of self-restraint to do the right thing.

"Graham, I can't keep this."

"You don't like it? We can go to the store and change it. There's still time before everyone arrives."

He had time. I had to be here, coordinating everything, but that was beside the point.

"It's not that. The dress is gorgeous. But taking it wouldn't be right."

There was fire in those hypnotizing irises. Even though there were at least two feet between us, I suddenly felt as if we were close enough to touch.

"I beg to differ."

"Graham."

"I want to see you in that dress."

I nearly swallowed my tongue at this—mostly because it sounded like what he meant was *I want to take it off you.* His gaze traveled up and down my body. I hadn't checked, but the dress seemed my size, which meant Graham had watched me very closely.

"When did you even buy it? Stores don't open this early."

"I have my ways."

Private opening hours—got it.

He was bossing me into accepting this dress, just as he'd bossed me into spending the night here…There were no two ways about it. I had the hots for this bossy man.

"Okay, I'll wear it. Thank you."

"Welcome. You like this room?"

"I love it. I've already put out my toiletries and pajamas in the bathroom, so I don't have to unpack during the night."

"And here I was, hoping you slept naked." He leaned in. "I don't either."

"I didn't ask." I cleared my throat, suddenly feeling very squeamish and very hot. My nipples tightened.

"But I'd be happy to take off my clothes for you."

Other body parts tightened too. I was hanging onto my wits by a *very* thin thread. "Graham, I need to get ready before the champagne is delivered."

I pointed to the door, and with a quick nod,

he took off. The room felt empty without him. I turned to look at my dress, trying to sort through everything I was feeling. This wasn't the time for me to get overwhelmed, so I decided to take things one step at a time. Step one: I was going to rock this dress.

Chapter Twelve
Graham

Amber and Matt radiated happiness. They'd arrived at the same time, because she'd decided she wasn't going to do the whole "groom must not see bride before" nonsense, much to the chagrin of her mother.

"How are you holding up?" she asked while we were waiting for the music to start.

"Me? It's your wedding."

"Yeah, but this must bring some unhappy memories for you."

What could I tell her? That I wasn't looking forward to hearing the vows, because every time I heard "I do" I saw my divorce papers flash before my eyes? I wasn't going to dim her happiness with my negativity.

"Don't worry about me."

"I can't believe we didn't manage to convince Nana to come for the wedding."

"She's stubborn." She was also terrified of flying. I'd offered to take a few days off and drive her myself, but she wouldn't budge.

"You don't make road trips across the country in my old age."

The woman was sharper than ever, but she didn't like to travel. She'd instructed me to send her pictures as things happened.

Once the ceremony started, it took a lot of effort to keep my focus on Matt and the wedding party instead of searching for Lori in the crowd. I lost the battle quickly. One sweep around the perimeter revealed that Lori was standing next to the piano. She was wearing the dress I bought her, and she was magnificent. A friend of mine owned a shop on Rodeo Drive and she'd helped me choose the dress. It fit Lori perfectly, highlighting the curve of her hips, her full breasts. I knew I should have paid attention to the minister, but I couldn't. Her green eyes were cast downward. Only when Amber and Matt started reciting their vows did she look up. Something clenched in my chest when I realized she'd teared up. When she caught me watching her, she shrugged one shoulder, as if saying, "What can you do?" and smiled through her tears.

She had to be attending at least a wedding a month, and yet the vows still moved her to tears. Despite the rejection she'd suffered, she was a believer through and through. For one split second, Lori made me a believer too. I was confident that Matt and Amber would make it to their sixtieth anniversary and surround me with nephews. I planned to claim the role of uncle, even if we weren't related by blood. But this was the first time since my divorce that I dared to believe that maybe they weren't a unique case. Maybe Elizabeth and I just hadn't been a good fit. Still, we'd once exchanged vows too, and it all ended with shouting, accusations, and Elizabeth repeating every chance she got how disappointed she was in how our marriage turned out.

After the ceremony, Lori ushered the wedding party to the photo session and the rest of the guests inside the tent.

While the photographer was splitting us into groups, I engaged others in conversation, but I couldn't help looking away every time I caught sight of turquoise. Lori was the only one wearing that color today. She moved around the tent constantly, talking to servers and the rest of the personnel. In the hour it took us to finish the photo session, she hadn't sat once.

She bossed around anyone who wasn't giving one hundred percent to their job. Crazy as it sounded, watching her all fierce and in charge turned me on. Lori was a strong woman. I liked that a lot. I went straight to her after the photographer announced we were free.

"Lori, are you going to be on your feet all day?"

"Of course."

"No breaks?"

"I'll call Milo at nine before he goes to sleep, but otherwise no." Her devotion to him got to me every time. *Every single time.* "I have to make sure everything runs smoothly."

"Everything *is* running smoothly."

"Yeah, but that's because everyone knows I'll be busting their balls otherwise."

Her words went straight below my belt. A dirty vision flashed in my mind.

"Nice dress," I said on a wink.

"Thank you. A well-meaning gentleman bought it for me."

"Is that so? How about toasting with him?" I pointed to one of the servers circulating with glasses of champagne on trays.

"I don't drink while working."

I saw my opportunity right then and there. She could have a drink with me *after* work.

"Can you believe it's the wedding day already? Sometimes I get so caught up in preparations that I'm surprised when the day finally arrives."

"You've done a great job."

And her job ended today, but I was nowhere near ready to stop seeing her. She smelled sweet and citrusy, like last night. And like last night, I wanted to pull her closer. Only I wouldn't let go of her now.

"Damn earrings," she muttered. One of her curls had entangled with her earring again, but I didn't trust myself to touch her with so many people around us.

"I'm going to the bathroom. I need a mirror to untangle this without pulling my hair out. See you around. I'll keep an eye on you during the speeches." Her warning was laced with humor. I took the bait.

"Or what, you'll bust my balls?" I challenged.

On pure instinct, I moved a step closer, and Lori tugged at her bottom lip with her teeth.

She sounded breathless when she said, "You bet I will."

She turned around, and I watched her until she disappeared from view. I couldn't wait to be alone with her, to have her all to myself.

Chapter Thirteen
Lori

By the time the main course was being served, I couldn't feel my toes. I'd been on my feet for twelve hours, but the wedding wasn't going to be over for another five. At nine, I slid out of the tent to call Milo. Afterward, I took advantage of the fact I was alone and took my first mini-break, enjoying the cool, salty air. I'd snapped a photo of the wedding rings and sent it to my cousin Pippa. She called me a few seconds later.

"Hey! Thanks for the pic. I always like to see my creations out in the wild."

"They're beautiful. So, when can we expect the special collection?" My cousin had created a limited edition collection of engagement and wedding rings a few years ago, and it took off. Now they wanted to grow that segment to a permanent line.

"I'm thinking next year. We still have to finalize details and contracts."

"Can't wait. How are things in San Francisco?"

"Oh, you know. Sebastian and Logan try to boss us around. Emphasis on try," she said, referring to her older brothers. "Christopher and Max try to teach my girls every trick in the book."

I laughed, imagining how that went. There was a strong twin gene in our family. Christopher and Max Bennett were identical twins, and they'd used their likeness for many pranks as kids. It seemed common sense to teach Pippa's twin girls to do the same. I'd last seen the Bennett clan at Landon's wedding, and I missed them.

"So, business as usual," I concluded.

"Pretty much. By the way, I've heard interesting reports about a certain best man." I could hear the joy in Pippa's voice. I wondered which of my sisters had ratted me out.

"Pippa Bennett-Callahan! Are you prying?"

"Of course. And proudly owning up to it."

"Well, I'm working this wedding now, but I'll call you next week and fill you in."

"Okay."

As soon as I clicked off the phone, I realized the DJ was playing dance music, when my indications had been to switch to low-key chamber music while the guests ate. With a sigh, I headed back inside.

"Andrew, the guests are eating the main course," I said when I reached his booth.

"Sorry, Lori. I got carried away." He switched to a low-key tune. I headed to the bar next, in the far right corner of the room.

"Dylan, how is the ice supply?" I asked the bartender. We'd ordered enough ice for the entire event, but we only brought out one ice bag at a time, for cosmetic reasons.

"I still have some left. I think I'll need a new one in about twenty minutes."

"Why don't you go and get it now while everyone is eating? I'll stay here in case anyone needs something."

He nodded and disappeared through the personnel door. We'd set up a lounge area in front of the bar, comprised of five leather chairs and a small coffee table in between. I sat on one of them and felt my skin prickle with awareness. Graham was watching me again; I was sure of it. I'd caught him looking at me often tonight.

I chanced a glance across the room and immediately found him, even though he wasn't in his seat. I felt even more wired to him than yesterday. That invisible thread linking us was growing stronger, and I had no clue what to do about it. Maybe he could feel that too, because each time we talked tonight, he'd kept a respectable distance, as if he didn't trust himself to be too close to me. Our gazes crossed. It was a good thing I was sitting because my knees weakened a little. I could swear his gaze was more molten each time he looked at me. He was an excellent best man. His speech had been fun and heartwarming, and he'd dutifully danced with each bridesmaid.

I'd tried to ignore the twist in my gut each time one of them had leaned in too close, or laughed with him. The maid of honor had been particularly possessive of him, monopolizing him for double the number of dances the other bridesmaids had. Yep,

I'd counted. I was certain Jackie hoped they'd honor the long-standing tradition of the best man and the maid of honor getting it on during the wedding night. My gut twisted some more at the thought. It shouldn't bother me, but it did. I hadn't been so attracted to a man since before I had Milo. I could still feel the heat of his lips on mine, even though it happened twenty-four hours ago. Yeah, I'd counted that too.

A waiter showed up next to me. On his tray, he carried a plate with the main course and a glass of orange juice.

"Your dinner, Ms. Connor."

Even though Amber had been generous enough to treat me to the entire menu, I hadn't had time to touch the appetizers. I was starving, but I was afraid that a full belly would drain me of energy. As if he could sense my hesitation, the waiter said, "I have orders not to leave until you accept the dinner."

I didn't have to ask to know who'd given the orders. Warmth spread through me. Not the kind that was sparked by a kiss and simmered on the surface, lighting up my nerve endings. It was the more dangerous kind. The kind that went deep into my bones and was impossible to shake off.

"Thank you." I took the plate and the glass. Eating at the coffee table wasn't elegant, but I'd promised Dylan I'd stay here until he returned with the ice.

I didn't dare look at Graham again. I didn't think I could meet his eyes right now and not give myself away. I wanted him. I wanted him so much that I wondered again if it wasn't smarter to head home after all.

As the evening wound down, it appeared that someone else wanted to stay here too. Jackie was complaining loudly about going back to the city so late. Graham didn't extend her the offer to spend the night here.

A funny thing happened once the guests started filtering out. Despite having been on my feet the entire day, energy spiked in my veins.

"I can't feel my feet," Amber complained after the very last guest left. She put a hand on my shoulder, beaming. "Thank you for everything."

"My pleasure."

"Should we start taking down the decorations now?" she asked.

"That's my job. Don't you even think about it. You two hop in that fancy car waiting for you and go to your fancy hotel room. Don't you have a wedding night to celebrate?"

"Yes, yes we do!" Matt exclaimed.

Amber waved her hand dismissively, but winked at her husband. "Where's the hurry? You already knocked me up. Already sampled the goods."

Matt's eyes widened. Graham seemed suddenly very interested in a napkin he'd picked up off the floor. I pretended I didn't hear anything.

"Amber, I've got everything under control here. I'll tip the staff and then see to the decorations in the morning. Off you go."

She relented, and as Matt took her hand, Graham said, "I'll walk the two of you to the car."

Once they left, I tipped each member of the staff, thanking them for their work. I kept looking over my shoulder, checking if Graham had stepped back inside the tent. Usually, I was exhausted at the end of a wedding, but now I was so wired that I felt like tap dancing. After the staff left, I went by each lighting installation and turned it off. When I had two left, I heard someone step inside the tent. I would have known it was him even if we weren't the only ones left on the property. I recognized the strong, confident rhythm of his steps.

As I turned off the switch, the tent went darker than I expected. I realized Graham had turned off the last light at the same time. Some light was still filtering in from the house, but the semidarkness invited naughty and illicit activity. I couldn't believe my mind had gone there already.

Graham broke the silence first. "You did a great job today."

"Thanks, and back at you. You were an excellent best man."

"Does that mean I passed the test?"

"With flying colors."

He stepped close enough that I could see his smile. It was the closest we'd been for the past few hours, and I was suddenly very grateful he'd kept his distance during the party, because his proximity made it hard to think.

"You danced a lot," I said.

"Comes with best man duties."

With one hand, he undid his bowtie and popped open the top button of his shirt. There was something incredibly sexy about the fact that he felt comfortable enough around me to do that. That one button he'd undone didn't reveal much, though. I wondered how much relaxing it would take for him to pop open another one, give me a glimpse of his skin. Hell, I wouldn't say no to a peek at a nipple either. What were we talking about? *Oh, that's right. Dancing.*

"You seemed to have fun dancing. The girls certainly did."

He was silent for a beat, then moved even closer.

"Do you know how hard it was to stay away from you tonight, Lori?"

I sucked in a breath.

"You were the only woman I wanted to dance with, and I couldn't have you. The whole night, I've been fantasizing about making everyone leave so we could be alone."

I couldn't form an answer. All thoughts fled me. All my muscles were strung tight. He brought one hand to my belly, and I knew he could feel the tension coiled in my body.

"You're so tense, Lori. I want to ravish you." His hand moved higher. "I want to taste you, make you mine."

He brought his mouth to my ear, moved his hand from my belly up to cup my face, and kissed me. I moaned when our tongues collided. His sheer masculinity made my entire body thrum, lighting me up on the inside. It felt out-of-this-world good, just like before. Was it possible that I'd forgotten what it felt like to be kissed? No, I just hadn't been kissed by someone who was so good at it. And deep down, I knew no other kiss would ever match Graham's.

I searched in vain for my arsenal of excuses. I couldn't think. All I could do was feel. When he brought me flush against him, and his erection pressed against my belly, I lost all decency. I wound my fingers through his hair, tugging and demanding. His passion lit me up. He cinched my dress up until his fingers were on the bare skin of my thigh. He slid it to my ass and hoisted me up until l felt the tip of his erection against my center. I almost came, and my panties were still on.

"I want you so much, Lori. I don't know what not wanting you feels like anymore."

"I want you too," I admitted, voice low, almost a whisper.

He kissed me again, and I lifted one bent leg onto his thigh, opening up, grinding against him. I needed more friction. *Oh my*, this was too much. Feeling his fingers digging into my ass cheek, his hard chest pressing against my breasts, teasing my sensitive nipples, the length of his cock rubbing against my clit—

I exploded the next second, coming so hard that the leg I was standing on shook. The one I'd lifted spasmed. Graham held me tight to him while I regained my breath. I couldn't believe I'd just climaxed. It usually took me about fifteen minutes to relax and work myself up to a high point. Embarrassment gnawed at me, but Graham put me at ease with one sentence.

"Lori, you coming like that was so damn sexy."

He took my hand, and we moved onto the pathway leading up to the house. As we stepped inside, I heard a buzzing sound. Graham took his phone out of his pocket, tossed it in the bowl with keys at the right of the entrance.

"Don't you want to take that? Could be important."

"Lori, that phone could be on fire and it wouldn't stop me."

Okay then.

Up the stairs we went, then into the master bedroom. He kissed me against the door, his hand tugging on the zipper of my dress. A shiver ran through me. My muscles tensed.

"What's wrong?" he murmured.

"Nothing," I said quickly.

"Lori, I can feel you thinking, stressing. You go all rigid when you're nervous. Talk to me."

"I haven't done this in a while." I glanced out the window, at the ocean, not quite able to meet his eyes. The moon hung low, its glow amplified by the reflection in the water. Graham cupped my cheek, turning my head until our eyes locked.

Chapter Fourteen
Lori

"I'll make it so good. I promise. Do you trust me to do that?"

I nodded, and he kissed me again. He started with my mouth, moved over to my shoulder. "I've fantasized about undressing you all night." He undid the zipper of my dress, slipped a hand on my bare skin, blowing my inhibitions to smithereens. "Since I saw this dress, all I could think about was taking it off you."

I needed him naked. I wanted to admire that gorgeous, bronze skin. I wanted to touch and taste. With eager fingers, I got to work on the buttons of his shirt, until I freed his torso. The reality was more delicious than all the fantasies I'd had. I ran my hand across his steely muscles and placed open-mouthed kisses on the expanse of his chest. He interrupted my exploration before I could have my fill, though I was starting to suspect I couldn't ever have enough of him.

He rid me of my dress next. Taking one step back, he took me in from head to toe. I felt exposed in my lacy bra and panties, but the hunger in his gaze put me at ease. And when he captured my mouth and pulled my ponytail free, fisting my curls, heat coiled low in my belly. I rolled my hips almost involuntarily and slammed right into his, trapping his erection between us. Even through his pants, I could feel how much he wanted me. Through the haze of lust, I felt him kneel before me, taking off my pumps. He kissed my legs, moving to my inner thighs. As he moved farther up, I felt heat gather between my thighs, adrenaline coursing through me, like a buzz that wouldn't quiet. I'd never felt so aware of my body, so alive.

Hooking his thumbs in the elastic band of my panties, he tugged them down, exposing me further. Without warning, he swiped his tongue over my center, and I saw stars.

"Graham!"

He moved up, kissing the top of my breasts next. My nipples were pressing painfully against my bra. As if sensing that, he undid the clasp and kneaded my bare breasts, swirling his tongue around one nipple, then moving to the other. I felt every lash of his tongue between my legs as if my peaks were wired to my clit.

A bolt of energy zapped through me, making me rise on my tiptoes and brace my hands on his biceps. When he groaned against my skin, I clenched my thighs. The emptiness inside me was becoming unbearable. I pushed his pants down with one hand, and Graham kicked off his boxers next. At last, he was naked. He was glorious. Utterly glorious. He led me to his king-size bed, and when I climbed on it, my first instinct was to cross my legs.

He cuffed my ankles, spreading me wide open, climbing between my thighs, and lowering his head right above my center.

He nuzzled my clit with the tip of his nose, pulling one fold between his lips, then the other. I nearly came again. My back arched, and I fisted his sheets to keep from tugging at his hair. His back wasn't in my reach, but I thought I might scratch him if it was. This man brought up wild impulses in me that I didn't recognize.

"Graham, that's perfect. Oh, God, it's so good."

When he shifted his weight on the mattress, I looked between us and saw he was rolling on a condom. I swallowed hard at the size of him. He kissed up my belly, between my breasts, until his face was level with mine. A tremble of anticipation rocked me when I felt his erection against my inner thigh.

He gripped himself at the base, flicking the tip around my entrance, circling my clit, until I was panting and trembling in earnest and utterly soaked. Then he pushed inside me. He gave me just the tip, but a strangled sound tumbled from my lips, somewhere between a gasp and a moan. He moved in slowly, barely half an inch with every thrust, giving me time to adjust. He unleashed an inferno inside me. I didn't want it slow anymore. I wanted all his passion, without restraint. I rolled my hips, taking him in to the hilt. Feeling him so deep inside knocked the breath out of me.

"Lori, fuck. Oh, baby."

"Wow."

He lowered one hand, slipping it under my ass, digging his fingers into one cheek on every thrust, kissing me feverishly. I felt full—so impossibly, blissfully full—with his tongue in my mouth, his cock inside me, his pelvis pressing against my bundle of nerves with every thrust. I'd never known pleasure like this, white-hot and all consuming. Our rhythm was feral, and I'd moved from fisting the sheets to tugging at his hair. I dragged my lips over every inch of him I could reach, and it wasn't enough. I wanted to savor him. This man was pure perfection. His arms and shoulders were corded with muscles, which flexed on every thrust. I licked a morsel of taut skin, then took one nip with my teeth. Graham let out a low growl. He'd *liked* it.

I felt my inner muscles spasm, tightening around him as an orgasm teased my nerve endings. I didn't have time to prepare myself for it. I climaxed the next second, crying out Graham's name, gripping his shoulders. In the throes of passion, I felt him widening inside me. He was right near the peak. I held him close to me as he came, thrusting hard. For a second, I couldn't breathe. My muscles protested as we lay wrapped around each other.

When he rolled over to take care of the condom, my skin was suddenly cold in all the

places he'd touched me before. He moved to the edge of the bed, with his back to me. What was I supposed to do now? Hop in his shower, or go to my room? I wanted to feel those strong arms around me a tad longer, but I didn't want to overstay my welcome. Was this a one-night thing?

"Should I go to my room?" I asked, fiddling with the pillow. Graham straightened up.

The easy, natural silence from before turned loaded. My stomach clenched tighter with every beat of silence.

Even though the door was closer to Graham's edge of the bed, I moved toward the other one. He half turned then, and something in his gaze made me stop moving.

"I'd like you to stay, Lori. You don't want that?"

"I do."

"That's settled, then. Let's shower together." His voice carried a hint of demand now. The tightening in my stomach loosened.

"Okay."

He held out his hand for me, and I moved toward him. He had a curious expression on his face. It looked a little like relief, a lot like desire. On the way to the bathroom, he walked one step behind me. I hadn't thought much of it until I felt his hand slide down one ass cheek, giving it a little squeeze, then a tiny *smack*. I whipped around to face him.

"Hey!"

"You're too tempting." He hooked an arm around my shoulders and pulling me close. "Couldn't resist. Can you blame me?"

"Yes. Yes, I totally can." We were only a breath apart, smiling against each other's lips. Giddiness bubbled up inside me and didn't subside while we showered.

Graham's bathroom was almost as large as his bedroom. We were surrounded by shiny black tiles and silver specks of color. The bathtub was large enough to throw a party in it. The shower had more than a dozen programs.

"This is fancier than a spa," I said. "Which program should we use?"

"Your choice."

"Really?" I clapped my hands then got to work. The first button I pushed shot out a jet so strong it nearly plastered me to the wall of the shower. "Maybe not this one."

I looked closely at the signs painted on each button, but it was like trying to decipher Chinese letters. *Okay…* so trial by error it was. I played some more, settling on one that had a comfortable pressure. While the warm spray of water descended upon us, I rubbed the sides of my neck.

"Neck massage?" he asked.

"Yes, please." As he flipped me around, I counted my lucky stars for his gentlemanly manners. A minute into the massage, he flattened himself against my back and rubbed his erection slowly against my ass cheeks. I pretended nothing out of the ordinary was happening, up until he slid one hand to my breasts.

"That's not my neck." I was fighting to sound

serious.

He tugged at my earlobe with his teeth. "Seemed to also require my attention."

"How could you tell?"

"Close observation."

"Other places you think *require* your attention?"

He slid his hand further down until he brushed my clit. It was a feather light touch, but I buckled, gasping.

"You're still so wound up, sweetness. I could make you come all over my hand."

"That sounds so dirty," I said breathlessly. I braced myself for more of the sweet torture, but he flipped me around instead and kissed me slowly, tenderly.

"The things I want to do to you, Lori," he whispered when he pulled back, rubbing the tip of his erection against my belly. My knees became weaker with every rub. There was no mistaking the feral glint in his eyes. Clearly, he was making *serious sexy plans* already. I hadn't even thought beyond some messing around, but clearly, it was time to think bigger—*sexier.* I wasn't sure my body could even take more pleasure tonight, but I trusted Graham's abilities to ravish me.

And by God, did he ever ravish me.

"You corrupted my plan to sleep," I informed him a while later as he propped a pillow on the headrest and leaned against it. He pulled me to him until my back was flat against his chest. The circle of his arms was officially my favorite place in the world. Steely muscles, smooth skin. What was there not to love?

"This is better than sleep."

"So much better," I agreed. "I love this view. The moon and the water…."

"I like looking at the water. I house hunted for a property in this area for a long time. Finally bought it off a celebrity, even though the villa's not really my style. I thought about renovating, but it's too much hassle. The view sold me on the place. I grew up smack dab in the middle of the city, but I spent my vacations with my grandmother in Tampa. She lives near the beach. My best memories are from there. You'd like Nana."

"She still lives in Tampa?"

"Yeah. I tried talking her into moving here, but no chance. She moved there after divorcing my grandfather and is running a restaurant she bought. I think LA has too many unhappy memories for her."

His confession caught me by surprise. I hadn't expected him to share something so personal.

"You see her often?"

"I fly to Tampa on every major holiday."

"That's sweet."

I wasn't sure how things would be between us in the morning, but for now I wanted to enjoy this sexy man. As we lay like that, a low rumble echoed through the room.

"Someone's hungry." I rubbed my back against his stomach. Then I rubbed my own stomach, adding, "This someone is hungry too."

"Let's raid my kitchen."

"I don't eat this late at night. Calories count twice."

He cradled my legs between his thighs, rocking me while he pushed my hair to one side, kissing the back of my neck. Our closeness felt incredibly intimate.

"Lori, you're absolutely gorgeous. But if it eases your conscience, think of this as early breakfast."

His lips curled against the back of my neck. He was the devil. He really was. Was there anything he couldn't talk me into?

"You sure know how to spin words."

He took my words as a yes, which they were, and pulled me out of bed, dragging his knuckles against the side of my breast, then my ass, as if he had free reign to touch me. Which he had.

My skin turned to goose bumps, partly because he was touching me so shamelessly, but also because I felt a little exposed.

"Do you have a robe? Or I can use a towel to cover myself."

"I want you naked. It's a requirement."

"Really?"

"Yes."

I crossed my arms over my chest, pretending to be offended. In fact, I was weighing the pros and cons. I'd feel self-conscious parading naked around his house. But the heat in his gaze told me that he liked what he saw. This gave me leverage to ask for the same in return. A naked Graham definitely trumped any self-consciousness. *Oh, yes, I think I'll do just that.*

Discovering my naughty side was fun and… unexpected. Talk about Val and Landon not knowing how to have fun, but it seemed I'd forgotten too.

"I'll consider giving in to your request if you don't put on clothes either."

"Deal."

Damn! That had been too easy. I suspected I could have gotten a much better deal if only my negotiation skills were sharper. I tried my luck.

"I don't know…." I drew out the words, tracing a small circle on the carpet with my toe.

"You're not getting out of this room with your skin covered. I'm upgrading this to rule status."

"Fine."

He pulled me flush against him, kissing me. My body sizzled at the skin-on-skin contact, at the way my curves molded against his chest. We were a perfect fit. As we descended to his kitchen, one thought circled in my mind: I didn't want this night to end.

Chapter Fifteen
Lori

I woke up with a start, blinking at the sight of the restless ocean stretching in front of me. I must have fallen asleep after we got back from the kitchen. Before I had a chance to mull over last night, or to wonder why Graham wasn't in his bed, I glanced at the clock and immediately panicked. I'd overslept!

Tatiana from the decoration company was scheduled to have arrived half an hour ago. I looked around for my clothes before realizing I only had last night's dress here. My overnight bag was still in the room I'd left it in when I arrived. I wrapped myself in the towel I'd used last night after showering. Then I clutched my dress, shoes, and underwear to my chest and skittered out of Graham's bedroom.

I changed into jeans and a yellow polo shirt at top speed, tied my messy curls into an even messier knot, and headed downstairs. I couldn't believe I'd overslept. I never overslept. True, I never spent the night entangled with a hot and delicious man, either. How had I not heard the alarm?

I'd always been a troubled sleeper. It was rare for me to sleep deeply, but last night had definitely been an exception. I didn't know if it was because our sexy activities had worn me out, or because being held by those strong arms had felt so good. I wondered where Graham was. He'd told me he was an early riser, but since we'd gone to bed so late last night, I'd thought he'd sleep in.

When I stepped outside, I saw that Tatiana and her assistant, Bella, were already done taking down the decorations. Their *Bridal Boutique* branded truck was almost filled to the brim with boxes.

The team for the tent was also here, and they'd already disassembled half of it. Graham was helping too. What a sight that was—arms stretched, muscles flexed. He was wearing jeans, so I couldn't make out the finer details of his ass muscles, but I knew they had to be flexed too. Why couldn't he be one of those who wore jogging clothing around his house? That tight spandex would leave nothing to the imagination. On second thought, it was better that he didn't, because Bella and Tatiana were enjoying the view as much as I was, and they didn't have to know just *how* defined and lean his muscles were.

Oh, boy! Was I really being possessive and jealous? Yes, yes I was. I'd been jealous last night when Jackie had all but climbed Graham, and my possessiveness hadn't dimmed one bit after having spent the night with him.

I cleared my throat to announce my presence.

"Morning," Graham said. When he cast his bright blue eyes on me, he took my breath away. For a moment, I forgot we weren't alone. I took in his tousled hair, his full lips. Now that I knew how soft they were, how thoroughly they explored my body, I couldn't look at them the same way.

"Hi, Lori," Tatiana said, snapping me back to reality. "Wasn't expecting to see you at all. Graham said your conference call might take all morning."

It took a second for me to understand what Tatiana meant. Graham had covered for me.

"Oh, I got lucky. Didn't take so long after all. Here, let me help you with the boxes. Sorry I couldn't help packing."

Tatiana waved her hand. Bella shrugged. "Didn't take long at all."

We loaded the last of the boxes all together. Working side by side with Graham and occasionally coming so close that I could smell his body wash was a special kind of torture. When our arms accidentally touched, a bolt of heat ran through me, spreading from the point of contact all the way to my toes. I glanced sideways at him to check if he'd felt the sizzle too, and I startled when I realized he was watching me, gaze a tad darker than before. *Oh yeah, he'd felt it too.*

After Bella and Tatiana left, Graham said, "I'm going to make some sandwiches. Want some?"

"Yes, please." I glanced at the guys who were dismantling the tent. "Don't want to leave them alone, though. If I leave them to their own devices, they'll make a mess of your yard."

Graham smiled lazily, like he knew that concern for his yard wasn't the only reason I wanted to stay out here.

"I'll bring the sandwiches out here. We'll eat together."

"Sounds great."

I tried to compose myself as he headed back to the house, but I'd suddenly developed a lazy eye. The man was truly a work of art. I might as well get my fill while I could.

I slipped into full-on planner mode once he was out of sight, and good thing I did, because one of the guys had been about to throw one of the tent poles straight onto the flower bed.

"Careful there," I admonished. "Not over the flowers. Plenty of space next to it."

Both men grunted but did as I asked. This was why I insisted on watching over the disassembly. After one of the first weddings I'd organized, I received an angry call from the mother-in-law who'd hosted the wedding on her property because two of her precious alabaster statues had been manhandled by the vendors who'd come to take back their things. I'd paid for the damages. Since then, I'd made it a point to oversee the post-wedding activities myself or have one of my assistants do it. I jumped at the sound of a low chuckle. Graham was a few feet behind, holding two plates. I relieved him of one.

"Thanks. I didn't hear you."

We moved a little farther away, between two giant palm trees, where there were two rattan armchairs and a table.

"I can't sit. Standing keeps me awake," I

informed him. I practically inhaled my sandwich while also keeping an eye on the guys as they dismantled the tent.

"That stern look is a good one on you. I like seeing you in action," Graham said.

"Policing people isn't my favorite part of the job, but you got to do what you got to do. I can't believe I overslept. Why didn't you wake me up when Tatiana arrived?" I asked, placing the empty plate on the rattan table.

"Thought you could use the extra sleep. You need to be in top form for your trip to Universal Studios."

"You're right. I don't want to be a zombie. Milo needs my full attention."

Graham placed his plate next to mine, then shifted his position until we were face-to-face and tilted his head slightly.

"What about what you need, Lori?" He dropped his gaze to my lips. Why did he have to say my name like that? "I have a good idea of what you need, and I'll give you just that."

"Is that so? Without asking me if I want it?"

"I would, but I think you're afraid to want it. Even more afraid to admit it."

Wow. His words were *so* true.

"You have me all figured out, don't you?"

"No, but I'm learning. Last night was the start." He cupped my face, brushing the corners of my mouth with his thumbs.

"I'm working," I whispered, wondering if this

would rile him up. Oh yeah, it did.

"If you say that again, I'll take you in my arms and carry you away in front of everyone."

"No, you will not."

"Try me."

"I can wrestle you, Frazier. I have three brothers," I said smugly. "I've had plenty of practice sparring with them as a kid, and I take working out seriously, so I'm in great shape to kick your ass."

He pulled me behind a palm tree.

"I'd love to see you try to wrestle me." His voice was low and a little gruff, sending a current of awareness right to my nipples. His cheeks were covered in stubble, and it made him look, if possible, even hotter.

"If we were alone, I'd sink into you right here, right now."

He kissed me then, his mouth hot and warm on mine. My body responded to him in a visceral way. I touched those fine muscles, lingering with my hands on his shoulders, then moving to his arms. Every inch of my skin seemed to come alive as this sexy and funny man did delicious things to me.

***

Graham

I tore my mouth away from hers only because I'd make a spectacle of us both if I continued.

"Let's set a date for when I can cook for you

and Milo."

She immediately tensed in my arms.

"What's wrong, Lori? Talk to me." Was she pushing me away?

"I haven't thought through how to explain all of this to Milo."

"What do you usually say when you introduce a date?"

"I haven't dated in years, Graham. Dating is daunting enough for an adult, but parading men in front of a kid is not the best idea."

It took me a few seconds to absorb what she was saying, and then I felt a wave of affection for her. Not attraction. Affection.

I'd suspected her dating life took a back seat when she said it had been a while last night, but I hadn't realized she'd meant *years*. She wasn't pushing me away. This was simply new for her. I could work with that. Fuck, I had no clue what I was doing here either. I'd stuck to superficial entanglements after my divorce, but this was something else.

The thought of letting her go was scarier than the thought of getting hurt. I was man enough to admit that. This wasn't only physical attraction. It had never been just about that. I wanted to get to know Lori better, even at the risk of getting burned. But could I risk hurting her? And her son? Elizabeth's words rang in my ears. That I hadn't been the husband she'd wished for. Could I do better? I wanted to.

"You won't be parading men," I assured her.

"Just me. I'm very territorial."

She gave me a small smile. "Milo needs stability. He gets attached to every man in his life, like my brothers, or his soccer coach. Substitutes for the father he doesn't have."

That gutted me, because… what did I know about being a father, after all? Nothing. I hadn't had stellar examples, and kids didn't come with instruction manuals. But I knew Lori was right. Stability was important.

"I understand what you're saying."

"You do?"

"Didn't have much stability myself, so yeah. I understand exactly. We both have our issues, Lori, but what we have is special."

I pulled her against me and skimmed my hands up and down the sides of her body, lingering on her delicious breasts.

"You're very convincing," she murmured, nodding. I claimed her mouth and kissed her until I felt her rise on her tiptoes. I nudged her knees open, rubbing against her. "If you keep doing that, I'll forget what I'm actually here to do," she whispered.

"That's the plan, baby."

"You make me want to be wild. But I have to go back to supervising the guys. I need to leave here in an hour."

Instead of letting her go, I kissed her again.

"What are you doing?" she muttered.

"Giving you an incentive to come back. I know how to play my cards."

"Oh yeah?"

"Yeah."

"Well, you'd better behave. I'll call you tonight after we finish at Universal Studios and we'll set up a date for that dinner. Sometime this week?"

"Okay. I'll leave you to handle things here."

I stepped back, even though those lips were tempting the hell out of me. I wanted to pull her close again and kiss her hard, lift her in my arms, and take her inside the house. I'd sink inside her before we'd even make it to the bedroom. I hadn't gotten nearly enough of this woman last night. Not just her body, but the way she'd filled my house with her laughter and her warmth. A selfish part of me regretted not keeping her up until morning. I'd wasted those last few hours sleeping instead of enjoying her.

A strong breeze came from the ocean, ruffling her hair, bringing a few strands in her face. On instinct, I pushed them away, tucking them behind her ear. Lori darted the tip of her tongue between her lips. Her nipples pushed against her shirt, suddenly greeting me. I rubbed her earlobe between my thumb and forefinger, touching her bare arm when I lowered my hand.

"Go, before I get other ideas," I said.

I shoved my free hand in my pocket to keep from touching her again. She turned around and walked toward the workers, her hips moving seductively with every step. Did she have any idea how innately sensual she was? Did she know how crazy it was driving me to let her walk away from me?

"Guys, extra care with the flowers. Please! I told you already." She was magnificent, strolling around, dishing instructions. She was a strong woman, raising her son alone, making her own way through life.

I walked back inside the house, bringing the plates to the kitchen. Looking at the counter, I smiled. We'd fought over the last bite of our snack last night. I'd let her win. I climbed the staircase, making a beeline to my bedroom. The bed was unmade, and seeing the rumpled sheets brought another smile. The house hadn't seemed too big last night with Lori in it.

I usually spent Sundays going out for a run and watching soccer games. Occasionally, I also went over pressing sponsorship contracts, but as a rule, I avoided working from home. From there, it was an easy path to becoming a workaholic, and I didn't want that kind of lifestyle. The club was rendering millions in profits the way I ran it, which was by working a solid nine to five, with the occasional phone call or meeting after hours. I didn't need or want more money.

Today, I'd broken that rule. After completing my run and watching the third quarter of the latest game, I scrolled through my e-mails, answering the most pressing ones. And I still couldn't stop thinking about Lori. Last night had been incredible. I'd effortlessly opened up to her, and I felt deep in my bones that my life was going to change in a fundamental way. I wanted to make that change. I was so deep in thoughts that I barely heard my phone buzzing. Amber's name flashed across the screen.

"You're on your honeymoon. Don't you have better things to do than call me?"

"Wanted to make sure everything went smoothly today."

"Everything's fine. You wouldn't even know there was a wedding here."

"Graham, I know I've said it before, but thanks so much for everything. And this honeymoon, you shouldn't have. It's too much."

Ah, there it was. I knew we'd been having this conversation.

"Enjoy it."

"You've been sneaky about it."

"Was the only way." I hadn't given them any details about their honeymoon, just made it sound as if they'd be getting a weeklong getaway in a spa resort in the Los Angeles area. It was half true. They were in a resort… in the Bahamas. I got to my feet and headed outside, descending on the beach.

"So, Lori's gone already?" she asked.

"Yep. Three hours ago."

"Counting the minutes too, huh?"

"That obvious?"

"Saw how you were looking at her last night, but I was too busy enjoying the spotlight to call you out on it."

"Right."

"You going to see her again?"

"Definitely."

"I sense a 'but' in your tone."

"No *buts,* only… can I ask you something? Do you think I could make a good father?" I shoved a hand in my pocket, fingering a coin I found there. My feet sank a few inches in the warm sand. For a second, all I could hear were the waves and seagulls chirping in the distance. I wondered if I'd only said that in my head. I'd never voiced that fear before.

"Graham, you're a great man. I've known you for almost twenty years. You're not like your dad or your grandfather. Get those ideas out of your head, or I'll call Gran."

The corners of my lips twitched. "Don't call Gran. She'll hand me my ass."

"And you'd deserve that for doubting yourself. We're not doomed to repeat our parents' mistakes, you know. Or I'll end up with a bad perm after the age of sixty, or a slight wine addiction. Or both. Imagine the horror."

"I already have a divorce on my resume. First move in following in the steps of my infamous forefathers."

"No. That was the wrong couple at the wrong time. You and Elizabeth weren't compatible. Sometimes it takes time to realize that. I have to go, or Matt will start wondering what I'm up to."

"Enjoy your honeymoon."

"Oh, I intend to. It's either that or feel guilty that you're spending so much money on us. I've decided to enjoy it."

"Good girl."

After saying goodbye to Amber, I sat on the sand and scrolled through the photos on my phone, pulling up the one Lori sent me, with her and Milo at the concert. That little boy had her eyes, but his hair was a light brown.

You made this little boy very happy, Lori had written after the concert. And last night, Lori had definitely had fun. But was I what they needed long-term?

Chapter Sixteen
Lori

When I arrived at Val's house, Milo begged me to stay a little longer because he hadn't finished painting. My sister was resourceful. She had him painting with a squirt gun. Seeing my son reminded me of Jeff's e-mail. I was mad at myself that I still allowed him to affect me so much.

"What are you doing with this boy? Every time I pick him up, he wants to stay longer."

"Won't give my secrets away." Val shrugged one shoulder as she went inside the house. She reappeared carrying two plates of her delicious cheesecake.

"Val, you're killing me."

"You've been on your feet all night, woman. Indulge a little. Plus, you know what Dad used to say. *Your sweatpants will never be tight if you don't wear any.*"

We sat at the wooden table in front of Val's house, watching Milo have fun.

"How was the wedding?" Val asked, twisting her hair into a loose ponytail. Even when she had no makeup and wore sweatpants and a white cotton T-shirt hanging off one shoulder, my sister was chic.

"Beautiful. I'm a little sad it's already over."

"Did something happen with Graham?"

"I slept with him," I whispered.

Val made a sound that had me worrying she'd swallowed her tongue. "Wow! I was not expecting that. How was it?"

"It was perfect. I didn't even know it could be *so good*." I laughed at Val's eager expression. I was dying to share some details, but I couldn't bring myself to talk about spicy activities with Val. I'd call Hailey later today. She'd eat it all up. I'd give her a heads-up to have popcorn ready.

"You're not going to give me any details, are you?" she asked.

"Nope."

She shook her head. "I still can't believe it."

"You put something in that perfume."

She batted her eyelashes. "That's an idea for an advertising slogan." She clapped her hands twice before drumming them on the table. My sister's mind was a dangerous place. "Oh, Lori. I'm so happy for you. You deserve this so much. "

"He's so sweet. And sexy. And perfect. He's… too much."

Val studied me while she munched on her cheesecake. "You've got it bad."

"I do," I admitted. It was scary as hell. This morning, when we'd talked so honestly, I'd been a little less scared. Now, however….

"When are you bringing him to Friday dinner?"

"What? I don't know. Why?"

"So I can check if he's got it just as bad," she said, like it was the most natural thing in the world. "Also to make it clear what's at stake here. If he hurts you, I will pummel him. I don't care that he's Jace's boss. I have moves, and I'm not afraid to use them. And Hailey can do a lot of damage with those heels. That's without even counting our brothers."

I undid my messy bun and trying to smooth my fingers through my hair. "Slow down, kick-ass lady. Don't scare him away yet. You were so laid back about it before the rehearsal dinner. Why the change of gears?"

"Well, that was before… this." She gestured at my face. "Goofy expression, dreamy eyes. This isn't just fun for you."

"You know I can kick ass too if needed, right?"

"Of course, but it never hurts to have backup. Now, let's talk about fun stuff. In the mood for some sexy lingerie shopping? I know an excellent website."

"Why are you giving me dangerous ideas while we eat cheesecake?"

"Because every dangerous idea seems like a good one when you're eating cheesecake."

I laughed, wholeheartedly agreeing. I didn't know if it was something in the cake, or the fact that sitting with my sister and eating something delicious made me relax too much, but Val had always been able to talk me into buying the craziest things over cheesecake.

"Text me the website, and maybe I'll buy

something later."

She rubbed her hands, pointing to the bench on her porch, where her laptop stood. "If you want us to look together, I won't say no."

"Nope. Punishment for giving me dangerous ideas in the first place."

Her phone chimed, and she checked it quickly. "Hailey and Jace are on their way."

"On a Sunday? How did you manage that?"

"I told her I baked a cheesecake, of course. Jace was with her, so now they're both dropping by."

They both arrived a short while later, and I instantly knew something big had happened. Hailey was radiating. Her hazel hair was styled in loose curls. She was wearing a yellow maxi dress, a denim jacket, and big silver hoops for earrings.

"What gives, sis?" Val asked. Hailey placed her hands on her hips and twirled once.

"I, fellow Connors, am no longer a business consultant. As of next week, I'll be working with a PR firm here in LA, rubbing elbows with Hollywood's best."

"Wow, congratulations," I said.

"Why didn't you say anything on Friday?" Val asked.

"I got the signed contract back this morning. Didn't want to say anything until all T's were crossed and all the I's dotted."

"You knew?" I asked Jace.

"No. Dropped by to try and talk her into brunch, and that's when I found out."

Sometimes I thought our youngest sister had come into the world with that shield of badassness wrapped tightly around her. When we were little, she'd occasionally let me actually be a bigger sister and clean her messes. As an adult, she typically never let anyone know she had a problem until she solved said problem. Case in point: she hadn't told anyone she'd even applied for this job.

I was happy Hailey had switched from consulting. The job had required her to fly out on location from Monday to Thursday, so she'd lived in LA only part time. She never missed Friday night dinners, but she was typically so exhausted that she slept through her weekends, not allowing for any shenanigans, whether of the sisterly variety or not.

"PR firm?" Val whistled with appreciation. "Hats off to you."

"It'll be a lot of fun, but also a lot of work. The rich and famous get into messes often enough. My boss said a lot of new clients come to us because they like the company's track record with getting A-listers out of hot water."

"Sounds stressful," I chimed in.

"What can I say? I thrive in high-pressure environments. And dealing with an A-list scandal is at least fun, compared to spreadsheets and PowerPoint presentations about Key Performance Indicators and Liquidity and so on."

"So… since you're be rubbing elbows with celebrities, can you get me and Val tickets to the Awards? Oscars, Emmys, Grammys?" I asked, batting my eyelashes.

"Are you kidding? Yes, yes, and yes. We've been dreaming of going to award events since we were kids. We're going even if I have to smuggle you two in."

"Atta girl," I said, hugging my baby sister at the same time as Val.

"Girls, aren't we getting a little too old for Connor sandwiches?" Hailey asked, sounding out of breath, but hugging us back just as hard. Dad had coined the term on a memorable spring morning, when he'd found all six of us trying to hug Mom.

"No, definitely not," Val said. I squished Hailey harder.

Jace watched us with a devilish grin. "Well, sister dearest, I'm happy you joined the dark side. Now I can finally let the shit hit the fan. I'll have someone to get me out of it."

"You'd better never, ever require my services, or those locks of yours will suffer," Hailey said.

"That's how they teach you to solve a crisis?"

"No. I save those techniques for people sharing my DNA."

***

Milo and I left after everyone had another slice of cheesecake, and I'd pulled Hailey aside to spill the details from last night. Milo's energy was endless. I took him to Universal Studios every few months, so I already knew the ins and outs of the place. It was crowded, but we had Front of the Line Passes. We visited our usual spots, the theme worlds of Jurassic Park and Harry Potter.

Milo's favorite attraction was the one I liked least. The Revenge of the Mummy boasted an indoor roller coaster. We went on it twice. My stomach behaved during the first ride, but lurched into my throat during the second one. It remained there even after we climbed off.

We were heading to a puppet show booth when my phone vibrated in my bag. I prayed it wasn't one of the vendors informing me some of their inventory was missing. It had happened on two occasions, and we'd never known who'd been the culprit: a staff member or a guest. Vendors liked to blame the servers, but I'd seen guests eyeing the decorations with a little too much interest. The strangest things could happen.

Speaking of strange things, my stomach cartwheeled right back into its place when I noticed Graham had sent me the message.

Graham: Lori, I can't stop thinking about you. I'd love to see you and Milo this evening and spend time with both of you. I'll probably screw up often, and I want you to tell me when I do—it's the only way I can improve. It's a leap for both of us, but I want to get to know you and Milo better.

Graham didn't wear his heart on his sleeve, so I appreciated his text even more. I tried forming a good enough answer, but my mind was blank.

Lori: I'm speechless.

Graham: :-) No pressure. It took me an hour and three drafts to write that. Are you still at Universal Studios?

Lori: Yes. We're heading to a puppet show. Taking a break from the roller coasters, thank God. I don't think my stomach will recover until dinner.

My phone buzzed again, but I couldn't read the message right away, because we'd arrived at the booth. There was a lot of commotion, with six- to-nine-year-olds crowding in front of the counter, and parents standing in the back, eyes on their offspring. Milo slipped his hand out of mine, joining the crowd of kids. Only after I stood in the back with the rest of the parents did I glance at the phone. An electrifying buzz had taken residence in my chest.

Graham: What are you doing for dinner?

The buzz extended to my fingertips. I typed back quickly, not giving myself time to overthink anything.

Lori: I was planning to take him for a burger and fries.

His answer came a minute later.

Graham: I make some mean burgers. I'm good with fries too. If you prefer, for now we can just say I'm your friend, or Jace's boss. I promise not to kiss you in front of Milo ;)

The boldness of him, I swear. I was feeling like a girl with a crush on her prom date.

Lori: We're in. Does 7 work for you? Want

to come by our house, or should we come to yours?

Could I have been more cautious? Maybe. Was there a chance this would lead to heartbreak? Definitely. But I wanted this more than I'd wanted anything in my life.

Graham: 7 is perfect. I'll come to yours. Text me the address.

Chapter Seventeen
Graham

Milo and I bonded over soccer. He'd started firing questions the second Lori opened the door. He showed no sign of stopping while they gave me a tour of the two-bedroom house. The kitchen was separated from the dining area by a sliding wall made out of stained glass.

"And I thought I'd heard every soccer-related question," Lori murmured as we took the dinner ingredients from out of the shopping bags. I only needed Lori to provide me with salt, pepper, and oil.

She smacked her forehead. "I ran out of olive oil the other day. There's a convenience store one block away."

"Want me to go?"

"Mooom, please don't make Graham go. I have to talk with him about the foul in the last game." Milo was perched on a stool, clasping the edges with both hands.

"I'll go. It's close," Lori said.

"I'll get started here."

After she left, Milo hopped off his chair, leaning against the counter while I was slicing potatoes. His soccer knowledge was impressive.

"Can I have orange juice?" he asked when he paused for a breather.

"Sure," I said automatically… but then I wondered if I should have given it more thought, because Milo kept glancing over his shoulder at the entrance door while he took the orange juice out of the fridge, as if he was sneaking around.

He put the carton back right after he poured himself a glass, which he asked me to rinse after he drank it. I became even more suspicious. Somehow, I didn't think seven-year-olds tidied up after themselves unless they wanted to cover their tracks.

"Do you go to the stadium to watch every game?" he asked.

"Not all of them. We could go together sometime. If it's okay with your mom."

"Can-I-have-popcorn-while-we-watch? And-ice-cream?" he asked, all in one breath it seemed. Were those trick questions?

I didn't know what the protocol was, but common sense dictated I should ask Lori first before committing to anything. Said common sense flew out the window when Milo put his hands together as if in a prayer. How much harm could some popcorn and ice cream do?

"Pleaaase."

Then he widened his eyes. How could I *not* say yes to that? I had to ask Lori.

"Sure."

By the time she returned, I'd already sliced all the potatoes and the oven was the right temperature.

"You've had orange juice," she exclaimed the second she saw Milo. Turning to me, she explained, "Ground rule: no sugary drinks allowed in the evening."

"Duly noted," I said.

Milo's grin was contagious. That little marauder had me in the palm of his hand. He'd charmed me faster than even his mother had.

"Milo, go wash your hands and then set the table," Lori instructed. Milo left the room without arguing. I couldn't help smiling.

The corners of Lori's mouth twitched. "He played you."

"No, he didn't." I tried to hold my ground, but hey, she'd busted me, so why not man up and admit I'd been played by a seven-year-old? "How could you tell? He put the carton back in the fridge and I washed the glass."

"Never wipes the corners of his mouth. They were a little orange."

"By the way, I also agreed to buying him ice cream and popcorn when I take you both to a game."

"I was gone fifteen minutes. How did the shit hit the fan so quickly?"

"Babe, his eyes were this wide." I held out my fingers like goggles in front of my eyes to demonstrate.

"Ah, he brought out the big guns. You'll grow immune to it."

Didn't seem likely. Milo had me wrapped around his little finger. But I didn't want to waste time challenging her assumption. I had other things on my mind. I glanced over my shoulder to confirm that Milo wasn't on his way in. We were in the clear. I backed Lori against the counter.

"What are you doing?"

"I'm about to kiss you. Have a problem with that?"

She wiggled her ass a little. "Not at all."

I brought her sweet face close to mine and sealed my mouth over hers. This was heaven. *She* was my heaven. I'd seen her this morning. How could I need her so much already? At this stage, we were just supposed to get to know each other better. I was supposed to take her out, show her and Milo a good time, but not go around promising him things, bonding with him. My rational side was warning me that I was already in too deep with Lori, that I should stomp the brakes. My instincts bulldozed over my rational side. Holding her in her kitchen and kissing her was exactly what I wanted to do.

"Stop that sound," she whispered as she pulled back.

"What sound?"

"I'm not sure. Was it a growl? Was it a groan? Sexy as hell, anyway. Makes me want to climb you."

"Jesus, Lori. How d'you expect me to control myself when you say that?"

"Maybe I don't want you to control yourself." She gave me a sassy smile, but moved away as we heard Milo gallop through the house.

"What are all those herbs for?" she asked

while Milo set the table. He was proficient enough that it was clear he did it quite often. I was impressed by Lori's education skills. You wouldn't have caught me dead doing a chore at his age.

"Thyme and oregano. They're great with fries."

"And what kind of cheese is this? Cheddar?"

"No. Something better. You'll see."

"You should be a chef," she said.

"It's my hobby."

"You're a pro at it."

"I considered going to culinary school in my twenties, after college." The buns were almost roasted. Everything else was ready.

"What made you change your mind?"

"I loved the club more than cooking. I worked there straight after college. When my grandfather died, my father took over. He'd never worked before, so he made a mess of things, nearly bankrupted the club. He convinced Nana to put up the restaurant as collateral for another debt of his. She nearly lost it. That happened about three years ago. It's when I took over, before Dad could do more damage."

"Why do I get the impression you don't get along with your dad?"

"Because I don't. I didn't get along with my grandfather either. He put Nana through a lot with his cheating. Dad didn't do much better in that department."

"How did you save the club and the

restaurant?"

I hesitated. "I had a trust fund from my grandfather. I hadn't used it before on principle, and it was enough to get out of trouble."

What was it about this woman that made opening up so effortless? I usually changed the subject when asked about this, but with Lori, I didn't want to hold back or pretend. I wanted to show her all sides of me. And if she didn't like them? Better to find out now than later.

Using my trust fund to bail out the restaurant and club had driven a deep wedge between me and Elizabeth. She didn't speak to me for five weeks after I told her.

She'd always pestered me to use the trust fund for our own benefit, even though we had more than enough money. But we'd always had wildly different opinions of what "enough" was.

"That was clever," Lori said. There was no judgment in her tone, but that could change in time. For now though, she seemed to like the man I was. It made me want to back her against that counter and kiss her until she begged for more. She winked and blew me an air kiss when Milo wasn't looking. Sassy woman. I'd show her who was in charge here as soon as dinner was over.

***

Lori

The cheese was to die for. Seriously. The fries

too. During dinner, Graham and Milo dove right back into their soccer talk. Graham answered every question in detail, and they'd been debating a penalty for the past five minutes. I loved that Graham paid attention to what Milo was saying, instead of just pretending to. People thought kids didn't notice, but they did.

"We have fries left," I announced once we'd cleared the plates.

"I want more fries," Milo said.

"Give me a minute. I have a trick." Graham rose from his chair and headed to the kitchen. I couldn't spy on what he was doing through the colored glass, but I thought I heard the oven door open and close. A few minutes later, he set fries with melted cheese on the table. They were divine.

This man was a wizard. How could he make food taste so good? We reached for them at the same time and Graham interlaced our fingers for a brief, sweet second, as if he couldn't help touching me.

"Best fries ever," Milo declared. Making me happy was nice. But making Milo smile? That was the way to my heart.

Once the last of the fries were gone, Milo started firing off questions again, but he was yawning and rubbing his eyes, signs that he was tired.

"Milo, say goodnight to Graham, then go brush your teeth and shower."

"I don't want to go to sleep yet. Graham and I are talking."

Graham grinned at me. I grinned back.

"Buddy, I'm going to leave too. I have to wake up early tomorrow, just like you. Responsible men go to bed early, so they can wake up early."

"I want to be a responsible man," Milo parroted back, squaring his shoulders and standing straighter. He bid Graham goodbye before heading to the bathroom. I started on cleaning the table, and when Graham gathered some plates, I shook my head.

"No, no. You cooked. I'm cleaning."

Graham came next to me, bringing a hand to my waist and tucking me into him. I nestled against him as best as I could. I'd been craving his nearness and his body warmth the entire evening.

"I had a great time tonight, Lori." He cupped my cheek, his fingers feeling warm against my skin.

"We had a great time too."

"You've got a lovely boy."

"Thanks."

As Graham leaned forward, Milo called from the bathroom, interrupting our moment.

"I'm going to see what he needs. His bedtime routine takes about twenty minutes."

"I'll wait."

"Are you sure?"

"Yes."

"Okay."

Milo talked nonstop.

"Graham is so cool," he said while putting on his pajamas. "He knows all about penalties. And he likes to talk. Can we have burgers with him again?"

"Yeah, we will."

"Yay!"

My heart squeezed as Milo slid under his covers. He was already starting to hero-worship Graham. Was I doing the right thing here? Risking not just my heart, but Milo's too? The two of us had achieved a precarious balance. Was I being selfish, choosing to bring someone else into our little world?

When I closed the door, Milo was already half asleep. He went out quickly, and once he fell into slumber, he slept through the night.

I closed the door connecting the corridor between the bedrooms to the living room and found Graham still in the kitchen. I joined him, sliding the stained glass wall closed too.

"He's asleep," I announced.

"That was fast."

"He's always been like that. He likes you, by the way."

"I was hoping he would. I like him too, and in the near future, I'd like for us to tell him we're dating."

"We will," I assured him.

Graham moved toward me until he stood so close to me that our chests almost touched. This man was more potent than anyone had the right to be.

He feathered his thumb across my lower lip, then my upper one, and I felt the gentle touch straight between my thighs. The world around us seemed to blur as he pulled me into a kiss. He traced my lips with the tip of his tongue before exploring my mouth. He wrapped one hand in my hair, tugging a little. A white-hot bolt of energy ran through me. I bucked my hips in reflex and discovered Graham was hard.

"See what you're doing to me, Lori?" he asked in a low, molten voice when we pulled apart.

"You're insatiable."

"No, you just have this effect on me." He kissed my forehead. "Now, be a good girl and don't tempt me."

"Or what?" I challenged. His eyes were hooded, and judging by the wood in his pants, he was close to the edge. What would he do if I pressed too much? I'd never been one to thread too close to the danger line, but Graham had this inexplicable effect on me. He made me want to dare more.

"I'll sweet talk my way into your bed."

"You think I'm that easy?" I pretended to be offended. Graham saw right through me.

"No, but I'm not the only one who wishes we could spend the night together."

Well, the jig was up. Pretending was one thing, but I didn't lie. Besides, I wanted to see his reaction when I admitted it.

"True. I keep daydreaming about tasting you… everywhere."

Graham exhaled sharply. He backed me into a corner of the kitchen, roaming his hands everywhere. God, I wanted him to touch me more. Why was I wearing so many clothes? I wanted those talented hands directly on my skin. As if reading my thoughts,

Graham snaked one hand under my sweater, then under my bra, rubbing my nipple between his fingers. I braced my palms on those strong biceps.

"I want a taste of you, Lori. And I'll have it."

He pushed my shirt up then unclasped my bra. He drew his thumb around the outer edge of my peaks before giving my nipple a lash of his tongue. I drenched my panties. He smiled against my skin.

"Does this make you wet?"

I nodded.

"Say the words. I want to hear them."

"Y-yes. It makes me wet," I stuttered in between flicks of his tongue. He pressed two fingers against the crotch of my jeans, rubbing the fabric against my sensitive skin.

"Do you want to come, Lori?"

"Oh, God, Graham. Yes."

He was moving his fingers fast, and even through the denim, every time he touched my clit, tremors spread through me. Then he took the hand away.

"Why did you stop?"

He brought his lips up to mine. "Because I want to touch your skin. I want my fingers inside you when you come."

When I felt him undo the fly of my jeans and lowering the zipper, all my nerve endings felt on fire.

"I will make you come, Lori. Hard and fast."

I clenched from his dirty words and dug my fingernails into his muscle-laced arms when he touched my center. He teased my folds first, dipping one finger in between them before nudging my clit. He was kissing my neck, nipping gently with his teeth. With his other hand, he grabbed my ass, hoisting me farther up. He moved his fingers rhythmically, rubbing me until I came apart, clinging to him, burying my face in his shoulder.

"Orgasm number one," he whispered in my ear.

"There will be more?"

In response, he slid a finger inside me, then another one, pressing the heel of his palm on my clit. I bit into his shoulder, muffling my cry. My knees nearly gave out when the second orgasm rocked through me.

"Woman, you're so sexy it's killing me."

"Mmm..." was all I could say as small tremors of aftershock spread through me. He held me for a few minutes before stepping back and washing his hands at the sink.

"Earth to Lori... everything okay?"

I nodded, still feeling a little lightheaded. "Oh yeah. Better than okay. Still on cloud nine. Might take me a while to return to earth."

"I should go." His lips opened in a gorgeous wide smile as he made his way out of the kitchen. I caught up with him in the foyer.

"Are you sure?" I moved closer, running my hand down his chest, stopping at his belt. He was still hard. Graham took my hand in his and brought it to his lips, peppering it with soft kisses.

"Yes, I'm sure. Otherwise, tomorrow

morning, you'll have to explain to Milo why I'm in your bed."

"I see. Well, have a good night. Thanks for the burgers and the fries."

"So I'm forgiven for the orange juice mishap?"

"Only if you don't do it again."

"Can't make any promises. No clue how you tell him no, especially when he looks at you with those *eyes*. He'll have me eating out of his palm for a long time. I can tell already."

Chapter Eighteen
Lori

From: Jeff Finn
To: Lori Connor
I have rights, and you know that. But I want to solve this amicably. Get in touch with me. You'll be sorry if you don't.

I'd gotten the e-mail late last night and, as a result, hadn't slept a wink. I was still fretting over it the next morning as I took Milo to school.

Usually, I dropped him off in front of the schoolyard, but today I went right along with him. He skittered to his friend Jilly the second he saw her. Ms. Higgins, the teacher, was already at her desk, so I stopped to greet her.

"Good morning, Ms. Higgins."

"Hello, Ms. Connor. To what do I owe this surprise?"

"Oh, no particular reason. Thought I'd walk with him today."

She beamed. "You have a great boy. Was the only one who got over 90 percent on the math test last week. I'll see you and your brother at Soccer Day on Wednesday?"

"Of course." I wasn't a fan of any parents' day, mostly because it brought front and center that Milo only had one parent. He never said anything, but I saw the way he looked at the other kids, and no amount of his favorite food or goofing around on my part cheered him up after that. Quality uncle time worked though, which was why I was grateful Will was joining us. Yep, I was one big cheat, but if it worked, why not?

My thoughts returned to Jeff. What did he want? He'd said he just wanted to catch up first, and now suddenly he brought up his rights?

One thing was clear, though—I couldn't ignore him anymore. I'd hoped the last e-mail was a fluke, but since he mentioned rights now, things changed. He wanted a fight? I'd give him one. He'd broken Milo's heart by not being a part of his life, and I wasn't going to let him do any more harm. I replied to his e-mail.

From: Lori Connor

To: Jeff Finn

Why are you bringing up your rights *now*? You've had no interest in Milo. Ever.

After I left the school, I hurried across town to meet one of my assistants, Molly. We were scouting new wedding locations today. The restaurant scene in LA was ever changing, and staying on top of our game required knowing the scoop on the newest wedding venues. Today, we had three promising leads. If they cut the mustard, we'd be adding them to our list. My level of enthusiasm was surprisingly low when I arrived. I loved scouting new locations, imagining how they'd look with wedding decorations, the potential happy couples. Jeff's e-mail was still looming over me.

"Hey, boss," Molly said. "I have something for you."

She pointed to the box in her hands. I didn't recognize the brand, but by the shape of the carton, there were sweet treats inside. If Molly started anticipating my needs for sugar, the girl had earned herself a raise.

"Gimme, gimme!" I took the box with grabby hands, and my mouth watered when I discovered slices of cheesecake inside.

"When did you buy these?"

"I didn't. They were delivered. Luckily I had to pick something up from the office this morning. First, I thought maybe you ordered samples, or a local business sent them of their own accord, but the delivery guy said specifically they were from Graham Frazier. Weekend went well, I take it? He was satisfied with… the wedding?"

I nodded as I helped myself to a slice of cheesecake. Goodness, this was the elixir of life, right here. Molly was eyeing the second slice, and I realized common decency dictated that I had to share. I held the carton out for her, keeping my fingers crossed that she'd decline my silent invitation. No such luck. She downed the second slice before I even finished my own. Still, even the sugar rush from one sweet treat was an excellent mood booster. *Graham had been thinking about me first thing this morning.*

I was smiling when we stepped inside the restaurant. Oh yeah, this one was a winner. I felt it in my bones from the first sweep across the room. Floor-to-ceiling windows that allowed in plenty of natural light, a spacious dance floor. They even had a fountain in the patio that would make an excellent backdrop for photos. It had all the makings of a dream location.

"Ms. Connor, Ms. Black, nice to meet you." Joanna Worthington, the location manager, strode to us, shaking our hands.

"This is lovely," I said earnestly. "Can you give us a tour?"

"Of course."

"Is it okay if I take pictures while we're at it?" Molly asked.

Joanna hesitated for a moment. "Of course."

Every restaurant had a photo gallery online, but they were often only from the best angles, and I wanted to show our clients all angles. Nothing like falling in love with a location when you looked at their website and then discovering you'd only seen the good bits. Best to know everything from the get-go. While Molly clicked off the camera, I committed to memory the numbers Joanna was rattling. I didn't like them much, but I did like the location enough to persuade her to lower them.

"I'll be honest; you're charging a lot for the menu. Even your cheapest version is fifteen percent above comparable offers."

Joanna pursed her lips. Molly hid her face behind the camera. She liked to say I had all the grace of a bulldozer when it came to pricing.

"We're committed to offering our customers the best."

A rehearsed answer, but not necessarily a bad one. It wasn't good enough either, though.

"I know as a new business, you want to break even as soon as possible. But as someone who reviews dozens of wedding menu prices a week, I can tell you that the higher prices will work against you. Now, if you were to include a few standard alcoholic beverages in that price, we could work something out."

Joanna's lips were a thin line now, but I continued before she could protest.

"I don't need an answer now. I'm going to put some new packages together this week. If I don't hear from you by Wednesday, I'm going to assume you don't want to be included."

Joanna nodded, her body language somewhat steely, but I was expecting that. Still, a little time pressure went a long way.

People took forever if they didn't have a firm deadline. I hoped Joanna would cave to my request because I loved her restaurant. If not, Molly and I would find someplace else. There were restaurants at every corner in LA; it took a lot of determination and stamina to find the best ones, and I had both in spades.

"One of these days, I'm going to film you when you go in shark mode," Molly said once we were out on the street. "You had an extra edge today. That cheesecake did the trick, huh? Or was it the man sending them?"

"Careful, Molly. Attributing my edginess to outside factors is the best way to get under my skin," I said with humor.

"Oh, but it is honest."

We headed to a small coffee shop across the strip to review the visit. I always liked to talk about a new location right after we scouted it, while the details were still fresh. The scent of baked goodies filled the air, and I smiled, remembering Molly's comment. She was right… sort of. It hadn't been the sugar that had lifted my mood so drastically, but the fact that Graham was just so unexpected in the best way. When Molly went to the restroom, I seized my chance and texted him.

Lori: The cheesecake was delicious. Thank you. To what do I owe the surprise?

Graham: I wanted you to start the week well.

Well, damn. What could I say to that? A second message popped up before I could swoon further.

Graham: And I wanted to sweeten you up so you'd say yes to a lunch date.

I laughed and checked my calendar, but it wasn't looking good. A lot of clients, current or potential, wanted lunch appointments because they could leave their workplace for an extended break.

Lori: Early afternoon snack on Wednesday or Thursday? My lunches are booked for the rest of the week.

Graham: Thursday works. I'm attending a team meeting on Wednesday.

Lori: What are we doing?

Graham: You'll see.

When Molly came back, she pointed between the phone and my face with a triumphant expression.

"If you tell me that grin is work-related, you're full of it."

I laughed, pointing at her notebook. "Molly, don't try to turn this into gossip hour."

As we went over the details we'd discussed with Joanna, my thoughts kept wandering to Graham. Yep, I wasn't too proud to admit to myself that I was daydreaming. But I was also afraid it was all too good to be true. While reviewing the photos Molly took, I chased those ugly thoughts away. He'd sent me cheesecake so I'd start my week well, and I was going to see him on Thursday. I didn't know what he'd planned, but I was determined to enjoy every glorious minute of it.

***

Over the next few days, Graham and I kept exchanging messages. One evening, after one of Jace's games, he even talked to Milo on the phone and they discussed every goal and foul.

After the school event on Wednesday morning, Will had to hurry back to the station, but we were grabbing lunch together later. As luck would have it, Val texted to ask if I wanted to eat with her, so I suggested she join us.

When we arrived at his station, it was bustling with activity, as usual. Policemen ventured in and out, and stacks of paperwork were being carried from one desk to another in the open office space.

We stood by the elevators, trying to locate our brother in the crowded room. He and his partner had a designated desk, but neither was sitting at it.

"Testosterone overload," Val whispered, gazing after a tall and handsome blond policeman. "What is it with men in uniforms?"

I elbowed her. "Why don't you find out? Bet some are single. Will would be over the moon that you're finally dating someone he's probably already researched."

Val laughed but shook her head. "I'm using enough “mind” real estate worrying about Will fighting crime; I don't want to worry about the man I'm dating too. I want to date someone with a *safe* job. Why couldn't Will take a leaf out of Jace's handbook and pick a safer career?

"But pro soccer players get in nasty accidents all the time."

"That's supposed to put my mind at ease?"

A few minutes into our wait, one of Will's coworkers, Theresa, spotted us.

"Hey, girls. Waiting for Will? He's been in the

captain's office for a while."

"Is he in trouble?" I asked.

She leaned in conspiratorially. "Not at all. Our captain wants to promote him."

"Now look at that!" Val exclaimed. "We didn't know."

Just then, Will stepped through the door at the far end of the room, waving at us and striding in our direction. Theresa took off with a wink. Val and I exchanged a glance. Yep, teasing was officially on the table.

"Sorry I kept you waiting. Captain wouldn't shut up," he said, kissing us each on the cheeks and pushing the elevator button.

"No problem. We've heard some interesting rumors," Val said.

"Which you failed to mention this morning," I continued. Will was glancing from Val to me, a smile tugging at the corners of his lips.

"Or Friday at dinner. I don't remember him mentioning he's going to be promoted," Val said.

"Hey, maybe promotion is a bad word and we don't know it."

Will was grinning openly now. "You two going to ride my ass during the entire lunch?"

"Maybe," I conceded as the elevator dinged and the doors opened.

We walked inside the elevator, and Will waited until the doors closed to speak.

"Captain's trying to persuade me. I don't think it's for me."

"Why not?" Val asked.

"I don’t like deskwork, and the promotion would come with a lot of handshaking and paperwork."

The elevator opened, and we all remained silent as we walked through the station.

When we stepped out in the blinding sun, Will continued. “I like the work in the field, catching criminals, so they’re not a danger to anyone anymore. It still eats at me that the culprit in Mom and Dad's hit and run was never caught."

Val straightened up, expelling a breath. I'd always known this was what partially motivated Will to join the police force.

No one spoke on the way to the Mexican restaurant we'd chosen as our lunch spot. I had no idea what to say, and by the looks of it, neither did Val, which was worrying. My older sister always knew what to say.

We sat in a corner of the restaurant, and a waiter took our order right away. I wanted chili con carne. Will and Val went for beef burritos.

"How was the school event today?" she asked after the waiter left.

"Same as usual," Will replied. "By the way, I overheard a conversation between Milo and another kid. Milo asked him how it felt to have a dad and said that his had left when he was little because he didn't love him and his mother."

"What?" Val and I asked at the same time. I never badmouthed Jeff in front of him. Never.

Whenever he asked about his father, I was vague on why he wasn't part of our lives.

"He must have heard us talk," my sister muttered, mirroring my thoughts. Damn it! How had I been so careless? What was going through my boy's mind? Or heart? I had half of my chili con carne left, but I all of a sudden lost my appetite.

"Jeff has sent me a couple of e-mails," I said. I shared everything with my siblings. They'd always been my rock, and I valued their advice.

"You mean beyond the yearly booty call?" Val asked through gritted teeth.

"Yes. I ignored the first e-mails, but then he said he had rights and wanted to do this amicably."

"One of these days, I'm going to find something to charge that bastard with," Will grumbled. "Or take matters into my own hands and give him *another* black eye."

"He abandoned Milo. What rights exactly does he think he has?" Val asked through gritted teeth.

"I replied and asked him just that. But he didn't reply back."

"Typical of him," Val said. "Don't lose any sleep over this. We're here for you, okay? Anything you need, tell us." Val took one of my hands in hers, as if feeling that anxiety was gnawing at me. I couldn't explain why I was nervous—legally, I had the upper hand. But a pit formed in my stomach every time I thought about the semi-threatening e-mail. After finding out Milo had overheard me insulting Jeff, I couldn't help but feel like I was failing at parenting.

"Let's circle back to the promotion," Val suggested, smiling sweetly at Will. I knew her effort was partly so she'd take my mind off my troubles. "Where the captain fails, we can succeed."

"Yeah, unlike him, we know what works on you. Also, we're related, so we have a have an ace up our sleeve—we can pull out the emotional card."

"You girls give yourselves too much credit," Will informed us.

"Might we remind you that we have a documented history of talking you into things? Remember when we convinced you to play laser tag with us after you swore you'd never do it? And we beat you?"

He slapped his forehead theatrically. "Not that again. You've been holding that over my head for too long, so I've got to come clean. I let you win that one."

I'd *suspected* that might have been the case for years now, but hearing it out loud still stung. I took great pride in our one and only victory.

Val chose the path of denial. "He's trying to save his own ego. We'll let him think we've bought it."

Chapter Nineteen
Lori

"Wait, why are we getting into your car? Are we driving somewhere? Why didn't you tell me to meet you there?" I asked when I met Graham the next day. He'd asked me to drive to the stadium, only to now inform me we were driving in his car to another location.

"Because I'm whisking you away."

"Oh." I fidgeted with my thumbs behind my back, smiling sheepishly. "Well, whisk me away, Frazier."

He pulled me flush against him, kissing me until I tingled in intimate places. Did he not know what danger an under-sexed and under-kissed woman was? He couldn't kiss me like that in public, or he was risking me jumping him like I had in that tent and my kitchen.

As we climbed into the car, I wondered if we were heading to the beach, or if he had a restaurant in mind. The truth was, it didn't matter. I was just happy to spend some time with him. We'd talked on the phone every day this week, but nothing beat admiring those fine muscles, that sculpted jaw.

"We're going to a park I love," he informed

me. I beamed, looking out through the window, at the people, the cars. I was being whisked away to a midday date in a park. Could life get better than that?

"How did it go with the new wedding location?" he asked.

"Joanna replied this morning. She agreed to my prices." I'd told him about Joanna's restaurant on the phone, and now I filled him in on the details.

"I like seeing you so excited. You light up."

I relished his compliment. We talked a little about everything until he pulled the car in front of Griffith Park.

We climbed out of the car, and he headed to the back, opening the trunk and retrieving two blankets and a huge lunchbox.

"What's in the box?" I asked.

"Our afternoon snack."

"You… prepared this?" My voice was high-pitched, but I had the strangest feeling I was actually dreaming all of this. Maybe I'd dozed off at my desk researching groom costumes for Chihuahuas.

"I did."

Graham took my hand and gave it a small squeeze, kissing my forehead. Not a dream, then. He led me through a narrow passage flanked by greenery. The smell of patchouli was thick in the warm day. The path opened up in a beautiful clearing. Enormously old California oak trees lined the other end of the clearing. This was one of my favorite parks. Central Park in New York had nothing on it. Griffith Park was five times bigger and contained some of my favorite landmarks: the Hollywood sign, Batman's cave, and even an outdoor theater.

"Let's go under those trees," Graham said.

"Sure."

He didn't let go of my hand as we crossed the clearing. I loved the feeling of my hand cocooned in his warm, much larger one. The grass was high, tickling my ankles. The only sounds surrounding us were birds chirping and the rustle of leaves. It was a sunny end of February day, which caused a conundrum. If we sat in the shade, it could become chilly, but if we sat in the sun, we'd start sweating. When we reached the trees, he laid out the blanket in the shade, pointing out that we could cover ourselves with the second blanket if needed.

"My lady, if you please."

"Why, thank you."

I sat on the blanket, stretching my legs. Graham lowered himself on his haunches, unloading the box.

"I made grilled cheese sandwiches and French pancakes with peanut butter and raisins."

"You made them?"

"Yeah."

I wouldn't have cared if he'd bought our snack from a fast food joint, but knowing he'd taken his time to prepare this made everything even more special—and surreal. Was I really here with this handsome man? Could this really be my life?

"What are you thinking about?" he asked,

sitting next to me.

"That this doesn't seem like my life," I said honestly.

"It is." He kissed the side of my head, then moved his lips lower, feathering them on my cheek before resting them on my neck. I shifted my position until my back was flat against his front.

The grilled sandwiches were delicious.

"Where did you learn to make these?" I asked after my third one. I wasn't even that hungry, but they were addictive.

"Nana's recipe."

"I'm already in love with Nana," I declared, munching happily.

"She loved showing me her recipes. Said she hadn't managed to teach my dad, but wanted to do things differently with me."

"Is *she* close to your dad now?"

I felt him go a little rigid, and regretted the question. I wanted him to open up to me, but in his own time.

"Not exactly."

"And your mom?"

"She passed away a few years ago. I wasn't too close to her either. My parents divorced when I was two years old. I lived with Dad, except summers, which I spent with Nana. Mom had visitation rights, and I saw her every other month. She remarried and had two more kids, but I'm not close to them. I've seen them a couple of times in my life."

My heart clenched for Graham the boy. I

couldn't imagine what that must have felt like.

"I'm sorry."

"I got used to her not being in my life. I missed her, but I got used to it. I overheard Dad tell Nana once that he wasn't equipped to be a single dad. I actually believe he just didn't know how to handle it. I told you not everyone was a great parent like you." He wrapped his arms a little tighter around me. Graham threaded his hand through my hair, moving it to one side and planting a kiss at the back of my neck. "I like how strong and independent you are."

"Thanks."

After finishing the sandwiches, we dug into the pancakes.

"Oh my God. You're a wizard, not a cook. Pancakes can't be this good."

Five minutes later, the pancakes were gone, and my belly was about to explode. We cleaned up with some wet wipes from my purse, and then I rested my hands on Graham's thighs, moving my palms in small circles. The sun had shifted in the sky, and so had the shade, so my feet were now lying in the sun. A gentle breeze swayed through the trees. This was heaven.

"Do you want ice cream? I hear there's a joint somewhere in the park," he said.

"Mmm, no space. Thanks to a gorgeous man, I'm already full."

Graham laughed softly in my ear. "I see. Tell me more. You like him?"

"Oh, yeah. He's quite something."

"Does he make you smile?"

"Often."

"Good. If I ever stop making you smile, I want you to tell me, okay?"

I stilled. "Why would you even say that?"

He didn't respond, so I turned around, trying to gauge his expression. His lips were set in a thin line. "Does it have to do with your divorce?"

Something flickered in his eyes, and I knew I was right. "Want to tell me about it?"

For a brief moment, I thought Graham might brush me off, but then he said, "When we divorced, Elizabeth threw it in my face that her happiness wasn't a priority for me. We were married for three years and didn't see eye-to-eye on anything. She was an aspiring actress, and I think she believed marrying me would be more glamorous. She wanted us to attend every movie-related event in town, travel constantly. I tried, in the beginning, because I knew networking was key in the industry. But I couldn't keep up with all the events, all the parties she wanted us to attend so we'd be seen by key people. And as for traveling, it started to wear me out at some point.

Eventually, she attended more and more events on her own, travelled alone. I don't blame her; it's what she wanted. But we spent more time on different continents than together. I flew to visit her every other weekend, but it wasn't the same. We were married for three years, and during the last two, I think we didn't spend more than a couple of months together."

"So things… fell apart?"

"Yes."

"Sounds like you were too different to compromise."

"You could say that. We wanted different things in life, and neither of us realized it until a few years into our marriage. Or maybe I just don't know how to do relationships right."

"I don't think that's true. You're close to Amber and Matt. You've charmed me and Milo like a pro."

I was humbled by his openness. I also didn't know what to say to reassure him. These were early days, and I didn't know him that well. Plus, I had fears of my own. Graham kissed up and down the side of my neck, but where the kisses had been light and playful before, they were more sensual now. His lips lingered longer, and when the tip of his tongue came in contact with my skin, a current of awareness zipped right through me.

"This wasn't my best idea," Graham said. It gave me immense pleasure that his voice was rougher. "Should've taken you somewhere private. We can do that now."

"I knew it. You've lured me here under the pretense of a date, when all you want is to have your wicked way with me."

"No pretense, sweetheart. I like spending time with you—talking to you, holding you. But I also like to sink deep inside you, and I won't apologize for it."

I was officially on fire. Using nothing but words, he'd transformed me into a bundle of need. I shifted on the blanket, turning so I could look at him. His gaze was molten.

"You cannot do this," I informed him.

"What?"

"Turn me on, just like that. I could teach you a lesson, you know." I moved my hands upward on his thighs, so he'd get the message. "But I'm not that cruel. I can't send you back to work with blue balls."

He threw his head back, laughing. "You're something."

"I can be a little devil," I confirmed. "You ain't seen nothing yet."

"Is that a threat?"

"Yes. Yes it is." I added a scowl to drive my point home, but Graham merely laughed again. Then he pulled me even closer in his lap, kissing me, the heat of his body seeping into mine.

Kissing like this, slow and deep, felt incredibly intimate. It was also arousing as hell. I felt every stroke of his tongue against mine between my legs.

"I cleared my afternoon," he said.

"You did?"

"Yeah. When you said you had time until five, I cleared my schedule too."

"Just for me?" I asked.

"Just for you."

Ah, hell. That made me *ridiculously* happy. He gave me a sexy kiss, pulling my ass farther into his lap until we were grinding against each other. I was so hot for him that I felt I was going to break out of my skin. He was hard, and his fingers kneaded my ass cheeks possessively over my dress. He skimmed his fingers up my body, laying them at the sides of my neck. He kissed one corner of my mouth then moved to the other.

"How about we move this party to my house?" I whispered, shuddering.

"I love your ideas, baby."

***

Graham

"All for us!" Lori exclaimed when we stepped inside her house, twirling once. I loved her energy. I loved everything about this woman. I tucked her to my side and kissed her neck, inhaling her subtle citrus smell before descending to her shoulder.

"I could do this all afternoon." I traced her collarbone with my fingers, then skimmed my palm down her arms, feeling her skin turn to goose bumps under my touch.

"I think some other parts of me need your attention too."

"I think *you* need to learn the value of patience." I moved on to her other side, nuzzling her neck with my nose, then repeating the movement with open-mouthed kisses.

Lori cinched her dress up, revealing more of her legs… and then garters. *Fuck, fuck, fuck.* She was wearing garters all this time? I swallowed, fighting the urge to tear off all her clothes right this instant.

"You were saying about patience?" Lori whispered seductively, pressing her ass against my erection.

"I'm starting to think you planned to seduce me from the get-go."

Lori laughed softly, then yelped as I scooped her into my arms. "Oh, I like this."

I carried her to her bedroom, setting her back on her feet at the side of the bed. I pushed away her dress straps, pressing my thumbs over her bare shoulders. I wanted her bad. I wanted her now. She stepped out of my reach, lowering the zipper on her side. A growl tore from me.

"You're driving me crazy."

"You're responsible for making me rediscover my inner seductress. Now you have to suffer the consequences."

"Lori…" I said warningly, but she held up her finger.

"I want to show them to you. Sit on the bed."

I growled again, more desperately, but sat.

She pushed her dress down as slowly as she could, revealing a sexy outfit one inch at a time. She was fucking out-of-this-world sexy in those stockings.

"Come closer," I beckoned. When she didn't move, I said in a gruffer voice, "Come here. I need to touch you."

I opened my legs wide, and she stepped between them. I ran my fingers up and down her thighs.

"You bought these for me?"

"Well… I liked them. And I thought you'd like them too."

I moved one hand between her thighs, stroking two fingers over the scrap of fabric covering her entrance. Her knees buckled. She was aroused. I could feel it through the panties.

"You're beautiful, Lori." A black scarf hanging from the open door of her dresser caught my attention. It looked like silk. “Close your eyes.”

“Why?”

“Just close them.”

I rose from the bed, taking the scarf in my hands, coming up behind Lori. I pushed her hair to one side, running the scarf along her spine. She arched forward.

“What is that? What are you—”

“Shhh… enjoy it. And keep your eyes closed.”

I ran my hands over the cups of the bra, then undid the clasp in the center. I lavished her breasts with attention as soon as I freed them, all the while teasing her skin with the scarf: her forearms, her chest. Between her thighs. She didn’t know where I’d touch next, or where I’d lick. Her chest rose and fell with labored breathing, not only from arousal, but also anticipation.

I pushed her panties down, kneading that gorgeous ass of hers. I lowered her with her back on the bed, then took off my clothes as fast as possible. Lori let her bare thighs fall open invitingly. This woman was all mine.

I rolled a condom on before lowering myself on the bed. I gripped myself at the base, but instead of sliding inside her, I rubbed the tip against her clit. She jackknifed. A shot of energy so intense zipped through me I could swear my heart stopped for a second. I teased her nipples, alternating between a touch with the scarf and a lick until she was thrashing around.

"Can I open my eyes now?" she asked shyly.

"No. I'll tell you when you can."

Then I flipped her over on her belly, kissing down her spine, biting her ass gently, running my finger between the cheeks. She moaned in the pillow, tugging at the sheets. I spread her thighs wider, settling between them and lowering my head until it was level with her ass and pussy. Then I swiped my tongue over her folds until she exploded. I loved turning her wild.

"This was so good," she murmured.

"We're not done. You can open your eyes now."

I flipped her again then pulled her on top, so she was straddling my thighs. Cupping her ass, I lowered her on my cock.

"Oh, Graham, this is…." Her words faded on a gasp.

"This feels so damn good. I'm never letting you out of this bedroom."

She laughed, holding onto me. "Love that plan."

Our rhythm was fast and desperate, and I was touching every inch of her I could reach. I needed more. I was insatiable today.

"Baby, I need to fuck you hard," I rasped.

"Yes."

The wild came out in both of us then. I kept her hips up, moving into her from below, watching her beautiful breasts shift on every thrust. Her clit was colliding with my pubic bone, and she was so near to a climax that her legs were shaking. She was squeezing me tight, and I went in deeper, faster.

"Harder," she urged, exploding with pleasure when I obliged her. I thrust inside her through my orgasm, coming apart too. I wanted all she had to give. Then I kissed her, gently laying her on the bed.

"Did I hurt you?" I asked, only now realizing how rough I'd been.

"No."

"I was rough."

"I liked it."

"I didn't mean to be like that."

"You couldn't resist, huh? I loved it." I knew she meant it.

We showered, and when we left the bathroom, both clad in robes, Lori asked over her shoulder, "Do you mind if I put on some music?" she asked.

"Not at all."

Lori clicked a remote, and a slow song started blaring through the sound system in the living room. She swayed her head and neck to the easy rhythm. I pulled her to me, taking one of her small hands in mine and bringing my other hand to her waist. I swayed us both to the slow beat of the music.

I caught her dreamy smile when she glanced at the huge folder titled Wedding Portfolio on the coffee table. It brought back bitter memories for me, but I tried not to show it. She'd pick up on it, and I didn't want to get into it right now. I'd shared with her a lot today about my family and my marriage, and I was still feeling raw from it.

"This afternoon is the best," she whispered, looking up at me with so much warmth you'd think I was laying the world at her feet. This simple afternoon was making me immensely happy, and she seemed happy too. I was hoping, at least. I wanted this woman's affection. It scared me how much I craved it already, because it made me feel exposed. But that look in her eyes right there… I wanted more of it. Which was why, instead of taking things slow, I asked, "Do you have plans tonight?"

"Not beyond picking up Milo and bringing him back here."

"Let's do that together."

She hesitated, and I held my breath until she nodded. "Okay. What are you doing tomorrow evening?"

"I'm meeting some sponsors. Why?"

"My family gets together every Friday for dinner. Think you could come by next week?"

I loved spending time with her and Milo, so why not meet the rest of the family too?

I tucked a strand of hair behind her ear. "Definitely. I'd love to come with you."

"It's better that you won't be here for this one, actually. I'm going to tell them about us. I mean the girls know, but my brothers don't."

"Sounds like a plan." We hadn't talked about when to break the news to those close to us, but I'd already told the three people I cared about most that I was dating Lori.

"Nana, Matt, and Amber already know about us."

"And your dad?"

"I'll tell him next time we talk, but we don't have that kind of relationship."

"Sorry I'm being so nosy. I can't help thinking what a pity it is that you aren't closer. My parents passed away in a car accident when I was a kid, and I still miss them."

I held her closer, feeling her go soft in my arms.

"I'm sorry. Honestly, I wouldn't know how to build a relationship with him. After the fiasco at the club, we drifted apart even more. We speak once a month when I send him an allowance."

"Oh?"

"I promised to send him money if he in turn promised not to ask Nana for it. It also gives me some peace of mind, knowing he's set up financially. Means he can't get in trouble."

I knew she was tight with her siblings, and I hoped she wouldn't think I was a heartless bastard for keeping my father at arm's length. But her eyes didn't hold judgment, just warmth and empathy. I could learn a thing or ten from Lori, and I was looking forward to it. I twirled her once, and the tie around her robe loosened a bit. I saw my chance and unfastened it completely.

"What did you do that for?" she asked.

"You're so beautiful. Shame to cover you up." I switched up our dancing position, wrapping my hands around her waist, pulling her close enough that her breasts were pressing against my chest. Her nipples puckered when I lowered my hands to her ass.

"You're so good with your hands," she murmured. I lowered myself until I was level with her breast and drew a circle with my tongue around her nipple. Her hips surged forward. "You're good with your mouth too."

Straightening up, I captured her mouth. Her eyes flared when I pulled back.

"You bring out all my unladylike instincts," she said, bringing her hand to the tie of my robe and pulling at it.

"I like those instincts very much. I like everything about you."

"Is that so? Well, I love your mouth and hands. Haven't decided about the rest." She lowered her hand to cup my cock, stroking me up and down. "Love this too."

"You're still sore from earlier." I exhaled through gritted teeth, trying to keep my composure, but the movement of her hand was driving me crazy with lust.

"The good kind of sore, though."

"Still, what kind of man would I be if I seduced you now?"

She rose on her tiptoes, kissing my jaw. "The kind who liked the first time so much that he wants seconds? Don't worry. Your conscience will remain intact, because *I* am going to seduce *you.*"

"Give me your best, my lady."

Chapter Twenty
Lori

I planned to break the news to my brothers as soon as possible the next evening, because three of our Bennett cousins were also joining us, and I wanted to have *the talk* before they arrived.

Milo saved me the trouble. While Val told us the burgers were almost done, my son informed everyone how delicious Graham's fries and burgers had been. I supposed I should have considered myself lucky he didn't spill the beans to Will at the school event.

For a split second, you could hear a pin drop in my sister's dining room. Then Jace said, "Graham, as in Graham Frazier?"

"Your boss," Milo confirmed before I could even open my mouth.

"Sweetie, why don't you go wash your hands? They're dirty from playing outside," I said.

"But Uncle Jace and Will played too," Milo protested. For some reason, he considered washing hands a tragedy.

"They'll be washing their hands too," Val assured him. "After you."

"Told you," Will told Jace once my son was out of earshot. "She had that look last week, and on Wednesday."

"What look?"

"I believe you usually call it *gooey eyes*," Will said, with a fake shudder on the last two words.

"We're your brothers, not your next door neighbors," Jace informed me. "We can read through the lines. Damn, Will. All the responsibility is on you and Landon. I can't deck him… technically. But if he messes up, I'll forget he's my boss."

Landon shook his head. "Leave me out of your plans."

Will clapped a hand on Jace's shoulder. "Don't worry; I have your back. Have the police force on my side. I can think of worse things than speeding tickets if he messes with Lori and Milo."

I glanced at my sisters. "Help. How do we make them stop?"

Val shook her head. "No point. Let them get those brotherly instincts out of their system."

Landon nodded, and Maddie snickered. She and Landon might be married, but she still wasn't used to the madness that could be Friday night dinners.

"Can you look him up in your database or something?" Jace asked Will. "Check if he has any skeletons?"

Will seemed to seriously consider it, so I put my foot down.

"No, no he cannot," I said loudly. "Really,

Will. You can't abuse the system just because you're on the police force. You're not supposed to use the resources for your personal issues."

"You know me. I like to break the rules for a good cause."

The conversation changed course when Milo returned.

After dinner, I pulled Jace to the side. "I know Graham is your boss."

"He's my boss only in a manner of speaking. Honestly, I see the coach as my boss, not Graham. As long as I keep performing on the field, everything is fine. This isn't bothering me. I hope he treats you right."

"He does."

"Good."

"You'll be civil when I bring him over to dinner next Friday, right?"

Jace grinned. "Civil is my middle name."

Our Bennett cousins arrived shortly afterward, and we tabled the discussion. When Sebastian, Logan, and Blake stepped inside my sister's house, I kissed their cheeks and gave them a hug too, for good measure.

"Well, hello there, dearest Bennetts," Val said. As we all sat at the dining room table, she went on, "To what do we owe the pleasure of your visit?"

"We're changing the distributor in this area," Sebastian explained. He was the CEO of Bennett Enterprises, and Logan the CFO.

"Always good to meet them in person," Logan added.

"I just tagged along to annoy them." Blake leaned back in his chair, wiggling his eyebrows. Then he added, "Kidding. Alice and I want to franchise the restaurant business, and we had some interest here in LA."

"Impressive," I remarked. Blake and his sister Alice owned several locations in San Francisco.

Hailey parked a hand on her hip, tapping her foot. "So no one came just to visit us?"

Val waved her hand. "Never mind, we'll pretend you did. So, what's new in the family? Anyone popping out more babies? It's baby factory over there in Bennettland."

"Nadine is pregnant," Logan announced, referring to his wife. For some reason, he looked very, very smug. Hmm… interesting. All the men in their family had some mighty great egos, but I knew there was something more to Logan's smile. Sebastian shook his head, smiling, and Blake was semiglaring at Logan.

It took me a second to understand what was going on as I recalled a funny conversation from Landon's wedding.

"That's right. You two were in competition with each other for who'd have a second kid first," I said.

Logan's smile turned, if possible, even smugger.

"Well, Blake. Looks like you lost," I

continued, trying to contain my laughter.

Blake didn't seem fazed. "Clara and I aren't in a hurry. And Logan already lost the competition with Sebastian. He just chose an easy prey to compete with." Oh, yeah. The game was on. Now Blake was smug and Logan was glaring.

"I'm still in the competition," Sebastian declared.

I cleared my throat. "I remember Ava saying she was happy to stop at four."

Sebastian's lips twitched in amusement. "But my convincing prowess is unmatched."

Everyone laughed at that, and we chit-chatted about the entire family while we ate.

"Oh, by the way, Pippa has her eyes on you two." Blake pointed between Jace and Will.

"I knew it," I exclaimed. Their sister Pippa was an excellent matchmaker.

Will chuckled, turning to Jace. "We kind of got the gist of that at Landon's wedding. Nothing came out of her matchmaking attempts."

"Have you met Pippa? Failure doesn't discourage her. If anything, she'll try harder," Sebastian explained.

Will blinked. Jace ran a hand through his hair, looking somewhere between alarmed and amused. Closer to alarmed.

"We should give Pippa pointers," Hailey said conversationally.

Val nodded. "You're right. That would improve her chances of success."

Will turned to the girls. "You're not supposed to be on Pippa's side."

"She's family," Hailey protested.

"So what are Jace and I? Doormen?" Will gave our baby sister his most impressive I'm-a-detective stare. As usual, it achieved nothing.

"If it helps, I think Will's the next victim," Blake went on.

Jace fist-bumped the air. "Excellent news."

Will glared at him, and Jace had the grace to turn his shit-eating grin into an apologetic smirk.

"Sorry, buddy, but better you than me."

"I need backup here, not to be stabbed in the back."

Jace seemed to consider this. "Yeah, but if I do that, then I'll go down with you too."

"I always look out for both of us," Will insisted.

"These are just my self-preservation skills at work. As a cop, you should be proud."

Will remained dangerously silent. I could practically hear the wheels spinning in his mind. Oh, yeah. He was plotting his revenge, but it would take a while. That was okay. Brotherly revenge was best served after one put a lot of time and consideration in it.

"So, how come Pippa doesn't have her eyes on Val and Hailey? They're single," Will said.

Val explained that Pippa had said she'd done her best work on her brothers.

"I'd like to point out that I didn't need much

help," Blake said. "I knew a good thing when I saw it right off the bat, as opposed to these two." He threw his thumb in Logan and Sebastian's direction.

"So, basically, Will is toast." Jace was gloating a little too much.

Will surprised everyone by replying, "Well, she can have a go at it. I'm not opposed to a relationship, just haven't found the right person."

Well, damn. Honesty worked better than revenge.

Jace jerked his head back. "Are you telling me I'm about to lose my best wingman soon?"

"I'm sure your teammates can pick up the slack."

"Yeah, but as I said. You're the best."

It was time I added gasoline to the fire.

"Pippa and I should go into business. A joint venture of sorts. She match makes, I organize the wedding. She sells the couple engagement and wedding rings. It all comes full circle."

Hailey chuckled. Val was laughing openly, and Will's smile was even smugger than Logan's had been earlier. Jace was glaring at me.

I loved Friday dinners.

***

The next Friday, I was on pins and needles as Milo, Graham, and I arrived at Val's house, but I seemed to be the only nervous one. Milo and Graham were chatting about the dribbling video they'd watched when Graham was at our house. He'd joined us on some evenings, though he hadn't stayed overnight yet.

All my siblings were already there and we got introductions out of the way fairly quickly.

"Graham, I hope you like casserole." Val threw her thumb over her shoulder in the direction of the kitchen.

"I eat anything. Lori said you're an excellent cook."

Val was already succumbing to Graham's charm. "It's going to take another twenty minutes for it to be ready."

"Girls, how about some wine before?" Will asked, dangling a bottle of Merlot in front of us.

"Yes," Hailey, Val, and I said in unison.

Landon set a hand on his wife's shoulder. "Sparkling water for you?"

Maddie sighed, rubbing her baby bump. I couldn't wait for the baby to be born. The girls and I sat on Val's couch while Will poured us wine. Then he joined the guys. The lot of them, Milo included, started setting the table. To my astonishment, Graham joined them.

"Graham, you're a guest," I said loudly. "Come here and relax."

"I'm glad to do my part in earning my dinner."

"I like him," Hailey whispered.

"Me too," Maddie said in a barely audible tone.

"I'm joining the fan club, but why are we

whispering?" Val added.

Will cleared his throat. "Girls, are you just going to sit there, drink wine, and gossip the entire time?"

Hailey swirled her wineglass before raising it to her lips. "Yep. Excellent plan, wouldn't you say?"

"Think twice before you disagree, or I won't be feeding you," Val warned. That shut Will up. Jace, who'd opened his mouth, closed it. No one wanted to miss out on Val's casserole. Hailey and I would clean up after dinner. We had a mutual understanding: since Val insisted on cooking, the rest of us took turns setting the table and cleaning up.

Graham joked with my brothers, fitting in. Milo usually followed around one of my brothers, but tonight, he was glued to Graham's side. My boy was falling hard for him. I'd explained in kid's terms that Graham and I were dating, and his first question had been, "So we'll eat burgers and fries again?" I took it as a good omen.

"Earth to Lori!" Hailey waved her hand in front of me.

"Sorry, I drifted off. You were saying?"

"The event company my agency works with doesn't have time to take on a birthday party one of our clients wants to throw in three weeks on Thursday. I suggested your planning services. I know I should have asked before, but it was a spur of the moment thing. Are you interested?" When she mentioned the name of the client, my jaw dropped. He was a huge movie star.

"A Hollywood event? Wow. Of course I'm interested. We have other events that day, but my assistants can take care of them by themselves." I had full confidence in Molly, Valery, and Rose. This would be my first Hollywood event.

"Perfect. We'll coordinate our schedules and have a first meeting next week."

"Thanks!"

"By the way, the guy is as sexy in real life as he is on screen. Here, I've got some snapshots."

We gathered around her, peeking at her phone.

"Definitely sexy material here," I agreed. From somewhere in front of us came a low sound, like a growl. Graham was standing in front of us, feet apart, one brow cocked, bottle of wine in his hand. He'd clearly come to refill our glasses.

"Who's sexy?" he demanded.

"A movie star," I responded, at the same time Hailey said, "Her next potential client."

"He's got nothing on you though," I added quickly, trying to assess that glint in his eyes. Naughty for sure… but also feral. I felt delicious tingles *everywhere*.

"We'll talk about that later." His voice sounded a little rough, like he was trying to disguise yet another growl. *Oh la la.* I foresaw some sexy activities in the *very* near future.

After pouring us wine, Graham returned to the guys.

Val blew out a breath. "On a heat level from

one to ten, I assume bedroom gymnastics are somewhere at twenty?"

Ah, I could have mercy on Val, but where would be the fun in that? I might not feel comfortable sharing sexy details with her, but I could definitely confirm her question. Hailey and Maddie were looking at me with equal enthusiasm.

I nodded once, rubbing my hands together wickedly and wiggling my eyebrows. They got the message. Nonverbal communication was second nature in the Connor household, what with a seven-year-old running around. Plus, certain conversations were not meant to be carried out loud when the room was so full of testosterone.

I observed Graham over the rim of my glass, drinking *him* in. He was wearing a white polo shirt that stretched over his muscular torso. The sleeves cut right into his mouth-watering biceps. His abs weren't visible, even though the shirt fit him snugly, but I knew they were there, mine to explore later.

Val's casserole was delicious. She made it from one of Dad's old recipes, and it included peas and garlic, as well as caramelized onions. The vapors wafting around the dining table were enough to make one salivate.

After dinner, Hailey and I cleared the table. While we were loading the dishwasher, she asked me about Jeff. Val had filled her in about his semi-threatening e-mail. After I replied to Jeff's e-mail, I'd expected him to explain his request. Instead, he simply said he wanted to meet when he'd be in town in a couple of weeks, because he preferred to talk face-to-face.

"He's got some nerve," Hailey said.

"Who's got some nerve?" Graham's voice came from behind us, startling us. He was carrying some glasses, which Hailey stacked in the dishwasher.

"Milo's father," I whispered.

"You're in contact with him?"

"Not exactly. He e-mailed me. I ignored him at first, but he kept insisting, so I replied. He says he wants to meet in a few weeks when he'll be in LA."

"Don't worry, sis. We have your back," Hailey said. Graham drew his brows together. He looked… mad. My insides churned. Why was he mad?

Chapter Twenty-One
Graham

Milo fell asleep on the drive to Lori's house. We didn't wake him up when we arrived. He rested his head on my shoulder when I scooped him up, and he didn't even budge while I carried him to his bed. He was the cutest kid.

There was no reason for me to linger in Lori's living room afterward. We'd agreed that it was too early for me to spend the night here, even though I wanted to. We were meeting tomorrow morning, and I'd scheduled a phone call with Nana in ten minutes, but I didn't want to leave yet.

"What's wrong?" she asked.

"Nothing."

"That's not true. You've been different since after dinner."

She'd caught on to that? I'd been hoping she wouldn't. I wanted to let the issue slide away, mostly because I wasn't sure exactly why this was bothering me so much.

"Graham?"

"Why didn't you tell me your ex contacted you?"

"I don't know; I didn't think about it."

"You told your entire family, but not me."

"Of course I told my family," Lori said slowly, as if she didn't understand where I was going with this. If I was honest, neither was I. I felt out of my depths, and I wasn't used to this feeling. "I tell them everything. It's second nature to me."

"But telling *me* isn't."

"Graham, we've known each for—"

"Almost two months." My voice came out harsher than I'd expected. "I didn't know you two were in contact."

"We aren't. He e-mails once a year when he's here on a conference or something, and I turn him down."

"You *turn him down*? You mean he wants to hook up with you?"

"Keep your voice down," she said through gritted teeth. I hadn't even realized I'd raised my voice. Fuck, what if I'd woken Milo up? I ran a hand through my hair, processing this and trying to remain calm. But I wasn't calm, damn it. Was this a red flag? I'd taken a giant leap of faith here. If she didn't want to share things with me, was I just being a fool?

Then Nana called, at nine o'clock on the dot as we'd agreed. "You should take that."

"We're not done here."

"We can continue this lovely conversation tomorrow. *If* you think you can keep your voice down."

I'd pissed her off, damn it. And I didn't have my temper under control, which was why I nodded and let myself out of her house. I answered the phone as I climbed in my car. I'd driven here.

"Hi, Nana!"

"What crawled up your ass?"

I chuckled, feeling myself calm down. Nana knew me like the back of her hand. Of course she'd picked up on my tone. I relayed my conversation with Lori to her, because frankly, I could use some perspective.

"Graham, I see her point. You've known each other for a couple of months, but she's been a single mother for seven years. It makes sense she'd tell her family. I'm guessing she doesn't know how to... accommodate you in her life. Work together. Don't insist on why she didn't tell you. Make her understand why *you* want to know."

"What if I'm taking things too fast?"

"You have been impulsive since you were a little boy, but your impulses have mostly led you in the right direction."

"Except for my marriage."

"That's why I said mostly. But what you've got going with Lori, it's good for you. I can hear it in your voice."

"I fucked up in there. I raised my voice... she got mad." In the darkness and quiet of the car, things began to clear up.

"We all make mistakes from time to time. It's important to learn from them."

"Any other advice?"

"Pay attention to the little things. It's always

the little things that make us feel appreciated. Sharing the workload in the house. A surprise dinner. A message during the day asking how our day is going. Men think it takes the world to keep women happy, but the truth is, it's simple. Bring her and the boy here. I want to meet them."

I saw my chance then and there. "You'll have to fly to LA for that."

"Don't think I don't know what you're doing, young man. I know your tricks."

"Not a trick. Just using my cards right."

"Why are you so stubborn in getting me there?"

"Because when you retire, it would give me great piece of mind if you'd move here. Can I get you to at least consider that?"

"I'll find myself a nice nursing home when I feel like it."

"I wouldn't let you go to a nursing home!"

"I'll have you know they're not such bad places. Sophie and Annabelle showed me some pamphlets. If you've got a nice group there, it feels like you're in a camp."

Sophie and Annabelle were part of her posse, which was comprised of a dozen geriatrics in total. I wouldn't admit it even under torture, but they were an intimidating bunch. I knew there was no point insisting on the topic of the nursing home right now. I'd circle around to it another time; try another angle.

We talked for about ten minutes, and afterward, I sat in the car for five more, contemplating my next move. I wanted to fix things with Lori tonight.

***

I knocked at her front door. The light in the living room was still on, so I knew she hadn't gone to sleep. When she opened the door, she eyed me warily.

"You want to fight some more? At least tell me exactly why we're fighting."

"I'm sorry for my outburst earlier. Jesus, I don't want to fight. I want to know these things so I can protect you and Milo. I want to be important to you." That was the crux of it, I realized. Her green eyes softened. I seized the chance and moved closer to her.

"You are important," she whispered. "I'm just not used to sharing my life with anyone outside my family."

I kissed the tip of her nose, and moved to kiss one eyelid, then the other, feeling tension seep out of her.

"Want to talk about him? I think if I knew more, I'd understand better."

She nodded, leading us both to her couch.

"I met him when were in med school. I got pregnant accidentally. He wasn't thrilled, but for a while, it seemed things would work out. But when it came down to making plans for the future, he said he couldn't do this, that he wanted to focus on his medical career and broke up with me. And he did his med school in LA, only moved for residency. When Milo was about a year old, Jeff called me. I foolishly thought he wanted to make amends, but he wanted to get laid and thought I'd fall for it."

"If I ever meet the guy, I'll give him a black eye."

"I'm not going to hold you back. Can I ask you something?"

“Sure.”

“Are you in contact with your ex-wife?”

“No. Last time we spoke was at our divorce hearing. She moved to London after that, and neither of us wanted to stay in touch.”

“Okay.”

"So you wanted to be a doctor. Found out something else about you today."

"I did. But it wasn't doable with a baby. All those long hours at school, then the residency… so I switched gears."

"How did you come up with event planning?"

"Well, I’d always liked it. After our parents passed away, each of us was trying to do their bit in… you know… keeping the household together. Landon and Val were taking care of us while also running the pub we’d inherited and taking classes at a local college. Jace and Hailey were young. Will was watching us when Val and Landon weren't home. They didn't have time to deal with celebrations, so I started to as a teenager. Christmas, New Year, Easter, St. Patrick's Day, Fourth of July. Name any celebration, I was your girl."

"I see."

"Fun fact: if you ever plan a surprise party, don't tell Hailey. She can't keep a secret to save her life."

"Duly noted."

"So event planning sounded appealing. It was flexible, required no start-up capital. Now, I can't even imagine doing anything else."

"You're an extraordinary woman."

She shrugged. "I'm just like everyone else. I have my good days and my bad days."

"See? I need to know these things, so I can help you relax."

She laughed, snuggling closer to me. I buried my nose in her hair, breathing in her scent. It felt like home.

"You were doing fine with the grilled cheese sandwiches and the pancakes. Feel free to treat me to them anytime. How about tomorrow morning?"

"Is this your way of asking me to spend the night?"

She pulled back, poking my chest. "You're going to make me say it, aren't you?"

"Absolutely. You have no idea the kick I'll get out of it."

"What if I refuse?"

"You know how convincing I can be."

Leaning in closer, I feathered my lips over hers, skimming my hands down to her neck, pressing my thumbs over her sweet spots.

"If you do that, what I say doesn't count."

"Doesn't it?" I dragged my nose up and down her neck, moving my hands down to her chest. She growled softly when I drew small circles around the tips of her breasts.

"Will you spend the night?"

"I'll gladly accept your invitation."

I held her close and kissed her hard, happy we'd passed this milestone in our relationship. Lori crossed her legs around my middle, and I rose from the couch, carrying her through the house to her bedroom.

"I don't remember saying you'd be staying in my bedroom," she teased. I lowered her onto my body until her center touched my erection. She gave a little gasp, pushing her hips forward.

"I'm taking my chances."

"That wasn't an invitation." She tried to glare at me.

I kissed the tip of her nose. "Could have fooled me."

When we reached her bedroom, I closed the door behind us.

"Lock it," she whispered. "Just in case."

"And here I thought you were serious about banishing me to the couch." Chuckling, I locked the door, then focused on Lori, kissing one corner of her mouth, then the other before tracing her lower lip with the tip of my tongue. She shuddered as I lowered her feet to the floor.

"You have the sweetest lips, Lori. You know

where I want them tonight?"

"All over you?" Her tone was seductive and playful in equal measure.

"That's right, baby. But first, I'll drive you crazy. Turn around."

"Why?"

"You'll see. Turn around."

She swirled around, facing the bed. I lowered the zipper on her dress, letting the fabric fall to her feet. Her underwear landed on the floor next.

I brought her hands behind her, holding her wrists captive with my left hand.

"Graham," she whispered when I brought my right hand to her breasts and stroked her nipples. She tried to wiggle her hands free.

I brought my lips to her ear. "If you do that, I'll stop touching you."

She went still… until I moved my attention lower. I rubbed her clit in circles until she rose on her toes then rocked back on her heels. I couldn't get enough of her. I skimmed my hands down the back of her thighs, then on her inner thighs on my way up, dipping my thumb inside her opening. Then I followed that pattern with my tongue, until she broke out in goose bumps.

Turning her around, I kneeled in front of her, pulling her sensitive flesh between my lips and working her into a frenzy. I hooked one of her legs over my shoulder for better access, cupping her ass in my free hand, supporting her. She nearly rode me when she climaxed. It was fucking beautiful, the way she trusted me, the way she let loose. I kissed up her belly.

"Graham, I feel like I'm about to come out of my skin." I bit her shoulder lightly, moving my fingers over her folds, working her into a frenzy again. She rid me of my clothes so fast she almost tore a button off my shirt. Lori wrapped her hand around my cock, squeezing me good. Then she licked across the length, drawing circles with her tongue on the crown. I was painfully hard, and I needed to bury myself inside her.

I pulled out of her mouth, sliding on a condom, then laid her on her back on the bed, keeping her ass at the edge, placing both her ankles on my shoulder. I was standing, knees bent slightly, and pushed inside her.

"Fuck, Lori. This is so beautiful." I looked between us, at our union. I slid out and then back again slowly, watching her take me in, feeling her clench around me. She gyrated her hips, and I slammed into her harder, faster. Her body was a work of art, arching on my thrusts. I'd never tire of her. She was trying to be silent, pressing her lips together. But her groans were guttural, and the sound of skin slapping against skin surrounded us. When I felt her tighten around me, she brought a pillow close to her, turned her head, and bit into it. While she was still shaking with the aftershocks of the orgasm, I pulled out and flipped her around so she was on all fours.

“I'm not done exploring you tonight.”

I kissed along her back, nipping at her soft skin, kneading her ass cheeks in my palms before moving to drum my fingers on her inner thighs. My erection was rubbing between her thighs. When she pushed toward me, I entered her in one swift move. She was deliciously tight. I moved in and out slowly, working her up to another orgasm. When I saw her move one hand between her legs, I swatted it away, leaning over her until my chest was against her back.

“Don’t touch yourself.”

“Graham, please. When can I come again?”

I spoke against the back of her neck. “When I *make* you come.”

She spasmed around me, spurring me to move faster, love her harder. When I was close to climax, I brought my hand to her clit. She exploded, and I came so hard that my vision blurred.

After I took care of the condom, we fell onto the bed, regaining our breaths. Lying next to her, I pulled her in my arms. She peppered light kisses on my chest, laying her cheek right over my heart.

"It beats so fast," she murmured. We were silent for a long time, just enjoying each other.

After a while, she asked, "What did you think about the dinner tonight?"

"It was great meeting all of them. And I'll give credit where credit is due. Val is the best cook."

"I'd love to see you two in a competition. *Chef Graham* vs *Chef Valentina*." She twirled a blonde lock around her finger.

"We could whip up one for Christmas."

She stopped in the act of playing with her hair. Her gaze searched me, as if she wasn't expecting me to think that far ahead. I was surprising myself too, because I usually didn't. But how about her? My stomach was tight as a marine knot.

"I'd love to see that."

The knot loosened. I kissed her forehead and murmured a confession. "Tonight, I thought about my dad. Trying to patch things up, see if there's a basis on which to build a relationship."

"The Connor clan made quite an impression on you, huh?"

"Yeah." Sitting there, surrounded by the family, it was impossible not to think about Dad.

"Anything I can do to help?"

"I think I have to figure this out on my own. As a kid, I spent a lot of time with sitters. He was around more when I was a teenager, but I was too busy rebelling. I still blamed him for Mom leaving, and it didn't help that our house was a revolving door for his dates. Things cooled off completely when I went to college, and then became very tense when he got the club into trouble."

"Well, Dad used to say, 'Where there's a will, there's a way,' so I'm sure you'll figure it out."

I liked her vote of confidence. We talked about my dad for a little while longer, and then showered together. After we finished, Lori hovered in the bathroom, throwing me furtive glances.

"Are you waiting for me to leave?" I asked her.

She blushed. “Yes. I have to do some girl stuff, apply body oil, face cream.”

"Watching you oil up sounds like fun."

"Men." She practically shoved me out of the bathroom.

"What can you do? We're simple creatures."

"I'll lock myself in."

"I can pick locks."

"Wow. Will is going to be pleased to know I'm dating someone with that skill." She pointed at me. "Don't pick the lock. Trust me."

As I heard the door lock, I went to the bedroom, put my jeans on, and then headed for a glass of water. In the hall, I started to whistle before catching myself—what if the sound woke up Milo? I peeked into his bedroom to make sure he was okay. The little dude slept like a rock, hugging his pillow. All good here. I went into the kitchen and downed a glass of water.

Later, after Lori fell asleep in my arms, I wondered what exactly we'd tell Milo in the morning to explain my stay, but I shouldn't have worried. The little guy's only question when Lori told him that I spent the night was if I could teach him how to make grilled cheese sandwiches.

“You bet I can, buddy.”

“Awesome.”

“Well, since you two have breakfast covered, I'll be a lady of leisure and just watch you,” Lori said.

We spent the entire day together, heading to the zoo, and then to a movie. Watching Milo and

Lori together, I kept thinking about her ex. I didn't know what his intentions were, but I wouldn't allow him to hurt Milo and Lori more than he already had.

Chapter Twenty-Two
Lori

On the morning of my meeting at Hailey's agency, I arrived in my office to find a bouquet of flowers and a note.

For good luck. I'm sure you'll win them over.

Love,
Graham

I held the note to my chest, already feeling like I had this in the bag. I made a mental note to surprise Graham with dinner when he returned from his trip. The team was playing in Miami, and he'd flown with them to talk to local sponsors. I'd take a trip to the lingerie store before too. He'd definitely appreciated the goodies last time, but I didn't want to wait for an online order to ship. I picked up the wedding invitations I wanted to show the bride I was meeting this afternoon and then headed out.

It was the second week of March, and I'd always thought the city started feeling more alive around this time of the year. Tourists started pouring in, and even the locals seemed different. Even though the weather didn't vary too much between the winter and spring months, I think the psychological factor played a role. *Winter is finally over.*

Since Hailey's offices were in Beverly Hills, I was wearing a black pencil skirt, red silk blouse, and black peep-toes. I looked like I was heading to a cocktail party, but on this side of LA, *overdressed* was the universal dress code.

"Lori, I think this will work out just fine," Cameron Salvatore said two hours later, checking his watch. He was Hailey's boss, and we were currently in his office. I'd pitched him my idea and had named my price, and he'd agreed so fast it confirmed what Hailey had told me in private: I was way too cheap for Hollywood. She insisted I charge more, but I hadn't wanted to seem greedy, or like I was taking advantage because Hailey was my sister. Besides, why should I charge more than usual?

"You've got yourself a deal, Cameron."

"Hailey will be your contact person, of course, but feel free to e-mail me too if you need more assistance."

"I'll keep that in mind."

We shook hands, and as my sister and I left his office, I felt the familiar thrum of adrenaline take over. This would be my first Hollywood event, and I loved a good challenge. It was out of my comfort zone, but I loved pushing myself.

"Want a tour?" Hailey said, rubbing her palms

together.

"Sure."

We walked along the various cubicles and offices, all decorated in a blend of crisp white with sharp, dark lines. Pictures of celebrities adorned the walls.

"Have all these been the agency's clients?" I asked.

"No, but Cameron likes to play *as if*. He hung pictures of everyone whose handprints are on the Walk of Fame. Says it sets the right mood."

"He's smart."

Hailey nodded. "He is."

She introduced me to several of her coworkers, and I took in the atmosphere. Once I'd visited Hailey at her old workplace. Everyone there had looked on the verge of a breakdown. I had no idea how she'd managed in that environment for so many years, but Hailey was a tough cookie. Here, it was clear that they all worked at a frantic pace, but everyone had a smile for my sister. I knew this place would be good for Hailey because she was radiating in a way I hadn't seen her in a while. Her old job had been sucking the soul out of her. Here, she was appreciated.

"Want some coffee?" she asked.

"Sure."

The coffee station was encased in glass walls, so we had a view of the entire entrance area, which was decorated with new-age paintings and Greek god statues. Interesting mix.

Hailey poured us both coffee, and then we clinked our mugs.

"To the Connor girls taking over the world," Hailey said.

"Hear, hear. Thanks for arranging this meeting."

"No problem. Now all I have to do is get a celebrity to endorse Val's perfumes, and we're golden. World, watch out: we're taking you by storm."

I laughed. "You have it all planned out?"

"World domination? Since I was eight years old. Granted, I thought all I needed was Superman's cape or Wonder Woman's tiara back then, but my plan's more realistic now. Goal is the same."

"Dad used to say that." His words suddenly echoed in my mind. "If the plan's not working, change the plan. Not the goal. I didn't think you'd remember that. You were so young."

"And Dad's words were gospel." He loved to regale us with stories from his childhood, and of how he'd wanted to emigrate from Ireland to the States since he was a kid, the determination it took to succeed.

"But if Val wanted a celebrity to advertise her lines, she could probably pay one. Here's an idea. Bring it up Friday at dinner. Landon would be all over it. He's been trying to convince Val to take him up on the financing offer for ages."

Hailey lifted a brow. "And risk Val murdering me in my sleep? No, thanks. Besides, it's not the same thing. I'm not talking about paid advertisement. I'm talking about a celebrity trying on her stuff and then bragging about it all over social media—"

"Or in an interview." I realized what she was getting at. "It's different when they mention something casually and you can tell they really mean it, or when they talk about it because they're paid."

"Exactly. They have to try the stuff *casually*. And who better than yours truly to make it happen?"

"Hear, hear."

Hailey nodded with conviction, tapping her foot against the floor. She was wearing black peep-toes with a three-inch heel. I remembered she had a date this evening, and this was definitely not her date style.

"You have your date shoes tucked away somewhere for tonight?"

She grimaced. "I cancelled the date. Turns out he's engaged. Looked him up on Facebook."

"Yuck. Hate guys like him."

"Oh, but get this. He was angry with me for searching him up online. I mean, how dare I, right?"

"Want to come by for dinner tonight? Share a bottle of Pinot?"

My sisters and I had a wine system: Chardonnay to celebrate, Pinot Noir to drown our sorrows.

"Not worth wasting Pinot on him. But I won't say no to hanging out with you. Don't you have plans with Graham?"

"He's in Miami with the team." I sipped more

coffee, thinking about the past days with him. He spent the weekend with Milo and me, and Monday and yesterday night as well. Yesterday evening, he took me out on a date while Marlene, one of the mothers I run with twice a week, watched Milo at her house.

"What's wrong?"

I looked over my cup to notice my sister studying me. I might as well fess up. "Well, let's just say sometimes I wish I had your dating experience, assholes and all. I feel so out of my depths when it comes to this. Before Graham, it had been seven years. I actually spent more years *not dating* than dating. Last Friday when we returned from dinner, Graham pushed me to open up, questioned why I hadn't told him about Jeff. At first, I was mad, but then I was glad he did it. I realized I needed to be pushed, or I'd stay in the cocoon I've created for myself, and that can't be healthy for a relationship."

"You're going to figure things out," she assured me gently. My hope was that Graham wouldn't get tired of pushing. "Lori, trust me. You'll get the hang of this. You're the bravest person I know."

I blinked. "Me?"

"Yeah. I remember when you got pregnant. I was scared shitless *for* you. But were you scared? No. You calmly told Val and Landon that you couldn't go through with med school, but that you'd already thought of an alternative plan."

"You weren't there," I replied. Truth be told, I

had been *terrified*, but making plans had actually helped deal with the fear.

"Jace and I eavesdropped. Will pretended he wasn't listening, but I know he was."

"Of course."

"My point is, you know how to figure stuff out. Here are a few rules. Enjoy the time with your man. Don't feel guilty about taking time for yourself, and don't overthink everything."

That caught me off guard. "How do you know I was going to do that?"

"Because I know you. And it's my duty as your sister to tell you that you deserve to have a good time, with a good man. And Graham seems like a really good man."

"He is." In fact, his attention for me and Milo overwhelmed me a little.

Hailey patted my arm. "Glad we're on the same page. So don't be afraid to let yourself be swept away by him, okay?"

"I'm not afraid… so much anymore. Okay, I am. A bit. Great pep talk."

"Call me whenever you need one." She checked her smartphone. "I've got a call with a client in ten minutes. I should go prepare. See you tonight?"

"Absolutely."

***

When Hailey came over that evening, we

chatted until it was almost morning and made plans for a girls' night out with Val, which we managed to pull off a week later. Graham said he'd love to spend the time after dinner with Milo, and I wasn't going to lie, I was a little nervous leaving the boys on their own for the first time, but it made sense. Graham came over for dinner, and he was spending the night at my house anyway.

I met my sisters at Hailey's house. Will was also there, having just dropped off some supplies Hailey needed for light renovations.

"What are you girls up to?" Will asked.

We tried to tone down our we're-up-to-no-good expressions. We failed.

"Preparing for a girls' night out," Val said casually.

Will looked between us. "Should I keep my phone on hand?"

Hailey sighed dramatically. "One time. You came to our rescue one time, and you'll hold it over our heads forever."

Will was now sporting a shit-eating grin. "It's one of the small pleasures in life. The only weapon I have against you."

"We'll behave," I promised, even though we probably wouldn't. What could I say? We Connor girls liked to have our fun, and we hadn't had a night out in almost two years, what with Hailey's constant traveling.

We were absolute knockouts, if I said so myself. I wore a little black dress, and my hair was in an asymmetric braid. I'd tried to let it loose, but I looked as if I'd electrocuted myself. Val rocked a red strapless dress that showed off her legs, and Hailey wore denim shorts and a silk blouse that showed off one shoulder.

Tonight was ours.

We headed to an open-air bar in the Santa Monica area and congratulated ourselves for choosing a weeknight to go out because we easily found seats at a high, round, bar table right next to the waterfront. LA was party central, especially once spring rolled in, but if you knew where to go, you could always find places that weren't crowded. Since I kept a close eye on venues of all kind, gems like this one didn't escape my radar. The air was salty, the breeze chilly, and I was out with both of my sisters. After this, I was going home to a god of a man filling my bed. Life couldn't get better than this.

"I'm buying the drinks tonight," Hailey announced. "Are we starting with cocktails?"

We perused the menu and decided tonight would be screwdriver night.

While we waited for our order, we all put our phones on silent. It was one of our oldest rules, both for girls' nights and for Friday dinners: no phones. Otherwise the temptation to check a new message or e-mail was still there. It was hard to disconnect, especially since it seemed to be expected of us to be available almost twelve hours a day, despite working in different fields.

I discovered I had a text message from

Graham.

Graham: Can't wait to sink inside you later tonight. Want to know what else I'll do to you?

There was a second message too, because he'd apparently interpreted my silence as Yes.

Graham: I'll spread you wide and lick your clit until you come apart.

This man. Why was he sexting with me when I was out with my sisters? I typed back quickly.

Lori: Turning me on when I'm out in public is just mean. But I'll get my revenge later tonight. I'm turning my phone on airplane mode now. It's a girls' night out rule.

I slipped the phone in my purse, or I wouldn't be able to resist the temptation of sexting with him.

"We're not allowed to think about meetings or to-do-lists or the million things we didn't get to do today, okay?" Val asked.

Hailey and I nodded.

"To Hailey being back. We've missed you, girl," Val said when we got our cocktails and held up her glass.

"I've missed you too."

We barely clinked glasses when three guys approached us.

"What are you celebrating, ladies? Can we join in on the fun?" one of them asked.

Hailey answered right away. "Sorry, but this is a testosterone-free area. It's girls' night."

The guy smirked. "We can buy your drinks."

"We can buy our own drinks," Val said smoothly. "It's a closed party."

The guys shrugged, and finally left. "That was quick," I pointed out.

Hailey patted Val on the shoulder. "She had her scary face on."

"What do you mean? I don't have a scary face."

I laughed. "Yeah, you do. It works miracles, so don't overthink it."

Two cocktail rounds later, the party was on.

"You have to tell us your secret," Val insisted, referring to Hailey's ability to walk in sky-high stilettos for hours at a time.

"No secret. Just gritting my teeth through the pain. Eventually you don't feel it anymore."

"Do you think that if we get her properly drunk, she'll finally tell us the truth?" I asked Val.

"Nah, I think it's time to accept she might have superhuman powers."

We ordered another round, and I couldn't help but notice that one of the guys who'd approached us at first was glancing at Hailey regularly.

"Hotshot there can't take his eyes off you, Hailey," I said.

"I know. But he won't be doing more than looking. I dipped my toe in the LA dating pool last week and got burned on hot lava, so I'm just going to enjoy spending time with you girls tonight."

Val pulled her in a half hug. "LA is a tough

dating scene."

Hailey scrunched up her nose. "I dated while I was on location with projects, and I can confidently say dating isn't easy anywhere."

"That's very encouraging," Val said seriously. Or as seriously as she could after a few screwdrivers.

Hailey held up a shaky finger. Or maybe her finger wasn't shaking, but I was seeing double. No way to tell.

"Let's make a pact. That we'll move in together when we're old and wrinkly if we're still single. I can't become an old cat lady. I don't like cats."

Val blinked. "You're talking too fast. Did we have the same number of cocktails?"

"Yep. My tolerance is higher."

"More proof that you're not actually human."

"About the pact?" Hailey urged.

"I'm in. I'll massage your abused feet, you'll make sure I don't forget my teeth prosthesis around the house. I'm banking on your superhuman brain to be functioning better than mine."

I chuckled, and they both turned to me.

"Don't laugh at us poor souls just because you have a man who looks at you as if you walk on water, and he's skilled in bed," Val admonished.

My brain felt like mush, but… "I'm pretty sure I never talked to you about Graham's skills in bed." Then it dawned on me. I pounced on Hailey. "You tell Val what I tell you?"

"Someone has to."

I pressed the heels of my palms against my eyes, laughing. Oh, why wasn't I surprised?

One round of cocktails later, we'd officially reached our limit and were planning to head home.

"Should we call Will, just to troll him?" Hailey said with an eyebrow wiggle.

Val seemed to seriously consider it, but I still remembered what had happened last time we'd had that brilliant idea.

"Girls, should I remind you what happened last time we pulled this prank? We almost gave him white hair."

Will had offered to drive us home, and since we were opportunistic brats, we took him up on it. When he'd arrived, some guys were getting too friendly. Will flexed some of those over-protective brotherly muscles.

"Oh, yeah, you're right," Hailey said, as if only now remembering. "How about Jace?"

Val shook her head. "Nah, this isn't the place for him or he'll get ambushed by people asking for his pic or autograph."

We ended up parting ways in front of the bar, each hopping into an Uber. I relaxed in the back as the car took me home to Graham and Milo. I hadn't felt happier in my entire life. The house was quiet when I arrived, even though it was a little past midnight. I checked on Milo, who was sound asleep, then went in my bedroom, dropping my clothes on the floor and slipping in bed next to Graham, who was also fast asleep. Unfortunately for him, I was in no mood for sleeping. Plus, I was hot and bothered, just from watching him all gorgeous and muscly in my bed. I appreciated the view. It would be a pity not to show him how appreciative I was, right? I didn't think he'd mind, so I threw the covers to one side. I worked on him with my mouth. I'd barely licked him twice before he woke up.

"Lori!" he groaned, rolling his hips in my direction. "You're home."

"Yep. And I'm up to no good."

He looked straight at me while I took him in my mouth, bobbing my head up and down. Then he switched things up, pinning me against the mattress with his body.

He kissed my mouth, and I knew he could taste himself and the alcohol.

"You've had a few cocktails, haven't you?"

"More than a few."

"So I'd be taking advantage of you."

"I'm begging you to."

"Begging me?" He smiled against my lips, sliding his knee between my legs, parting my thighs. "In that case, how could I deny you?"

Chapter Twenty-Three
Graham

"Calendars are here," Amber's voice resounded throughout the corridors of the club as she made the rounds.

"Are you happy with them?" I asked when she barreled in my office, carrying a stack of calendars.

She pushed one into my hand. "Absolutely. Don't tell any of the boys on the team I've said this, but you're hotter than all of them."

Charity or not, taking my shirt off for this wasn't my brightest idea.

"They won't hear anything from me. By the way, I want you to expand on the benefits of the calendar in the club's quarterly planning session next week."

“Sure. Want to grab dinner? Matt’s picking me up in an hour.”

“Can’t.”

"Plans with Lori?"

"Milo. I'm picking him up from school and spending the afternoon with him. Lori has to work tonight." She had her Hollywood event this evening, and I offered to watch Milo. We had a lot of fun when Lori went out with the girls.

Amber nodded appreciatively. "I like the sound of that. I'm so glad you're giving this thing with Lori a real chance. After your divorce, I thought you'd be a serial dater until you got old, and then I'd have to deal with your grumpy ass."

I chuckled, shaking my head. Then a realization hit me out of the blue, shocking the hell out of me. For the past two years, I hadn't wanted to give my future much thought—probably because I agreed with Amber that I'd end up a grumpy, old sack of bones and still going out on meaningless dates. But now, I was cautiously optimistic about my future, hoping Lori and Milo would be in it.

"Your concern for my well-being is touching."

"Well, what are friends for? I haven't seen you this happy even when you were married."

I pondered her words, then realized the explanation was simple. "That's because I wasn't."

Elizabeth and I spent half the time fighting to reach a middle ground on anything, and most of our compromises made neither of us happy. Amber smiled at me. She and Matt had been wary of Elizabeth from the start, pointing out that we were too different.

"I'm happy for you, Graham. I'll let you get back to what you were doing. Need to get these to the boys. Practice should be over soon."

After Amber left, I turned my attention to the issue I'd been putting off all day—calling my father.

Almost three weeks had passed since my first Friday dinner with the Connor clan. When I sent him the last monthly payment, I tried to talk to him for longer than five minutes. He'd seemed pleasantly surprised even though it had been awkward as fuck, mostly because we hadn't had a real conversation in years. Now I was debating calling him, even though it wasn't the time for a monthly payment. After debating with myself for a few more minutes, I finally bit the bullet and dialed his number.

"Hey! How have things been?" I asked as he picked up.

"Graham? That you?"

"Yes."

"Your number's hidden. Did anything happen?"

"No, I just thought I'd touch base."

"Okay."

An awkward pause followed. Yeah, this wasn't getting easier.

"Where are you?"

"I landed in London. I'll fly back next week." He'd always been a globetrotter, so this came as no surprise.

"Passing through LA any time soon? We could watch a game together."

Another awkward pause followed, but he actually did sound animated when he said, "I can do that. I know the team's schedule and when they're playing at home."

"Let me know when you're in town."

"Will do. How's the weather there?"

"Sunny. London?"

"It's raining cats and dogs, like the English like to say."

Talking about the weather wasn't much, but we had to start somewhere. We exchanged some more pleasantries before ending the call. I was wondering when our conversations would stop feeling like pulling teeth.

It was time to pick up Milo, so I left the club. I almost stuffed the calendar in a trashcan, then thought better of it. I knew someone would have a field day with it, so I put it on the passenger seat.

Milo was waiting along with a few other kids in the small yard in front of the school building when I arrived.

"What do you want to do, buddy? It's just the two of us today," I asked as soon as I strapped him in the car.

"I get to choose what we do?"

"Yes."

His face morphed into a strange expression, like he couldn't believe his luck. He and Lori had loved testing out new restaurants with me, so I thought he might go with that.

"Can we go to the toy store?" he asked.

"Sure. Does it have a name?"

"Simba's."

I googled the address, then used the GPS app on my phone for directions. Milo chatted my ear off the entire drive, informing me about the toys of all his classmates.

Simba's was hands down the equivalent of nirvana for a kid. Milo's expression was priceless. I felt like I was reverting to my seven-year-old self too. It had a warehouse feel to it, with rows upon rows stocked chock-full of toys.

"Can I have this truck?" He pointed to a miniature red truck.

"Sure."

He placed it inside the small cart I was pushing. Ten feet later, his eyes went wide, his little mouth formed an O when we came to a stop in front of an assembly of superhero figurines.

"Look at Thor," he said excitedly. "And Captain America."

"I'm Team Iron Man."

Milo took each figurine in his hands, inspecting it before putting it back.

"Do you want one of each so you have the entire collection?"

"All of them?"

"Sure, buddy. Buy whatever you want."

I realized something was amiss when his eyes went wider than I'd ever seen them. Did Lori have some sort of rule about how many toys he was allowed to buy? I had to remember to ask her… for another trip. No way was I letting the kid down now. We loaded one of each in the cart and moved forward, coming to a stop only a few feet later. Milo pointed to a fire truck. His eyes went wide again, and suspicion gnawed at me. I was being played. I was sure of it. But I still nodded.

The section of outdoor entertainment came up next. We were surrounded by slides, swings, and tents. Milo inspected a small tent, which didn't seem suited for any sort of camping. The slightest wind could blow it away. A family of three was inspecting the tent next to us, and when they moved away, Milo immediately pointed to it.

"Can I have a tent in my room?" he asked. That was where saying yes to everything got me.

"Would your mother be okay with that?"

Milo averted his gaze, which was answer enough. The tent was small enough to fit. I was pretty sure Lori would hand me my ass for this, but when Milo sighed and cast those green eyes at me, I knew there was no way I'd say no.

"Okay. We're taking this, but then we're heading straight home, okay?"

That grin right there? Yeah, it was worth it.

"*Yes!* Wow. I will have a tent. I will be an actual explorer. Maybe my uncles will help me build it."

"I can help you."

"Really? Like a real dad?"

Wham. My chest twisted, and then twisted again. What was I doing, playing at being a father? I had no idea how to be one. What if I screwed this up? The better question was, what were the odds that I wasn't going to screw this up? But when this little boy smiled at me, I wanted to be everything he needed. I made myself a promise, right there and then, not to disappoint Lori and Milo.

I ruffled his hair, lowering myself on my haunches.

"Exactly. I'll build it with you. Do you know if your mom has a toolbox?"

"Yes. Uncle Will brought us a new one last year. I know where we keep it."

"Okay, buddy. Let's take everything home and I'll help you build it."

Like a real dad.

***

Turned out we'd both miscalculated. The tent didn't fit in his room, so we set it up in the living room. I hadn't manned up enough to send Lori a picture yet.

"You're the best explorer," Milo declared after we pretended to light a campfire in the living room. The fire was pretend, but the mess we'd made wasn't. We brought in twigs and leaves, and cleaning up was torture, because we dragged in dirt too.

"Do you have homework?" I inquired after we cleaned up as best as we could.

"Yes."

"Let's take a look at it."

"Do we have to?"

"If we want your mom to allow me to watch you again, yes."

Milo practically ran to his room, returning with a book and a notebook. We settled on the floor, and he showed me his math homework.

I'd saved a soccer club from bankruptcy and turned it profitable, and I'd minored in engineering. Surely a second grade math problem couldn't stump me? Except it did. Not so much the problem itself, but the way of presenting the solution. It was a simple geometry question, but explaining it to a second grader was different than explaining it to an older student. I spent twenty minutes on Google and thirty on YouTube until I understood what I had to explain.

"Milo, we've earned an ice cream," I announced once we were done.

"We're allowed ice cream for dinner?" The excitement in his voice was contagious. Shit. I definitely remembered a rule about sugar and evening, but I chose to fake selective memory loss just this once.

Chapter Twenty-Four
Lori

"I get now why planners charge three times their normal rate for celebrity events. It's because you do three times the work," I told Hailey the second she picked up. I was driving home from the birthday party, and she'd asked me to call after the event was over. "But it was exciting."

"Exciting enough to do it again?"

"Absolutely. But I'm going to rethink my rates."

I'd been running around like a crazy person ever since I took on the event. I'd realized this birthday party would be more work than even a wedding from the first meeting. By the time they changed the theme for the third time, I understood why the previous planner had bailed. I wouldn't lie; the thought crossed my mind too. But I didn't want to put Hailey in a bad position, and I made a point of seeing through what I started. Besides, if I wanted to work more celebrity events, I had to get used to the grind. Now, however, I was ready to sleep for a week.

"Do that. I told Cameron you've given us an introductory rate anyway, so he's going to expect a price raise."

"Okay. Thanks."

"I'm so happy I found this job, Lori. I'd forgotten what it was like to actually live in my house. I'm planning some changes around here."

"Oh?"

"A new coat of paint. A shoe closet."

"Wanna organize a Connor day at your house? We can bring sandwiches and do a group job of it."

"Nah, job is not that big. Though I was thinking about calling our brothers. Not sure which one to torture."

"How about all three?"

"Oh, you're giving me dangerous ideas."

"That's what older sisters are for. What are you up to tonight?"

"Netflix and a glass of wine. Not like others, who've got a sexy man waiting for them at home. Enjoy him."

"Oh, I will. And I plan to be very thorough about it."

I arrived at home shortly after finishing the conversation with my sister. Just seeing Graham's car parked in front of my house made my insides flutter, even though it scared me how much this felt like we were a family. What scared me even more was how much I wanted it.

When I opened the front door, my jaw dropped. There was a tent in my living room. *A tent.* I swept my gaze around the room, almost afraid of what else I'd find, and my chest warmed when I saw both Graham and Milo sprawled on the couch, *sleeping.* They looked so cute that I wanted to wake them up just to snuggle them. Tiptoeing around the room, I started picking up some toys that were sprawled around.

"You're back," Graham whispered, startling me. He glanced at Milo, who seemed sound asleep. "Let's not wake him."

"I'll carry him to his room," Graham offered. Milo slept like a rock while Graham took him in his arms. We tucked him in together, then returned to the living room, where I came face-to-face with the tent again.

"How did this happen?" I inquired.

"Simba's."

"Oh, God. What else did you buy?"

"Just superhero figurines and the tent. And a truck… and a fire truck." He was so sexy, walking barefoot around my house. His jeans were low on his hips, and a white T-shirt with short sleeves covered his torso. It was the kind he wore under his shirts—snug enough for every delicious inch of him to be on display. I had a prime view of his mouth-watering oblique muscles. Devouring him had to wait, though.

"You have to learn to tell him no. He's playing you."

"I know. But by the time I realized it, it was too late. And where's the fun in saying no?"

"So how much fun did you have, exactly?"

"We went crazy at Simba's, came back to build the tent, did some math homework, and went for ice cream."

"Wait, math?"

"Yup. Had to search for tutorials on the Internet. Haven't felt so stupid since I failed introductory engineering in college. But the Internet saved my ass."

Wow. I was too stunned to say anything more than, "Thanks for spending time with him."

"I loved it."

"Well, now I am going to look after you."

I felt him wrap his arms around me from behind. He spun me around until we were facing each other. I rose on my tiptoes and kissed his chin. On a feisty whim, I scratched him with my teeth a bit. Graham pulled back, then crushed his mouth to mine. I couldn't even begin to describe the feelings I had for this man, but I planned to show him, and to make him as happy as possible.

"I'm so lucky to have you and Milo in my life," he whispered in between kisses. That caught me off guard because as far as I was concerned, it was the other way around.

"That's true for us too."

Graham had slipped so easily into our lives that I was afraid he'd slip out just as easily, and my feelings for him were stronger every day. I'd never stood a chance. Who would? Look at those dimples, and the baby blue eyes. And that smile, huh? Who wouldn't fall for that? Well, I hoped that no one other than me did, because I was not going to share him. Nope, Graham Frazier was all for me. Anyone wanting a piece of him would see me in full catfight mode. I went to set my phone on airplane mode, so no messages from bridezillas or other customers would interrupt our time together. I groaned when I noticed an e-mail from Jeff.

From: Jeff Finn
To: Lori Connor
I'm in LA next week. Let's meet for dinner.

"What's wrong?" Graham asked. I showed him the e-mail, and his nostrils flared when he read it.

"I'm going to give a friend of mine a quick call, okay? She's a lawyer and I want her take on this."

He nodded curtly. I felt him pace the room while I called my friend Bridget, expelling a relieved breath when she answered. In quick words, I told her about Jeff's past e-mails, and asked if she thought meeting with him was a bad idea.

"In my experience, these types of calls come when the party is regretful or looking to make amends. I think you should meet him and keep an open mind."

"An open mind?" It sounded easy in theory, but he'd hurt us both so much.

"Yes. Go to that meeting; see what he wants."

"Okay, I'll arrange a meeting via e-mail. The least contact I have with him, the better."

"Let me know if there is anything else I can do."

After hanging up, I tossed the phone on my couch and massaged my temples. Graham was watching me intently.

"Lori?"

"My lawyer thinks I should meet with Jeff."

I paced around the living room, trying to shake off the growing unease.

"Lori, talk to me. I want to know what's going through your mind right now."

"I don't even know."

"What are you afraid of?" he asked softly.

"What if he's interested in Milo after all this time? Could he take him away?"

Logically, the fear was irrational. But I wasn't feeling rational. I was scared.

"No! Hell no, he couldn't. We wouldn't let that happen."

We.

"I mean, he's never even paid child support, so I can hold that over his head."

"I'm coming with you to meet him. We'll go together and see what he has to say."

"That isn't a good idea. You don't know each other."

"So what? When someone bothers my girlfriend, I want to be by her side. Unless you don't think I belong there." Graham's eyes were steely with determination, his jaw clenched. God, the last thing I wanted was to hurt him.

"Of course you belong there."

He looked at me like I was his to protect. Like he wouldn't take no for an answer. He came right up to me, wrapping me in those strong arms. Feeling him pressed up to me melted away some of that anxiety.

"We'll go together," I said.

He tightened his arms around me and brought his mouth down on me. His tongue teased my lips, and I parted them instantly, welcoming his heat. The contact electrified me to the tips of my fingers and toes. I braced my palms on his broad shoulders, then smoothed them down his chest, tracing the dents between his muscles. Would I ever be able to be around him and not touch him shamelessly? All evidence suggested the answer was *hell no*.

"I have something for you," he murmured when we came up for air. He let me go, went to the foyer, and returned with a calendar. I held out my grabby hands when I realized it was the team's calendar.

"Gimme, gimme. I didn't know it was out. Which month is yours?"

"March."

I flipped to March, and my knees went weak. He looked absolutely mouth-watering. With his shirt off, held in one hand over his shoulder in a casual way. His chin was dipped slightly, his gaze cast in the distance.

I groaned. "Now the whole country will know how hot you are."

"No worries, baby. You're the only one who can touch me."

"I should get started on that, right? Why salivate at the photo when I have the model in front of me?"

"As I said, I like how your mind works."

I took one last look at the calendar before tucking it away on a bookshelf. I smiled when I felt Graham's hands on my hips, turning me around to face him.

He took my face in his hands, whispering, “I love you, baby.”

***

Graham

I felt her tense, and my gut clenched. I hadn't premeditated saying it, but now that I did, I didn't want to take the words back. But my gut clenched tighter when Lori looked at me with uncertainty. Had this been too fast? Damn it, that was how I felt, and I saw no reason to hold back. I took it as a good sign that she wasn't pushing me away, but I didn't like the stiffness in her posture. "You're amazing, and I feel so close to you that I don't want to be without you."

"That's so sweet." She swallowed, and I could swear I felt her becoming tinier by the second, like she was folding in on herself. I kissed her hard, hoping she felt the same way about me. I wanted her love—I needed it. There were no two ways about it.

"Can you say it again?" she whispered when I

moved my lips to her cheek.

It dawned on me that she wasn't used to hearing the words—at least not from anyone she wasn't related to.

"I love you, Lori Connor." I peppered her neck with kisses. "You deserve to be loved." I moved to her cheek, and repeated, "You deserve to be loved." I took a deep breath and went on. "If you don't feel the same, I don't want to rush you. I'm okay with whatever you can give me right now. But I at least want to know if you imagine you could love me one day."

I wasn't sure what I'd do if she said no. Part of me wanted to take anything she had to give me, but if she didn't see this going where I did….

"I do love you. I just… I hadn't expected this."

She ensnared me in the circle of her arms, crushing her lips to mine. Something seemed to expand in my chest as relief and joy overwhelmed me. I felt Lori smile against my lips *while* I was kissing her, like she couldn't contain herself. Life couldn't get better than this. She loved me. I wanted our lives to be so entwined that she'd never be able to shake me off. I thought I couldn't get involved emotionally anymore, but I'd been wrong.

"Hey, want to see my bedroom?" she whispered. We were still standing in the living room, wrapped in each other.

"You want to take advantage of me, Ms. Connor?"

"Why, no. Of course not. I'm a lady. I was rather hoping you'd take advantage of me, Mr. Frazier."

We broke out in laughter. Lori tried to shush us.

"We'll wake up Milo."

We did our best to keep our voices down as we hurried to her bedroom.

"Wow!" she exclaimed once I'd closed the door. I'd arranged scented candles throughout the room. Fishing the lighter out of my pocket, I lit up each one, then turned off the lights.

"Any other surprises planned?" Lori asked in a husky voice.

"Lie down and you'll see."

She tilted her head. "Want me naked?"

"Very naked. And on your belly."

I watched her take off her dress and underwear then remove the cover on the bed. She cocked a brow at the large beach towel I'd laid out.

"Lie down on the towel on your belly," I instructed.

When she was flat on the bed, I took out the massage oil from the nightstand, poured some in my palms, and then worked her upper back, pressing on her shoulder blades. Then I moved onto the middle her back, rubbing along her spine.

"Mmm… you're so good at this. Why do you have to be so good?"

"To drive you crazy."

"When did you think all this up?"

I lowered my hands to her ass, kneading each cheek with great care.

"Last week, when you were running around on adrenaline. Thought you could use some relaxing once it was over."

"Are you even real?" she whispered.

I slipped a finger between her folds until I reached her clit, to prove how real it all was. She gasped.

"How was the event?"

"You want me to talk *now*?" she protested.

"Why? Is something distracting you?"

I pushed her ass in the air and strummed my fingers on her clit. When she bit into her pillow, I undid the buttons of my jeans. Watching pleasure consume her was the best foreplay. She came so hard that her entire body spasmed.

I held her until she calmed down, then flipped her on her back. I was so hot for her that I could barely see straight, so I kicked off my clothes and underwear. Lying on top of her, I explored her mouth. I was controlling the kiss, and in the slow dance of our tongues, I showed her how I was going to love her tonight. She fidgeted, rubbing her soft skin against me.

I turned my attention to her breasts, flicking my tongue over one nipple, then the other. The skin on her breasts turned to goose bumps. Her arms were covered too. I slid my hands to cup her ass and found some there as well.

"Do you have goose bumps on your pussy

too, babe?"

"Why don't you check?" she rasped out.

The answer was a resounding yes.

"Graham," she whispered when I descended to explore her body. I brought a hand to her pussy, and my eyes crossed when I felt how wet she was. I feathered my thumb in circles over her clit, feeling her press her feet deep in the mattress. She pressed her forearm over her mouth, but I still heard her groan.

"Oh, God. Graham." Her muffled voice set me on edge. I was dying to be inside her, but I wanted a taste first, so I settled my head between her legs, focusing on her clit with my tongue and my thumb.

Lick. Stroke. Lick. Stroke.

I licked her until her legs trembled, and then I couldn't wait anymore. But when I reached to the nightstand for protection, Lori shifted into a sitting position.

"Not yet."

She gripped my erection, and my hips buckled. Lori took her hand away, clamping her lips around the tip then lowering her mouth on me.

"Lori, fuuuck. Stop or I won't last."

She showed no signs of stopping, but I pulled back when my balls tightened almost painfully. I slid protection on and then positioned myself between her legs, teasing her by rubbing the crown against her inner thigh. Pleasure pulsed through me, and I wasn't even inside her.

"Graham, please."

I moved the tip down to her entrance, sliding it in an inch before pulling back and dragging it up to her clit. Lori brought both hands to her breasts, touching her nipples. I leaned over and licked where she'd touched. At the same time, I buried myself inside her to the hilt.

She gasped. "Graham, I need—"

"I know what you need."

She was tight and warm around me, and I knew I wouldn't be able to go slow. We both needed it hard and fast. She pressed her heels just under my ass cheeks as we both moved ferociously. We kissed each other's groans until the very end. In that moment, I wasn't sure I even knew my own name, let alone if we'd been loud or not.

We held onto each other until our ragged breaths turned to laughter. Lori pressed her forehead against my shoulder, speaking into my chest.

"That was intense," she murmured between fits of laughter.

"You could say that."

After we cleaned up, we slipped under the covers, and I could tell Lori was going to fall asleep in a matter of minutes. I, on the other hand, felt wide-awake. She blinked slowly, clearly making an effort not to drift away.

Kissing the tip of her nose, I said, "Go to sleep, Lori."

"Aren't you tired?"

"No."

I shifted her so that she could use my chest as a pillow. She sighed contentedly, shifting even more, half straddling me.

"I've always had troubles falling asleep," she murmured. "But not when I'm with you."

"Then go to sleep. I'll hold you."

She was out in seconds, and her shallow breath was tickling my chest. This, right here, was all I needed to be a happy man.

Chapter Twenty-Five
Lori

The meeting with Jeff took place one week later in a cafe in Silver Lake. I'd been giving myself mental pep talks all day, but I was still nervous as hell by the time Graham and I arrived. I'd been biting my nails and wringing my hands during the drive. Part of me was grateful Graham was with me; the other part wished he wouldn't see me in this state.

"Baby, we're doing this together, okay?"

I nodded, too nervous to reply. Graham kissed my hand before we climbed out of the car.

When we entered the coffee shop, I located Jeff at a table in the corner. Seeing him was a shock. He looked as if seventeen years had passed, not seven. His hairline had receded somewhat, and he'd grown a second chin. When he rose to his feet, I also noticed a beer belly.

"Lori, it's been too long."

Not long enough was what I wanted to say, but I just shook his hand. Jeff jerked his head back when Graham introduced himself.

"The LA Lords's Graham Frazier?"

"Yes."

"Man, I'm a big fan of the Lords."

"Glad to hear it." Graham's voice was curt and in no way invited further conversation.

"Lori, I'd like to speak with you alone."

I lifted a brow. "Tough luck."

We all sat down, and after an awkward silence, Jeff said, "You two are an item, I gather?"

Graham draped an arm around my shoulders.

"Yes, we are," I confirmed.

"Okay, um… what would you two like to order?" Jeff asked. "My treat."

"How about cutting to the chase?" Graham suggested, mirroring my thoughts.

"Cut me some slack, man. I'm trying to work up the courage." Jeff shrugged. My stomach twisted. Work up the courage to what? My thoughts flew to Milo. Jace and Will had taken him out for dinner.

"Why did you want to meet, Jeff?" I asked.

He set an elbow on the table, scratching his double chin. "So, as you know, I'm working in Denver."

"Okay…?"

"I ran into some trouble recently. A patient sued me for giving him the wrong treatment. My lawyer initially said we had a strong case, but now it seems like there is a real possibility I might lose my license for malpractice. The hospital already fired me."

Graham and I exchanged a glance, and I could tell he was asking himself the same thing. What did this have to do with me and Milo?

"If the hospital fired you, I'm guessing they

think the patient is right," I said.

"All I did was prescribe some drugs that had just hit the market. The pharmaceutical company gave me a fat bonus, and their statistics were comparable to older drugs. I couldn't know it wouldn't work."

"Or you could have prescribed one of the time-tested drugs. But God forbid you actually do something that is not in *your* best interest, right? That goes right against the *Hippocratic Oath*." I couldn't help the venom in my voice.

"Well, it's a done deal now. My lawyer says it's important I appear as a responsible person. She looked up my records, said it doesn't bode well for me that I wasn't taking care of my kid."

I stiffened. "Get to the point."

Under the table, Graham squeezed my hand.

"I know I haven't been good about paying child support, but it would help if you'd declare that I did."

I stared at him. He couldn't be serious. This was why he wanted to meet?

"You son of a bitch." That was Graham. I needed a few seconds to calm down before talking.

"You have the nerve to show up here and ask me to lie for you? After you ditched me when I was pregnant and ignored your son all his life?"

"Come on, Lori. That was a long time ago. And seeing the company you keep, it's not like you're still pining after me or need the money. Landon's rich as fuck anyway. Not like you ever needed my money. What's the harm in helping me out?"

"The harm is that I'd be lying. You are not a responsible person, and you have not paid one dollar of child support. I will not pretend otherwise."

"Lori, don't be like that. You know I could make things difficult for you. I have never exerted my paternal rights, but if I decided to—"

"You continue that line of conversation and you won't have teeth left in your mouth," Graham said. His voice was calm and composed, but it sounded lethal.

I wanted to punch Jeff myself. Not only didn't he care one iota about Milo, but he wanted to use him as a bargaining chip. Christ, I couldn't believe he'd become even more of a scumbag over the years.

Jeff swallowed. "This already ate up all of my savings. They find out I've been avoiding child support all these years, they'll be at my throat."

"Which is what you deserve," I said.

He lifted his chin, narrowing his eyes. "You have no idea what it took to put me through med school and residency. I worked hard for this career to let a bitch like you ruin it."

I barely blinked and Graham was already out of his chair, grabbing Jeff by his collar. I sprang to my feet, along with several other patrons. Two waiters were hurrying toward us.

"You're a fucking scumbag," Graham bellowed.

"Christ! What did that bitch do to have you so whipped?"

Next thing I knew, Graham's fist connected with Jeff's jaw.

"Jesus Christ, are you insane?" Jeff covered his jaw with one hand.

"Don't you dare talk about Lori like that in front of me."

"Take it from someone who knows—she's not worth the trouble."

That earned him a second punch. The waiters pulled them apart then, and I immediately hurried to inspect Graham's hand. His knuckles were red but not bloody. I looked up at Jeff.

"This conversation is over. You have anything more to say on the topic, talk to my lawyer. If I were you, I wouldn't. I can take you to court for that accrued child support."

He paled, but I wasn't nearly done. I wanted to let out everything I had on my chest.

"You decided seven years ago that you didn't want to be part of our lives, fine. But don't think you have any rights to make any demands or to expect anything of me. You're just being a jackass, showing up here, demanding I lie for you. As I said, you have anything more to say on this topic, contact my lawyer. I don't want to deal with you again."

Jeff's jaw went slack. He wasn't used to this side of me. In med school, I was young and naïve. Even when he called after being gone for a year, I still gave him the benefit of the doubt. I'd hoped he'd finally decided to man up and to face his responsibilities. One of my biggest flaws had always been believing everyone deserved a second chance, and a third.

Before Jeff had a chance to say anything, Graham spoke. "We're done here. You contact Lori again, you'll have bigger problems on your hands than a malpractice lawsuit."

I was shaking slightly. Graham must have sensed it, because he splayed his hand on my upper back. He tucked me closer to him on the way to the car. When we reached it, he opened the door for me.

"I'm sorry this was so shitty. How is your hand?"

"Not as bad as his jaw will be tomorrow. I'll put some ice on it. Don't you worry about me. You were magnificent. So strong and decisive." He caressed my cheek with the back of his uninjured hand, his thumb dwelling on my chin before moving to rest on one corner of my mouth. He kissed the other corner. I rose on my tiptoes, placing my arms around his neck, flattening my torso to his. I loved this closeness between us, even though I wished I could pull myself together already. I was still shaking.

"What's on your mind, sweet girl? You can tell me anything."

"Not feeling so strong now," I admitted. The words felt strange on my tongue. I wasn't used to sharing these things with anyone but my siblings. I hoped he wouldn't think I was a weakling.

"Lucky I'm here to make it all better." He feathered his lips from the corner of my mouth to the center, kissing the upper lip, then the lower one.

"And how do you plan to do that?"

He gave me one of his knee-weakening, panty-melting, mind-blowing kisses.

"Love your plan," I murmured when we came up for breath.

"This was just a kiss. The plan is more elaborate."

"Do tell."

"I texted Jace and Will. They're going to drop Milo off at home in a few hours. He talked them into going to a movie."

"Of course he did." I shook my head with fake dismay.

"Hey! The little guy is persuasive. You're the only one able to resist him. Don't be so hard on the rest of us mortals."

I turned the fake dismay into a fake glare. "If I'm not too hard, I'll find a real-sized boat in my yard next time to go with that tent."

He smirked. "Relax, baby. I'd never put it in your yard. I'd rent a garage."

I laughed for real now, a full belly laugh.

"I'll make you dinner, and then I'm going to work out all the tension from your system."

"Will I get a massage?"

"Yeah."

"And some sexy time?"

"Possibly."

I pouted.

"Is that all you care about?" he teased.

"Absolutely not. I appreciate all your qualities.

It'd be a shame not to put those delicious sexy skills to use though."

"You wicked woman. You're lucky I love you." He took my face in his hands, studying me. "Are you okay, Lori? The truth."

"I think so. This afternoon just brought back some unpleasant memories. I've always known Jeff was a dick. He surpassed himself today… showing up like this, asking me to lie for him. No interest in Milo."

"Were you hoping he would want to be part of Milo's life?"

I shook my head. "No, I'm not an idiot. I wouldn't trust him even if he tried. He's flighty and would only hurt Milo more."

"I wouldn't let that happen. You and Milo are family to me."

"I love you so much," I whispered.

"You handled everything great today. Now, let's go home."

During the drive, I tried to calm down, but I was unsuccessful. Seeing Graham's reddened knuckles didn't help. His lips were pressed in a thin line—he was no doubt rehashing the past hour in his mind, just like I was. It set me on edge. Seeing Jeff today brought back the ugly feeling—and the fear—of being tossed aside. I shouldn't have let it get to me, but I was only human.

Even after dinner, I wasn't feeling like myself. Graham told me as much.

"I'm not angry, or nervous, just… unsettled,"

I tried to explain. "Not sure if I'm making much sense."

"You do. Seeing someone who has hurt you before has to get to you."

I blinked, relieved he understood, that he wasn't judging me. "It did. I hope I never have to see his face again."

Hooking an arm around my waist, he brought me close to him. "I love your strength, Lori." He dragged the tip of his nose up and down my neck, making me shudder.

"Thank you for coming with me today, and for being here now." Facing things together, as a team, was new to me. My family had always been behind me, of course, but this… this was different.

"My pleasure." He placed open-mouthed kisses on my neck, descending to my shoulder. My hands roamed his chest, and then I couldn't help myself and slipped my fingers under his shirt, tracing the lines of his six-pack. Then I undid the button of his jeans, and the fly, needing to touch more of him. When I squeezed his cock, he tugged at my lower lip with his teeth. Heat zipped through me.

Graham pushed both straps of my dress off my shoulders, lowering the zipper on the back. I was glad to be wearing a simple beach dress. Easy to put on. Easy to get off. He tossed it somewhere behind him in the living room, raking his heated gaze over my almost-naked body. The lingerie was so tiny that it didn't cover much. He got his jeans and boxers out of the way, and then his erection was between us, touching my belly, hot and hard.

I opened my thighs, but Graham pushed them even wider apart as he stepped between them, guiding his erection lower, rubbing the length against my center. I still had my thong on, and the friction was making my legs quiver. With grabby hands, I took off Graham's shirt.

"Do you have a condom on you?" I whispered. "I don't think we're going to make it to the bedroom."

He laughed against my lips, then reached for his jeans. After taking a condom out of his wallet, he rolled it on under my greedy gaze. We made it to the couch, but no farther. He kissed me ferociously. His hands were everywhere. His mouth was driving me crazy.

"Baby, I'll be rough," he whispered.

"I like it rough, and fast."

He didn't even take off my lingerie, only pushed the scrap of fabric covering my center to one side. He ran his fingers across my opening, strumming them against the sensitive flesh. I lifted my hips in a wordless request. When he nipped my clit between two fingers, I nearly came. He slid inside me.

"Wrap your legs around me. You'll take me in even deeper."

I followed his command, bringing my knees to his sides then resting my heels under his ass. He pulled back, then pushed inside me again, filling me up, stretching me.

"Graham!"

Our lovemaking was wild and unrestrained. When he brought his palm to my lower belly, pressing down, the sensation of him relentlessly driving inside me became even more intense. Graham kissed the tops of my breasts, then pushed the bra up, releasing my nipples. Cool air hit my peaks, and then the lash of his tongue. He was making me burn everywhere, even where he wasn't touching me. Even my toes felt on fire. And when he strummed his thumb over my clit, I came hard. He grunted out my name, a raw, primal sound, until he climaxed. Then he went still over me, bracing himself on one arm, keeping the other on my waist.

His voice was rough when he spoke in my ear. "Nothing compares to this feeling. This, Lori, is everything."

Chapter Twenty-Six
Graham

"This is so cool!" Milo exclaimed for the tenth time, inspecting the miniature carton warehouse a week later. We'd been working on his school project for days.

"I'm sure it'll earn you first place." I'd been tinkering with it every evening, and I was proud of it.

"Boys, you ready? Milo, we have to leave or you'll be late to school," Lori called.

"Ready, Mom!"

He slung his backpack over his shoulder, then walked to the front door, holding the project carefully in both hands. Lori was waiting for him there.

After Milo skidded out the door, I closed the distance to Lori and kissed her.

"Now *that*'s what I call a good morning kiss," she murmured.

"Want to have lunch together?"

"Can't. A handsome man is taking me to a fancy dinner in two weeks, so I need to go shopping. Today is the only day I have time."

"A handsome man, huh?"

"Handsome *and* charming."

"Sounds like you like him."

"Oh, I really, really do."

"You looking forward to the dinner?" It wasn't just a fancy dinner; it was a party hosted by the club to celebrate this season's results. Everyone was bringing their partners, and I wanted Lori by my side.

"Very much. I plan to blow that certain handsome man's mind with my outfit, hence why I need time to hunt down a fancy dress."

"Have fun."

***

When I stepped inside the club one hour later, the receptionist pointed to the waiting area after greeting me. "That guy sitting there has been asking for you. His name is—"

"Jeff Finn." *What the hell?* "I'll take care of this." I crossed the lobby to him. He rose to his feet when he saw me.

"What are you doing here?" I barked. Lori had been on edge since the meeting with that fucker last week, and nothing I did seemed to take that edge away completely.

"Waiting for you. We need to talk."

"Lori told you to contact her lawyer."

"I'm not talking to Lori though, am I? Here to talk to you."

I had no interest in what he had to say, but I didn't want to attract any attention by having him thrown out. I also didn't want him to bother Lori.

"Let's go to my office."

I led us to the upper floor, closing the door behind me once we were in my office. I stood behind my desk and didn't bother asking him to sit down.

"What do you want?"

"I didn't like the outcome of our last meeting."

"Tough luck. Maybe you shouldn't have insulted Lori, just like you shouldn't have been an ass for the last seven years and paid the child support. Then you wouldn't have to ask Lori to lie for you."

"I didn't ask to be a father. Don't see why I had to pay anything."

"You're a fucking coward." I clenched my fists and my jaw. I detested people like him, who shunned responsibility. "If you think I'll put in a good word for you with Lori, you're wrong."

"A good word? No, that's not why I'm here."

"So why are you here?"

"You and Lori looked… cozy in that coffee shop. I bet you wouldn't want me to stick around and cause trouble."

"You can't cause any."

"That's debatable. If I showed up at Milo's school to introduce myself, or at Lori's house…"

My throat tightened. I forced myself to take in deep breaths and expel the air slowly. It didn't help calm me down.

"You go anywhere near them, and you're going to be very sorry."

He sat on the chair in front of my desk

uninvited. “But imagine how unpleasant that would be for Lori, and confusing for the boy too. You wouldn’t want that. I imagine Lori wouldn’t be too happy with you if you let that happen.”

“Get to the point. Why are you here?” I was talking through gritted teeth, and the idiot was smiling.

“I’ve got your attention. Good. Let’s talk about what you’re willing to do so I don’t pay anyone any… confusing visits.”

“What do you want?”

“I realized I can get a lot more out of this than a declaration from Lori. I want money."

"What?"

"My insurance will pay for the malpractice damage, but since I won't be able to practice anymore, I won't have an income."

"How the fuck is that my problem?" I stuffed my hands in my pockets to keep from throttling the idiot.

"I can *become* a problem, make Lori's life difficult, claiming paternity rights and so on."

"If she takes you to court for that child support—"

"She can get in line behind other people I owe money to." He shrugged. "You write me a check, I'll make myself scarce."

"You have some nerve, showing up here."

"The lawsuit is ruining me. I've put in one-hundred-twenty-hour weeks for years. I don't have much to lose here. I'm a desperate man. I have the nerve for much more."

It was all I could do not to physically drag him out of the club. Doing that wouldn't solve anything. Sure, Lori had a case against him in court. But I didn't want her to have to see his face ever again. That meeting was hard for her. I didn't want her to go through it again. This idiot had caused her enough pain over the years. And what if he did try to contact Milo? What if he showed up at the school? Giving him money felt like rewarding him, but if it meant he'd be out of Lori's life, I was happy to do it.

I took out the checkbook I kept in the top drawer of my desk and wrote down a six-figure amount. I handed it to him over the table. He jerked his head back when he read the sum.

"You ever contact Lori again, I'll get a restraining order against you," I said calmly.

He snorted, pointing at the photograph of Lori, Milo, and me that sat on my desk.

"Any comments, and I'll give you a black eye to go with that jaw."

"I got what I came for." He fluttered the check in the air, then turned around and left my office. My pulse was hammering in my eardrums. I was clenching my fists. I had to calm down, because I was attending a team practice and didn't want the players to see me like this. I descended to the team's training grounds, still feeling very much on edge. I was the first to arrive, but Jace stormed in seconds later.

"That Jeff jackass was here."

"Came to see me. Got rid of him."

"What did he want? I swear to God, if he doesn't leave Lori alone…." He sputtered. I hadn't ever seen Jace lose his cool. He was the most levelheaded on the team, which was why he had great potential for captain. When one of his teammates became hotheaded, I could count on Jace to calm him down before a referee had to step in.

"I took care of it. He won't be bothering Lori again."

He glanced at my hand. "Lori said you punched him the other day."

"Yeah."

After a pause, Jace extended his hand, shaking mine. "Welcome to the family."

When the coach and the rest of the team filtered in, I went to sit on the sidelines, in my usual spot. I barely managed to pay attention to the coach's strategic indications. I replayed the meeting in my mind. Damn it, I should have called a lawyer first, have papers drawn up so I'd have it in writing that Jeff Finn would never bother Lori and Milo again. I was usually good at analyzing situations from all angles. But upstairs, I'd acted on impulse.

My thoughts remained on Lori and Milo during the entire practice.

I hoped I did the right thing to protect the woman I loved and the boy I'd come to think of as my own son.

Chapter Twenty-Seven
Lori

Milo came down with a cold the following week, but he was in top shape by the time his spring break started the week after. Unfortunately, Graham caught the bug, and he still had it on Saturday. The club's dinner party was tonight, but I wasn't sure he was in any shape to attend. I took an Uber to his house early in the afternoon. If he wasn't feeling well enough to attend, then I'd just take care of him. My schedule was clear anyway. Milo's spring break had begun, and he'd gone with Marlene, her husband, and their eight-year-old son to Orlando. They wouldn't be back until Thursday. It was the first time I'd be apart from my boy for so many days, but he'd insisted on going, and I didn't want to be a hog.

I found Graham tucked in his bed, curled on one side, hugging a pillow half asleep. I crouched next to him. It was the third day of sickness, and he seemed much healthier.

"How are you feeling?" I whispered.

"Like I died three days ago and now I'm coming back to life."

I pressed my lips together. *Men.* You'd think he had leprosy.

"I'm sorry you caught the bug."

"How come you haven't?"

"I'm a mom. I have enough antibodies for two lifetimes. I'm going to the kitchen to make you some tea."

While I was busying myself around his kitchen, I heard a faint buzzing from his living room. His phone was ringing, the word *Nana* appearing on the screen. I ran upstairs with it, but Graham had fallen asleep.

When I returned to the kitchen, it buzzed again. I decided to answer.

"Hi, Na— Ms. Scott." I'd nearly called her Nana. "This is Lori. We haven't met, but—"

"Lori Connor? Graham's Lori?"

"Yes. He's down with a cold, and he's asleep right now."

"Can you tell him to call me back?"

"Of course."

"Thank you. You know, when he was a kid, I used to make a concoction for him when he had a cold."

"Can you give me the recipe?"

"Do you have anything to write on?"

I put the phone on loudspeaker and opened the application for notes on my phone.

"Yes I do."

I typed into my phone as she spoke, then held it to my ear again once she was done.

"Thank you. I'll check if he has any of the ingredients, and if he's missing any, there's a farmer's market a few blocks away. I'll go shopping there."

"He talks about you often, you know."

"He does?"

"Of course. About you and Milo. He's quite taken with both of you. Graham is a great man, Lori. Take good care of him." Even though her tone was still warm, it held a hint of warning.

"I promise."

We chatted for a while, and she regaled me with stories from his childhood. I loved this window into his past and was already making mental notes about all the ways I could tease him. Nana was giving me excellent ammunition.

After hanging up, I checked his fridge and pantry, but he was still missing a few herbs for the concoction, so I headed out to the farmer's market. By the time I returned and prepared the remedy, we were on a time-crunch. Graham was already awake when I brought it to his room. I handed him the mug, and he looked up in surprise.

"You know how to make this?"

"Now I do. Spoke to Nana."

"My nana?"

"Yes. I brought you the phone when she called, but you were asleep, and then she called again. I answered to tell her you were sleeping, and we started talking. She gave me the recipe. Found some things in your kitchen, and bought the rest from the farmer's market. You should call Nana back when you have the chance."

He took several sips and didn't say anything in

between. Had I committed a faux pas by answering his phone? I hadn't even stopped to consider that maybe I'd overstepped some boundaries. He downed the entire contents of the mug, set it on the nightstand, and slid lower on his pillow. He patted the mattress, and I climbed right next to him. I still felt a little awkward about the phone call.

These past two weeks, I'd sensed some unease on Graham's part; a few times he'd seemed to want to talk, then changed his mind. Maybe I was reading too much into everything. I'd been jumpy since the meeting with Jeff, and felt guilty that he'd driven Graham to violence. I hoped Graham didn't think this kind of drama was bound to happen again. My life was usually drama-free.

"Graham, did I do something wrong? Should I have not answered your phone?" He turned on his side, facing me. "No, not at all. I'm just surprised you went to so much trouble."

"It wasn't trouble at all," I assured him, detecting a hint of emotion in his eyes. Did he think he wasn't worth that "trouble"? I had to rectify that. I scooted closer to him, intending to prove my appreciation.

"So, what did you and Nana talk about?"

"You, of course. She told me many stories. I can tease you for years."

"I knew it. Should have been there for your first conversation, so I could save face."

"I'm fairly confident Nana would've dished dirt on you even so."

"Probably." He kissed my cheek. "I won't kiss your mouth, just in case."

"I came all the way here, and I don't even get a kiss?"

"I said I won't kiss your mouth. Didn't say anything about other body parts."

He scooted closer, kissing my bare shoulder and my neck.

"You're taking advantage," I informed him, failing to work any sort of severity in my tone.

"I'm a sick man; have some mercy." He was smiling against my skin.

On I went with my fake chastising. "You're a sick man taking advantage. I feel compelled to point that out. How will you learn otherwise?"

He pulled back a notch, wiggling his eyebrows. "I'm blissfully happy in my ignorance."

"Are you sure you're up for the party tonight?" I asked.

"Yeah. I'm feeling much better. I was only messing with you."

"Is that so?" I crushed my mouth to his, taking what I wanted. When I pulled back, all my lady parts tingled at his lusty expression. But we were on a tight schedule if we wanted to make it to the party. "We should get ready."

Besides, I had great plans for us after the party. We had my house all to ourselves… and I hadn't just bought a fancy new dress. What I was going to wear underneath the dress was equally enticing.

A short while later, I stepped out of the bathroom, dressed to the nines. I was wearing a green wraparound dress, with pearls at my ears and around my neck. I'd styled my hair in loose curls. Graham looked as if he wanted to eat me up.

"Fuck, you're beautiful, Lori."

"Thank you." I twirled around once, observing him coming closer out the corner of my eye. He hadn't dressed up yet, so he was only wearing boxers. That left *so* much skin on display. He circled my waist with his arms.

"Graham, we're supposed to be at the party in half an hour."

"Change of plans." Bringing his mouth to my ear, he whispered, "I'm thinking me inside you, loving you until you come hard."

I bit lightly into his shoulder when he bunched my dress up, trying to maintain my composure. He blew out a breath when he touched the lacy end of my stocking. Then he groaned when he realized I had no panties.

"I planned to surprise you after the party," I said coyly.

"You're not wearing panties."

"Something for you to keep in mind tonight. The dress is tight, no chance of flashing anyone the goods. But… you have to get dressed now."

His eyes flashed with mischief, and I knew he wasn't going to let me off the hook.

Half an hour later, we were officially late already.

"We messed up my hair," I called from the bathroom while he was suiting up. When I came out, hair styled again, he smirked.

I crossed my arms over my chest. "My lips are swollen."

"It's a great look on you."

I glared. He bit back a laugh.

"You look like you've been thoroughly kissed. Only you and I will know where those lips have been. Everyone else will just know you're mine."

I sent him an air kiss. "Why, you think one of those smoking hot players might hit on me otherwise?"

"They won't if they know what's good for them."

"I still have to refresh my makeup."

"I'll wait for you downstairs and call Nana in the meantime."

When I descended the staircase a short while later, I could sense the change in mood before even seeing Graham pace around the living room. There were deep frown lines on his forehead, and he kept shaking his head, as if he was having a silent conversation with himself.

"Graham, did anything happen?"

He stopped midstride, jamming his hands in his pockets. "Talked to Nana."

"Is she okay? She didn't seem sick when I talked to her."

"She's not sick." He started pacing again, rubbing one hand down his face. His shoulders looked stiff, as if a lot of tension had accumulated there in a short period of time. "My dad called her. He's in a financial shit-hole again and asked if she could bail him out."

"Oh!" I was too stunned to say anything else.

"He didn't tell me anything about it when I talked to him." Graham paced the room some more but didn't offer more information.

"You still want to go to the party?" I asked.

"I can't bail on it. We should go or we'll miss the dinner altogether."

Chapter Twenty-Eight
Lori

The restaurant was near Hancock Park, and we drove through a section on Windsor Boulevard lined with gigantic palm trees that were roughly four times taller than the nearby lampposts. I spotted the Hollywood sign in the distance.

Everyone was already at the restaurant when we arrived. Since the event was private, we had the place to ourselves. I felt like we were in an open space, what with the glass walls and ceiling, and all the greenery outdoors.

"Let's introduce you to everyone." Graham offered me his arm as we walked in. I gladly took it, snaking my arm around his elbow. My man was still tense, and there wasn't a thing I could do about it right now.

The management was sitting at one large table, the players at two others. They all rose to their feet as Graham introduced me. Some were here with girlfriends, but most were solo. Amber was here with Matt. I hugged them both. I hadn't seen them since the wedding and her baby bump was visible now.

"You look great. Married life suits you," I said.

"Won't complain. Do you organize baby

showers?"

"Of course I do."

"I'll pick your brain later on." She rubbed her belly. I wanted to chat with her more, but we still had to finish the introduction round.

"Hey, I think I know this one," I said when we reached Jace.

My brother stroked his chin. "Could be we share a last name?"

I grinned as he kissed my cheek.

"Jace, why didn't you introduce us before? I'd have scooped her up before Graham did," one of his teammates said.

"That's Gaston. Ignore him. We all do," Jace explained.

Gaston opened his mouth, but promptly closed it when Graham glared at him. I could tell the guys enjoyed getting a rise out of Graham. Our seats were at the management table, but everyone mingled, especially since it was an open buffet. Graham didn't relax all evening.

If anything, he seemed to become tenser as hours went by. It was all there, in his body language. The stiffness in his shoulders took hold of his neck too. Whenever I caught his eye, all I got were strained smiles.

I ate pastrami, crab cakes, and a finely diced tomatoes and cucumbers salad with lime juice. Dessert was the highlight, though. Jace came up to me when I was loading a second serving of cheesecake on my plate.

"The chef here deserves a hug. This cheesecake is the best," I said.

Jace shook his head mockingly. "Easy on the compliments or I'll tell Val."

"You will do no such thing. Unless you want your coach to know you routinely ignore your food plan."

"You wouldn't do that."

"Try me." I bumped his shoulder.

"Sisters. They sabotage even the best laid plans."

"And we take that role seriously. I'm proud of you, Jace." I had no clue in how many more ways I could show him that before it went to his head. He was the team's most valuable player, and had been celebrated tonight as such. That required a lot of work and dedication.

A pretty blonde waitress came up to us, carrying a glass on her tray. "Mr. Connor, I have your special order here. Should I bring it to your table?"

Jace shook his head, picking up the glass. "Thanks."

"Is there anything else I can get you?" She sounded a little breathless.

"No, that's all." Poor woman had stars in her eyes. Jace was doing what he'd done since he was a teen—charming the opposite sex. I'd realized that smile would be trouble ever since my high school friends had blushed around him, despite the age difference. That smile had grown even more dangerous after Jace became aware of its effect.

"Question: why is there dessert here if all the players are on a strict meal plan?" I asked after she left.

"Because everyone else isn't? Amber arranged this. She likes to torture us."

"Oooh, I forgot to give her my thanks for that calendar. Best idea she's had."

"Please don't. That'll just give her more ideas."

"That's the point."

Jace sipped from his glass, then took a deep breath. "I meant to ask: did Jeff bother you again?"

"No, not at all. Not even my lawyer heard from him."

"Graham must have scared him good when he showed at the club."

I tightened the grip on my plate, suddenly feeling like the last bit of cake I'd swallowed was crawling up my throat. "Jeff came to the club?"

"You didn't know?"

"No, Graham didn't mention it. When was that?"

"About two weeks ago. Graham was in a mood afterward. Seemed out of it for a couple of days."

What was happening? Why hadn't he brought this up? And why the hell would Jeff bother Graham? I glanced around, searching for Graham, and found him talking with a player on the other side of the room. My stomach shrunk to a tight knot. Why hadn't he told me anything? Had Jeff's visit upset him that much? Maybe I hadn't imagined

Graham's unease these past weeks. After Jace's teammates pulled him away, Amber and I talked about the baby shower, but I couldn't focus on planning anything. I wished this evening would come to an end faster.

Graham was still tense when we climbed in his car and drove off. The conversation with Nana had clearly rattled him, but I wished he'd talk to me about it. Whatever it was, we could work through it together. And even if there wasn't anything to work through, I wanted him to know he could talk to me.

During the drive, I kept wringing my hands in my lap, trying to decide on the best angle to tackle this. I was completely out of sorts. When we pulled in front of my house, Graham didn't turn off the engine. It was dark outside, and in the dim yellowish light cast by the lampposts, I couldn't make out his expression.

"I'm going to head to my place this evening. I'm not in the right headspace right now."

My stomach bottomed out. He thought that was the solution?

"I thought we were at the point where we could talk things out, no matter what they were. Don't close yourself off to me. Talk to me."

Graham bristled. I bit the inside of my cheek. Damn, that came out different than I'd intended. My tone was almost accusatory.

"Not much to say. I still have to figure out what to do."

I took in his body language. Shoulders hunched, head hung. I wanted to comfort him, but he didn't seem to want that. I wasn't going to let him pull away, though. I didn't want that kind of dynamic in our relationship. It wasn't healthy. Besides, he'd been the one who'd pushed me to share things with him until now. Why wasn't he reciprocating?

Since I had no idea how to tackle the issue with his dad, I switched gears.

"Jace told me Jeff stopped by the club two weeks ago. What was that about?"

I wanted to get to the bottom of this.

Graham straightened up in his seat. "I meant to tell you about that, but then I thought there was no point anyway."

"But what did he want?"

"Money."

"What?" Goddamn it! I couldn't *believe* Jeff. That was why I hadn't heard a word. My previous anxiety morphed into anger. That moron.

"He showed up saying that he'd be making a nuisance of himself if I didn't give him money, so I wrote him a check."

"Graham, that's... wow. That you'd do that for Milo, and for me… I'm grateful." I was stunned and humbled, but the whole thing didn't sit well with me. "But, I'd like us to talk about these things before making a decision. You can't decide on your own when the ramifications might affect me, and especially Milo. It doesn't work this way. I don't think that giving Jeff what he wanted was smart. He might come back for more."

"Can't seem to do anything right, can I?" He sounded pissed off, which instantly pissed me off too.

"That's not what I mean. I just don't like the lack of communication."

"I didn't want you to have to deal with him again. That meeting with him lasted less than an hour and you were upset for days."

"So the solution was to push me out? Like you're doing now? Is this how it's always going to be?"

"The two things aren't related. I was … I wanted to spare you another unpleasant conversation. If you can't understand why I'd do that, maybe you don't feel as strongly for me as I thought."

What? How is this conversation getting so out of control?

"I understand that the conversation with your nana has you out of sorts, but I'm here for you."

Graham rubbed his hands up and down his face, as if he was losing his patience. Then he gripped the steering wheel. "I keep thinking the old man will pull himself together, grow up. He's sixty. Scares me to even think we're related."

"You're nothing like him. You've been great to Milo, and to me."

"What's to say I won't screw up in the future?" He leaned his head back against the headrest, frowning at the windshield. I went very still, feeling as if someone was pulling the rug from under me.

"So, what? You think it's better if you don't try?" I ran a hand through my hair, trying to calm down and be rational. But I felt more irrational with every second. "Is this…too much for you?"

Graham turned to face me abruptly. "That's not what I'm saying."

"But is this what you actually mean?" *Had* it all become too much for him? Was it the thing with Jeff? Was the strangeness in the last two weeks because he had second thoughts about being in our lives?

No, those were crazy thoughts. I was just reeling because I was afraid of losing him. I had to keep it together.

"This isn't about you or Milo. Lori, you've got this all wrong," he insisted. My chest constricted instantly. Was he about to give me an *it's-not-you-it's me speech*, or was fear clouding my judgement?

"Let me explain," he continued.

I wasn't equipped to have this conversation right now. I wasn't rational, and I didn't want to overthink every word he would say. I needed to be on my own to process everything. I was so riled up that I couldn't think straight, let alone carry a conversation.

I shook my head and cleared my throat. "No need." He motioned to turn off the engine, but I held my hand up. "Don't. I want to be alone."

"Lori, you need to calm down."

He definitely wasn't calm either.

"Don't patronize me," I said.

"I wasn't—okay, you know what? Clearly, neither of us is rational right now."

"I agree. Goodnight."

"Goodnight."

I climbed out of the car and walked to the house without looking over my shoulder. Once inside, I peeked out the window. Three seconds later, he drove away. I released a long breath. What just happened?

Chapter Twenty-Nine
Lori

I couldn't stand still. I put on my jogging gear and went for a run, starting through the quiet streets of the neighborhood, then taking a detour in the nearest park, which was bustling with activity even this late in the evening. I didn't feel at peace anywhere. When I was alone, I wanted to be with people, and when I was surrounded by a crowd, I wanted to be alone.

Once I was back in my house, I showered. Damn it, I still had too much energy, so I did something I rarely did: I cleaned up the entire place. Not just your run-of-the mill sweep. I went at it with full speed, scrubbing every corner, even moving furniture around. The tears came midway through the cleaning process. I tried keeping them at bay, but the effort was taking its toll, so I let go.

While I was cleaning the rift between the kitchen tiles with a toothbrush, my thoughts flew to the breakup with Jeff all those years ago. I was two months pregnant, and he told me we had to talk. He was jittery, but he'd been so ever since I'd found out, so I didn't think much of it. I was nervous about the whole thing too, so I understood. Then he broke the news to me, that he was leaving me and the baby. He'd thought about it for weeks, and it was just too much responsibility for him. He wanted to become a doctor. He couldn't let this get in the way of his career. I pointed out that I'd already given up on med school, and I hadn't asked him to give up too.

"There will still be sleepless nights, Lori. Babies cry. They get sick. They need you all the time. I need to focus on school one hundred percent."

"You're an insensitive jackass," I said numbly.

"I can't do it. It's too much."

He'd thrown my entire life off course that afternoon. I couldn't believe he'd asked Graham for money. The bastard. I was going to find him and shove that check up his ass. He'd probably cashed it, but I was confident I could find something else to shove up there instead. But that wouldn't make the other matter any better. The question remained… *had* it all been too much for Graham? I pressed three fingers to my collarbone, trying to alleviate the pressure there. It felt like my chest was strung together in a knot that grew tighter by the hour.

By the time I finished cleaning the bathroom, the kitchen, and the living room, I was exhausted and fell asleep fully clothed. But my sleep was restless, and I woke up as if I hadn't gone to bed at all. After a cup of coffee, I resumed project *clean the hell out of this house*. I had the one bedroom and all hallways left.

My mood was even grimmer than yesterday, and the quiet was closing in on me. I wasn't used to being alone. I grew up in a full house, and as a mother, I'd rarely had "alone" moments. Twice, I almost called my sisters, then changed my mind. I wasn't sure what to tell them, mostly because I couldn't make sense of everything myself. Sister telepathy had to be a thing though, because Hailey called around lunchtime. I was perched on a ladder, sweeping dust from the corners of the ceiling.

"Hey, sis. What are you up to?" she asked.

"Cleaning my house."

After a brief pause, Hailey asked, "Is the apocalypse coming?"

"Hey! I've been known to clean the house… once in a while."

"Usually when you have a shitty week. Wanna tell me what's wrong?"

I descended the ladder, sitting on the last rung and hugging my knees. "Graham and I had a fight last night."

"I'm listening."

"It's all fuzzy in my mind, honestly."

"And maybe it'll all be clearer if you lay it out to me."

My Hailey, always with that sharp, analytical mind of hers.

"Okay, well… I think I felt that something has been off for a few weeks." I went on to tell her about Graham's encounter with Jeff, and the problem with his dad. I finished with all the crazy words we'd said last night.

"I don't know, Hailey. That conversation was insane."

"Good thing you stopped before it got even more insane. People tend to say things they don't mean when tempers flare."

The ladder was cutting into my back, so I moved to sit on the floor, resting my back against the wall.

"I didn't like that he just went rogue and gave Jeff money. I need to be aware of things that can impact Milo."

"Don't disagree, but I think his heart was in the right place."

"I know, but what if it was too much for him, though?"

"Okay, that's it! You can't be on your own. You'll think in circles and drive yourself crazy. Want to go to Annabelle's with me and Val? She said she received some new merchandise. It's always fun to poke around. And then we can hit up one of our favorites for a late lunch?"

Yes! God, yes! That's exactly what I need.

"But I thought you both had plans." I distinctly remembered both of them chatting about their weekend plans during Friday's dinner.

"They fell through," Hailey said.

I wasn't going to look a gifted horse in the mouth, so I jumped at the opportunity.

"Meet you there in forty minutes?" she asked.

"I might need an hour, not sure how the traffic is, but I'll leave right away."

"That's a plan."

After the line went static, I changed into a

sundress and twisted my hair into a French braid. My mood improved drastically. I was ready to get out of my quiet, lonely house. It was so spotless that it was unnerving. I had to mess it up a bit when I returned.

Annabelle's was a small shop in Pasadena, selling everything from incense to vintage jewelry trinkets, to scarves and hats, and occasionally even shoes. The owner, Annabelle, had gone to school with us. She always called one of us when she thought we might like her new merchandise. My mood lifted a notch when I neared Pasadena. I could see the Colorado Springs Bridge in the distance, with its beautiful Beaux-Arts arches. I loved the neighborhood; the way the old blended with the new in this part of the city was incredible.

I reached Annabelle's in thirty-five minutes. Her shop was on the ground floor of an old Victorian mansion that had a gray-tiled roof and pink facade. It smelled like jasmine incense when I stepped inside. Since this had once been a living quarters, the shop had multiple separate rooms. Annabelle was busy with a client in the main room, showing her a vintage pendant, but she pointed to the adjacent room where I found my sisters. They were the only customers inside, sorting through a pile of scarves and sipping teas. Annabelle always treated us to exotic teas. I kissed both my sisters on their cheeks and lifted the third teacup to my mouth.

"Ouch. It's boiling."

Val slapped her forehead. "Sorry. We mixed ours with lukewarm water, but not yours. Didn't want it to get cold until you arrived." She poured water from a small bottle in my cup.

I tested the temperature by taking a small sip. It was pleasantly warm.

"So how did you decide to come here?"

Val shrugged. "We figured it was a fun thing to do together."

Something wasn't adding up. "Wait a minute. How did you two know I had time?" They'd known I'd planned to spend the weekend with Graham.

Hailey tilted forward and looked at Val. "I'm out of stealth maneuvers today. How about fessing up?"

"We were supposed to get her to relax first," Val countered.

Hailey cocked a brow. "Well, we already burned her tongue, so that ship has sailed."

"What's going on?"

"Fine, let's tell her," Val said as I turned in her direction. "Jace called this morning, said we should check on you."

In retrospect, the fact that Hailey had listened to me so calmly instead of going into full mama-bear mode should have tipped me off that she already knew something.

"I filled Val in, but if you feel like it, you can tell us everything again," Hailey said.

"You're evil, making me rehash it."

Hailey wrapped a green silk scarf around my neck, narrowing her eyes before removing it. "No, I'm not. I think it helps make things clearer."

I couldn't argue with that, so I started my tale again while trying out scarves. When I was done, my sisters exchanged looks.

"I think Graham was simply having a rough moment," Hailey said.

"Lori, honey, sometimes we need time alone to process things. You do that. I do too," Val said gently, and I cringed a little, because she was using her *mother* tone.

"Or we just don't want to let others see us vulnerable. Maybe he didn't want you to have a front seat for that. But I don't think he was trying to push you away," Hailey explained. I ran my fingers over the delicate black embroidery on a fire-red scarf, trying to sort through my thoughts, but it was a pointless exercise. I simply had too many thoughts warring with each other.

Hailey arranged a strand of hair that had escaped from my braid. "I can't believe he paid off Jeff. Who does that?"

"I wanted to smack him and kiss him at the same time." I smiled at the memory. "He's a great man. And I love him so much."

"Not saying he shouldn't have talked to you about it, but damn. If that doesn't spell love, I don't know what does," Val said.

I nodded, deciding to hang onto that. "I should talk to him, but I'm… not sure how to go about it."

"Hell no!" Val exclaimed. "You're not talking to him until we get you to relax. Your back and shoulders are stiff."

Both my sisters were studying me, and then they hugged me tight at the same time.

"A Connor sandwich?" Annabelle asked, finally walking up to us. "Shit hit the fan, huh?"

"Yep," I said once my sisters gave me room to breathe.

"Well, let's see if the pretties I have here will get your mind off it."

"I know what we can do afterward," Hailey announced, holding up a finger. "We should head out for chips and guacamole."

Val nodded. "That's a plan. But first, let's part with our hard-earned money and buy all these pretty things. Nothing helps blow off steam better. I already want three scarves."

"Hey, how about a tattoo too? We can hit up a parlor around Venice," Hailey suggested.

I glared at her. "No need to get crazy. I'm not letting anyone come near me with a needle."

Annabelle surveyed the three of us, raising a brow. "Do I need to worry about you girls?"

Hailey waved her hand in dismissal. "Not at all. We've got a brother with a badge he's very fond of. If things escalate, it's his brotherly duty to save us."

Chapter Thirty
Graham

I was giving Lori a few days to calm down, some space to think everything through. The conversation in the car had gone to hell, and I didn't want to repeat the experience. I'd said some goddamn stupid things. The more I thought about it, the more stupid they sounded.

Simply put, Saturday had not been a good day. Years ago, when I'd made that deal with Dad, I thought it was the smart thing. He'd be set up financially and wouldn't be around to cause trouble. But trouble seemed to find him anywhere. Clearly, my way of solving the issue had just swept the problem under a rug.

I saw that now, and I was going to make some changes. I didn't know what they entailed yet, but I was working on it. The phone call with Nana had made me question myself and the way I handled things.

Hearing Lori question me as well didn't help. It wasn't an excuse, but it was the truth. Had I been wrong to give that jerk a check without talking to her first? Sure. I'd known it was a bad idea *while* I was signing the check.

He might come back for more in the future. Lori was right about that. The last thing I wanted was to disappoint her, or make her unhappy. I'd gone through that with my divorce already. I needed to explain all this to her.

I loved Lori fiercely, but she had to understand one thing about me. When something bothered the people I loved, I took care of it. Simple as that. I'd always done it, and I wasn't going to apologize for it. I hoped Lori would see that. If not…

There was no alternative. I refused to lose her. If she didn't understand, I'd explain it to her until she did. Whatever it took. I admitted my technique could use some refining, and so did my communication skills, but I wasn't going to lose her or Milo over this. Just the notion made my chest twist.

In any case, we still had things to work through if her first conclusion had been that this was *too much* for me. She'd seemed past logical reason at that point, but her words had to be based on an underlying fear.

On Wednesday I headed to the club early. The team was coming back from their away game later today, and I wanted to prepare a pep talk. We'd suffered a brutal defeat, which was an especially tough pill to swallow after a string of victories and the celebration on Saturday. I wanted the guys to know I believed in them despite that.

The mood was grim when I entered the club. The usual chatter coming from the PR and marketing department was a whisper. I poked my head inside to greet them.

"Come on, chin up. It was just a defeat. We'll get back on our feet in no time. Amber, do you have time to go out to the stadium and double-check if everything is ready for tonight?"

The stadium was rented for a concert this evening, and I wanted to verify for myself that everything was running smoothly.

"Sure thing." She rose from her seat, smoothing her palm on her belly.

At the stadium, we started by inspecting the stage. They'd started transforming the arena on Monday. Building the stage and the requisite light installations took time. We checked in with the sound technicians as well. Everything was running according to plan. The concert was sold out, so the stadium would be at its full capacity. Lastly, I went over the emergency evacuation plans with the head of security and floor operators.

"Let's sit down a bit," Amber said once we'd completed our tour. We headed to the chairs in the VIP section that had been arranged on the arena floor itself, in front of the stage.

"I tire so fast it's not even funny. And I'm sleepy all the time." Amber brought a hand to her mouth to cover her yawn.

"If you want to take time off—"

"I don't. I'm not sick, just slower than usual." After a few beats, she folded her arms over her belly.

"So… are you going to bring me up to date?"

"On what?"

"How did the talk with Lori go?"

I hadn't intended to tell Amber anything, but on Monday morning, she took one look at me and knew.

"Haven't spoken to her yet."

"I thought you wanted us to come out here as an excuse to gossip."

"God forbid we actually work, huh?"

"Why didn't you talk to her?"

"I'm giving her some time to cool off."

"How much time exactly do you think she needs?"

"I figured a few days would be good. I've got some things to explain, and I want her to be calm when I do that. I saw on your calendar that you have a meeting with her today. I want to go in your place."

Amber punched my arm. "I knew you hadn't really dragged me out here for work. Thank God. How do you know I'm meeting her?"

"You put 'baby shower planning' in your work calendar, which is synchronized to mine."

"Any reason you're hijacking my date instead of getting one of your own?"

"I want to take her by surprise." Their lunch date was in ninety minutes. That still gave me time to buy flowers. I wasn't big on flowers, but I wasn't about to show up empty-handed after our fight. "Where are you meeting, anyway? There was no mention of a location in your calendar."

"Griffith Park."

After she told me the exact location in the park, I kissed her cheek and took off. First stop, the nearest flower shop.

***

I wasn't going to lie; my palms were sweating a little when I entered the park. People were milling around in the alleyways, their chatter forming a constant background noise that was punctuated by horn blares now and again. As I drew nearer to the ice cream truck, I spotted her.

She was sitting on a bench with her legs crossed. Her dress reached midthigh, displaying her beautiful skin. She didn't see me approach because she was bent over a large folder that no doubt contained some samples or pictures for Amber. Her blonde hair was hanging over one shoulder, fluttering in the light breeze. She straightened up when I sat next to her.

"I was expecting Amber."

"I'm a much better date though," I said with as much cockiness as possible, hoping it would help her relax. A very small smile tugged at the corners of her lips.

I held out the flowers. "These are for you."

She closed the folder, pushing it behind her, taking the flowers in her arms. The vendor said she'd mixed tulips with roses and freesias.

"Thank you. They're beautiful."

I shifted closer to her. "I want to tell you many things, Lori, but I'll start with the most important one. I love you. I'm crazy in love with you. Occasionally, that might make me do crazy things. I know I'm a bit of a hothead, and that I act on impulse. But I promise to work on that, to talk things through with you. On Saturday, I wasn't pushing you away… not exactly. It's hard to explain what was going on in my head. I guess I was disappointed in myself, and I didn't want you to see that." On a deep breath, I added, "I didn't want to disappoint you."

"You didn't disappoint me, Graham. Not at all."

Lori buried her nose in the flowers, then lowered the bouquet a little, and seeing those sweet lips parted slightly, I went in for a kiss. Sighing softly, she opened up for me. I wanted to kiss her until she'd climb in my lap, but we were in a park. I had to consider that.

"I'm sorry I overreacted. That wasn't okay. You deserved better than that. I promise do to better. And I'm sorry I pushed so much," she muttered when I let her go. "I shouldn't have. I was feeling a little insecure, and I was afraid you were slipping away from me. I love your crazy love, and your protectiveness."

Hearing those words from her was all I needed to feel whole.

"But I'm strong. I want you to know that. Even if I look shaken, that doesn't mean I can't handle things."

"I know you're strong. It's one of the things I love about you." I played with a strand of her hair, then pushed it behind her ear. It was time to bring up something else.

***

Lori

"Whatever happens, I want you to know there will never be a day when I don't want you and Milo." He said the words gently, cupping my face in his big hands. "I understand why you have that fear, but I need you to trust me, to trust us."

"I do."

"Obviously, I know it was wrong to write that scumbag a check."

“I don’t like that he got money out of you. I don’t like it at all. I know you meant well. But you understand what I mean about making decisions together, right?” I asked.

“I do. I promise that I do.”

"So we'll work together in the future? Not just on this, but also the problems with your dad and Nana.”

"We will," he assured me. "But know this: my instinct will always be to take care of the things that might upset you. Tell me how I can make it up to you."

"You don't have anything to make up for, but if you insist, I can think of a few things," I said coyly, running my forefinger from the button of his polo shirt to his sternum. He looked at me with those blue eyes I adored. They were full of love… and heat. The latter sent a sizzle so hot through me that I involuntarily shimmied my hips. Graham slyly raised one corner of his mouth.

Could this man not tempt me like this in broad daylight? I knew he wasn't doing it on purpose, though. It was just his irresistible sex appeal.

"Yeah, I can think of a few things too." He pressed his forehead against mine. "I love you, Lori. And I have great plans for us."

"Oh? Care to share them with me?"

He pulled back a notch. "I think I'll leave you guessing for now."

I laid both palms on his chest, debating how I could lure this out of him. Blackmail? Nah, too early in the day for that. Seduction? That could work. But we were in public, so my plan was a bust. Besides, I liked surprises. That didn't mean I didn't want hints, though.

"You really aren't going to tell me anything, are you?"

"No, I don't think I will. You're adorable when you're curious. And I'm good at making you fret."

"Don't be so full of yourself. I can resist your charm if I have to."

His eyes flashed. I liked to provoke him even more than he liked to make me fret.

"When you put it like that, sounds like I don't

have much going for me."

"I didn't say I was immune," I pointed out, and then I started counting on my fingers.

"You've got a lot going for you. See, you have these unique talents in the kitchen, and the bedroom. Plus, you charmed my son and my siblings. That's no small feat. And you—"

He feathered his lips on my neck, and I lost not only my ability to speak, but also my trail of thought. When he placed open-mouthed kisses on my sweet spot, I squirmed and fidgeted. Then I felt the tip of his tongue slide across my skin too. Oh, this vile man. He wasn't going to sweet-talk me into anything anymore. Once the tongue was involved, I knew he was going to seduce me.

"Graham," I half whispered, half moaned. I was already hot and bothered, and he was only teasing my neck.

"I'm taking you home, Lori. I'll share my plan for this afternoon," he whispered on a growl. "Starts with you under me. I'll love you until you cry out my name. That's a promise."

"I love your promises," I muttered. We had the entire day to ourselves, since Milo wasn't coming back until tomorrow.

"I intend to make good on every single one of them."

Graham kept his promise and seduced me thoroughly that lazy afternoon at my house.

He was kissing every inch of skin that wasn't

covered with clothes. His hands were busy methodically ridding me of said clothes. Every morsel of skin he revealed, he traced with his lips.

He kissed up my left inner thigh, then the right one. Then he buried his mouth in between, stroking me with his tongue until my legs nearly gave in. I was standing in front of the bed, and I was afraid I'd topple on it any second now. My clit was on fire. With every lash of Graham's tongue, the heat spread along my nerve endings. Pressure was building inside me. He kissed my tender flesh until he brought me so close to climaxing I almost saw stars. But then he pulled back, laying me on the bed.

"Not yet, sweetheart. I promise I will make you come hard, but not yet."

I kissed his chest as he climbed over me, rolling lower to trace the line of his abs with my tongue, feeling his erection across my chest. Graham pulled me back up until our mouths were level. He captured my lips, sliding in his tongue, kissing me ferociously. This man wasn't just kissing me. He was making love to my mouth. I became so turned on from his kissing I felt I would combust soon. I brought Graham's hand to my clit. He slid two fingers inside me, groaning against my mouth when he realized how slick I was.

Pressing the heel of his palm against my clit, he moved his hand rhythmically, driving me crazy. My body was at his mercy: his tongue explored my mouth, his fingers filled me, his palm worked my clit. I exploded all around him, bracing my palms on those muscle-laced arms. I felt him move slightly on the bed, then heard him slide on protection before he pushed inside me.

"Oh, oh, oh… Graham." My inner muscles were still clenched tight from the orgasm, and Graham slid in a few inches.

"You feel perfect." Another inch. "Perfect."

I rolled my hips then, taking in all of him, reveling in the exquisite pleasure. He loved me until we were both satiated and spent.

"Mmmm… every afternoon should be like this," I declared a while later, after we'd showered and returned to bed.

"I can make it happen." Graham bit my shoulder lightly. His hands were naughty again. He was propped against the headrest, and I was lying with half of my back against his chest. One of his hands was circling my nipples, turning the skin on my breasts to goose bumps. The other was drawing small circles on my lower belly, inching dangerously close to my clit.

"Your hands are wandering a lot today," I admonished.

"They are, aren't they? Entirely your doing."

"How do you figure?"

He kissed one shoulder then the other. "You're the one tempting me."

"Oh, I see. So you're not going to claim any responsibility?"

His lips spread in a grin. "None whatsoever."

I moved one of my hands between his thighs, squeezing his erection. He groaned.

"You were saying, Graham?"

"Lori." His voice held a hint of warning, but I ignored it, pumping along the length until I was satisfied that he was just as hot and bothered as I was. Then I stopped touching him and swatted his hands away, turning so I was half straddling him, laying my head on his chest.

We stayed like that for a long while, and eventually, I asked, "What's on your mind, Graham? I can feel your wheels spinning."

"My dad. Wondering what's the best way to deal with him. I was thinking about asking him to work at the club again instead of just giving him money. Maybe it'll teach him about responsibility."

"I think that's a great idea."

"You do?"

"Yes."

"But I don't trust him handling any money."

"How about PR? I saw a few old interviews with him. He seemed good in front of the camera."

He kissed the top of my head. "That's definitely a good plan. Amber could keep a close eye on him. She'd love it. Thanks for the idea."

"Anytime. Thank you for talking about it with me." I wanted to give this man everything he needed: my love and support, my strength. I cuddled closer to him, then moved on top, propping my chin on his chest, looking up at him. Graham feathered his fingers up and down the sides of my torso, paying extra attention to my breasts. I squirmed against him. He groaned.

"You have more ideas, huh?" His voice was rougher now.

I licked my lower lip. "Plenty."

He cupped my ass with both hands, squeezing a little. "Why don't you show them to me right now?"

"I'm trying to decide which one to pick first."

***

A few days later, after Milo fell asleep in the evening, Graham brought up Jeff.

"My accountant said that he hasn't cashed that check."

"Wow. Why do you think?"

"Talked to one of the club's lawyers. He said Jeff's likely waiting for the malpractice suit to be over to cash it; otherwise, he could lose that money too. I want my lawyer to draw up a document for that scumbag to sign that he'll never bother you and Milo again, and if it's okay with you, I'd ask him to give up parental rights too. I'd like Milo to see me as his dad one day."

I swear my heart grew in size. "I'd love that, Graham. I'd love it."

Jeff didn't give in easily. His first reaction when we approached him with the document was to ask for more money. Then Graham and I brought out the big guns, setting up a meeting with Jeff and a sharp lawyer.

I made it clear to Jeff that not only would I drag him through courts for the accrued child support, but that we'd accuse him of extortion too. When the lawyer and Will—who'd insisted on attending the meeting and flashed his badge at every turn—explained to him that cashing Graham's check could constitute proof of extortion, which is punishable by two to four years in prison in California, not only did he agree to sign our papers, he also returned the check and gave up his parental rights.

"See, brother?" I teased as Will, Graham, and I stepped out of the attorney's office. "The badge does work on someone."

Will winked. "Works on everyone I'm not related to."

Graham kissed the side of my head, pulling me into a half hug. "Let's go pick up our boy from school."

Chapter Thirty-One
Graham

Two months later, I asked Lori to let me pick Milo up from a play date. My official story was that I was taking him to try out some new soccer equipment because he was outgrowing the one he already owned. We were going to shop for new equipment, but that wasn't all I had planned for today.

While I waited for Milo, I scrolled through my e-mails. There was one from the lawyer who'd handled our issues with Jeff. I'd asked him to keep us informed on the outcome of the malpractice suit. The final decision had been reached last week. Jeff lost every penny he had to his name, and the right to practice. He had it coming.

As for my father, I was trying out the new arrangement Lori and I came up with.

I'd told him that the monthly payments would stop. From now on, he'd pay his debts and earn a living as an employee of the LA Lords. He'd seemed pleasantly surprised that I'd allow him to be involved with the club again. My hope was that the job would make him grow up, especially because he'd be working under Amber's strict supervision in PR and didn't have any direct access to the club's funds. Our interactions were as awkward as ever, but Lori insisted that would change with time. Maybe it would work out. I wasn't holding my breath, but it felt right to make that change.

"Are we really going to the store?" Milo asked the second he climbed into the car.

"Yes, we are, buddy."

"Can we go to the toy store too?"

Since I was liable to be talked into buying the entire store if I said yes, I shook my head. "We promised your mom we'll all go together next time, remember?"

He jutted out his lower lip, but didn't press the issue. I loved the little rug rat. I couldn't wait for him to have brothers and sisters, but all in due time.

We arrived at the club's store about thirty minutes later. It was almost closing time, but I'd already arranged for Christie, the vendor on shift, to keep the store open longer for us. Milo was ecstatic as he tried on jerseys and shoes. He didn't need a new ball, but I bought him one anyway, because he'd been eying it since we stepped inside the store.

"What do you say to pizza for dinner?" I asked once we strolled out.

"I love pizza. Is Mom coming too?"

"No, just the two of us. I need to talk to you about something."

He eyed me cautiously. "Am I in trouble?"

"No, not at all." I ruffled his hair, but he didn't seem to relax.

"Okay. I love pizza."

"Me too, buddy."

I led him to an Italian restaurant one block away from the club. It was one of my favorites. They used wood for their pizza oven, and the smoky smell was thick in the air. They made the crust thin and crispy. The wall paneling imitated natural stone, which made for a relaxing ambience.

Since it was relatively early for dinner, there were few patrons. I was a regular here, so the owner, Enzo, came to greet us. He was thin with olive skin and black hair on which he'd painted green strands.

"Graham, finally getting to bring your little one here too." He patted Milo's shoulder. I liked the sound of that. *Your little one.*

"Yeah. I'll bring Lori around soon too. I promise." I turned to Milo. "What do you want to eat?"

Milo tore his gaze away from Enzo's hair. "Can I have lots of pepperoni on my pizza? And onions?"

"One pizza with pepperoni and onions for him, and one with cheese for me," I said to Enzo.

After he left, Milo looked at me expectantly. He was still nervous about what I had to say. I'd planned to wait until dessert to lay it all out for him, but I decided to switch things up.

"Here's what I wanted to talk to you about, buddy. Your mom and I have been together for a while now, and I love her very much. I love both of you, in fact."

He swallowed hard and fidgeted in his seat, but he didn't say anything.

"I want to marry your mother, and I wanted to first talk to you, man-to-man, ask if you're okay with it."

Milo cast his eyes downward to the tablecloth, fiddling with the fork between his hands. Something was clearly eating at him, but I couldn't figure out why. I could only wait for him to open up.

Eventually, he looked up, and asked, "So you will always be with mom and me?"

"Yes I will."

"You won't leave?"

Punch straight to the gut. He'd become tiny while he'd asked the question, hunching his small shoulders. I chose my next words carefully.

"No, Milo. I won't leave. I promise. I love you both, and I'd like to be part of your family."

He played with the fork in his hand some more. I could tell he had other questions, and I waited patiently.

"If you marry mom, will you be my dad?"

"Yes, I will be."

"So I can call you dad?"

My smile seemed to encourage Milo to smile too. "Of course. I'd love that."

"That's so cool. I never had anyone to call dad before."

Something twisted in my chest. I wanted to hug this kid.

"So you'll do dad things with me?" Milo

continued. "Come to parents' day? Buy presents for Mom on Mother's Day?"

"Yes."

"Can I tell everyone at school I have a dad now?" he continued, almost as if he couldn't believe it.

My chest twisted some more. "Absolutely. So, what do you say? Do you give me your permission to ask your mom to marry me?"

"Yes! You have my permission."

Epilogue
Lori
One Month Later

"Wake up, sleepyhead," a soft voice murmured. I yawned, but instead of opening my eyes, I scooted closer to the source and was met with Graham's *clothed* chest. What the heck? Per my request, my man was sleeping only in boxers, so I could feel him up every chance I got. But now he was wearing a shirt and, by the feel of it, jeans too, which meant he'd been up for a while. I blinked open one eye, then the other. Through the glass wall of his bedroom, I noticed the sun was high up in the sky.

"What time is it?"

"Ten."

"I love lazy Saturdays. But you had a meeting this morning. How come you're home?"

The word still felt a little foreign on my tongue, even though Milo and I had moved in here a week ago. Graham had asked us to move in a while ago, but we had to wait until Milo's school year was over. I liked my house, but... I loved the villa more. There was more space, and the view of the ocean was simply amazing.

"Moved it to Monday so we could enjoy the

morning together."

I detected an edge in his voice.

"Nervous about tonight?" I teased.

"Not at all."

We'd invited my family for a barbecue on the beach. They were set to arrive at six o'clock. Milo had a sleepover last night, and Will was picking him up on the way here.

That meant we had the entire morning just for us. Graham's gorgeous eyes twinkled. He was planning something; I could tell. But what?

He braced his forearms by my sides, caging me in. He kissed my neck, then kissed even lower, swiping his tongue over one nipple—because we'd negotiated a tit-for-tat arrangement when it came to pajamas; he'd sleep without a shirt only if I did too. At the moment, I was at a clear disadvantage. I was squirming by the time he moved to the other.

"What a way to wake up," I whispered on a moan. Graham moved farther down, skimming his hands over my waist and hips.

His mouth was marking a red-hot trail everywhere he kissed: my breasts, my stomach, my belly. When he nudged my thighs apart, I readily opened for him. He swiped his tongue once over my entrance, taking my clit between his lips. A bolt of heat zinged me. My hips swung upward of their own accord. A small tremor coursed through me, spreading from my center right to my toes.

"I want you," I muttered, lifting myself up on one elbow and reaching for his shoulder, tugging at his shirt. I pulled at the fabric until he relented and moved up until his mouth was level with mine. I took off his shirt as fast as possible, then the rest of his clothes. He trapped me under him, rubbing his erection against my inner thigh, teasing me. I rolled my hips invitingly, and he entered me the next second. He loved me slowly, slipping a hand between us, strumming his fingers over my clit until I exploded, taking him over the edge with me.

"I don't think my body can handle so much sexiness first thing in the morning," I whispered, curling in his arms.

"Practice makes perfect."

"I could definitely get used to it… with more practice. And since today is a lazy day…"

Graham pulled back a little, kissing my knuckles, motioning with his head to the door. "We still have some of your boxes to unpack. Thought we'd make some headway this morning."

I hid under the covers. "I think I'll go back to sleep now."

"Come on, lazy girl. You heard what Nana said."

"If you have to swallow a frog, do it first thing in the morning."

We'd visited Nana last month, and I adored that woman. She also gave great advice, so I should lift my lazy ass from the bed. But I wanted to try one more time.

"I have better ideas." I peeked from under the covers.

"Unpacking first."

I wasn't going to win this battle, that much I could tell. Perhaps it was a good thing, because if I had it my way, those boxes would remain unopened until Christmas.

"Okay, okay."

Twenty minutes later, I joined Graham in the living room. While sipping my morning coffee, I surveyed the small mountain of boxes tucked in one corner.

"I could swear it was smaller yesterday," I muttered when I finally dragged myself closer. On top were four identical small boxes that looked unfamiliar, but that wasn't saying much. I'd been in a frenzy while packing. I started with the first small box. It was empty except for a card with one word. "*Will.*"

I frowned, trying to remember if these were supposed to be samples of wedding keepsakes. Boxes with printed poems on a card were not uncommon. Both the box and the card were definitely elegant enough for it—rectangular, with a glittery texture.

I opened the next one, hoping it would shed some light on the mystery. Another card, another word. *You.*

My heart started beating a little faster. There were two other boxes. Out of the corner of my eye, I tried to locate Graham in the room, but he wasn't in my line of vision, so I surmised he was somewhere behind me. My fingers were shaky when I opened the third box.

Marry.

I covered my mouth with one hand, blinking at the word. Then I opened the fourth box, and arranged all the cards next to each other. *Will You Marry Me?*

I felt Graham come up behind me. He brought his mouth to my ear, and whispered, "Marry me, Lori Connor. You're the sweetest and strongest woman, and you have my heart. Nothing would make me happier than knowing you want to be my wife, that you'll trust me to make you happy for the rest of our lives. Will you be my wife? Will you and Milo be my family officially?"

"Yes, yes! Yes! I want to marry you."

He put an arm around my waist, flattening my back against his chest. Looking down, I noticed a ring in his open palm. A beautiful, princess-cut diamond set in a platinum band. Even without a ring box with the Bennett Enterprises logo on it, I knew this was one of Pippa's creations.

"This is my vow to you, and to Milo. I'll always put you first, and love you."

"Oh, Graham. I love you so much."

My hand was shaking when he slid the ring on my finger. My chest was so full of emotion that I didn't know what to do with myself. Turning me around, he pressed his mouth to mine. We kissed as if we hadn't kissed in weeks. It felt like our first kiss all over again.

I hadn't been expecting this. After all, he'd been wary of marriage when I met him. I'd accepted it because I knew it didn't mean he loved me less. Yes, strange line of thinking for a wedding planner, and especially for me, but I was happy living with him and loving him. I didn't need a ring on my finger. Of course, that didn't make me any less ecstatic for actually receiving a ring. When I felt him hoisting me up in his arms, I wrapped my legs around him on instinct.

"Where are you taking me?" I asked, holding on tight.

"Upstairs to celebrate. We can unpack later."

***

My family started arriving at about five thirty. I was waiting for everyone to be here before I showed them the ring. Val and Hailey were the first ones. Val had brought her signature homemade barbecue sauce, and also some perfume samples for us to test and give our opinion. Landon, Maddie and their newborn daughter Willow arrived next.

“She's lovely, isn't it?” Maddie said as I cuddled Willow.

“Oh, yeah.”

“Can't believe she's finally here. Though my belly still looks as if Willow's in there.”

"You are beautiful." Landon kissed her cheek, and Maddie affectionately rumpled his hair. I loved seeing my brother so happy. Every time I saw them, they seemed even more in love.

I dashed to the door to greet Will, Jace, and

Milo, who'd just arrived.

"Hey, big boy! How was the sleepover?" I asked.

"He barely wanted to come with me," Will supplied.

"We watched all the Harry Potter movies." He wrapped his little arms around my waist in a hug. "We didn't sleep."

"At all?" I shook my head in mock disapproval. "I'll have a word with Lionel's mom and dad at soccer day next week." We had soccer days even in the summer vacation.

"They want to meet Graham. I told them he's coming with us. He is, right?"

"Yes, he is," I confirmed.

Milo grinned, letting go of me as Val called his name, and dashed toward her.

"So, my presence at soccer day is no longer required," Will said.

Jace pointed his thumb at Will. "If you ask me, he's sad about it."

I knew Jace was teasing him, but in truth, Will *did* look a little dejected. I slapped his arm playfully.

"Hey, you're always welcome to come. Or, you could always find yourself a girl and get the ball rolling."

Will smiled devilishly.

"Hey, how about moving this party to the beach?" Hailey called out. "Let's get the grill started. I'm starving."

After grabbing plates and supplies, we all

descended to the beach. The sun cast a warm glow, but the breeze was almost chilly. This was officially my favorite place in town: hearing the waves lap against the shore, feeling the soft sand under my feet.

While part of the group was in charge of the grill, others were setting the table. Graham and I were on bonfire duty. We wanted one for effect and roasting marshmallows.

Once everyone was taking a break, waiting for our dinner to be ready, I cleared my throat and held my hand out for everyone to admire my ring. I'd kept my hand in my pocket and out of view until now so they wouldn't notice the ring accidentally.

"We got engaged this morning." Graham kissed my temple as everyone came forward to congratulate us. Milo was the first one, followed by my brothers and Maddie. Val and Hailey hugged me at the same time. But as the girls pulled back, I studied their expressions carefully. They didn't seem surprised. I realized neither seemed the others.

"You already knew, didn't you?" I asked.

"He asked my permission," Milo piped up.

"And he talked to all of us at Friday night dinner about a month ago when you were out of the room," Landon added.

"We helped with the ring," Hailey said on a grin. "That was fun."

Will and Jace each gave me bear hugs, and I briefly wondered when these two would settle down. Our soccer star wasn't quite ready for that. Our hotshot detective on the other hand… I'd seen the mopey look on his face at Landon's wedding, like he was secretly hoping his turn would come soon. When Will's turn came, he was going to fall hard.

I sized my man up and down, and then I pulled him away from the group.

"You planned this thoroughly," I whispered.

"I did."

"You've been full of surprises lately."

"I have a lot more up my sleeve."

Lacing my arms around his neck, I pulled him a little closer, smiling against his lips. "Then it's a good thing I agreed to spend a lifetime with you."

Other Books by Layla Hagen

The Bennett Family Series

Book 1: Your Irresistible Love (Sebastian & Ava)

Sebastian Bennett is a determined man. It's the secret behind the business empire he built from scratch. Under his rule, Bennett Enterprises dominates the jewelry industry. Despite being ruthless in his work, family comes first for him, and he'd do anything for his parents and eight siblings—even if they drive him crazy sometimes. . . like when they keep nagging him to get married already.

Sebastian doesn't believe in love, until he brings in external marketing consultant Ava to oversee the next collection launch. She's beautiful, funny, and just as stubborn as he is. Not only is he obsessed with her delicious curves, but he also finds himself willing to do anything to make her smile. He's determined to have Ava, even if she's completely off limits.

Ava Lindt has one job to do at Bennett Enterprises: make the next collection launch unforgettable. Daydreaming about the hot CEO is definitely not on her to-do list. Neither is doing said

CEO. The consultancy she works for has a strict policy—no fraternizing with clients. She won't risk her job. Besides, Ava knows better than to trust men with her heart.

But their sizzling chemistry spirals into a deep connection that takes both of them by surprise. Sebastian blows through her defenses one sweet kiss and sinful touch at a time. When Ava's time as a consultant in his company comes to an end, will Sebastian fight for the woman he loves or will he end up losing her?

AVAILABLE ON ALL RETAILERS.

Book 2: Your Captivating Love (Logan & Nadine)
Book 3: Your Forever Love (Pippa & Eric)
Book 4: Your Inescapable Love (Max & Emilia)
Book 5: Your Tempting Love (Christopher & Victoria)
Book 6: Your Alluring Love (Alice & Nate)
Book 7: Your Fierce Love (Blake & Clara)
Book 8: Your One True Love (Daniel & Caroline)
Book 9: Your Endless Love (Summer & Alex)

The Lost Series

Lost in Us (James & Serena)
Found in U (Jessica & Parker)
Caught in Us (Dani & Damon)

***

Standalone USA TODAY BESTSELLER
Withering Hope

Aimee's wedding is supposed to turn out perfect. Her dress, her fiancé and the location—the idyllic holiday ranch in Brazil—are perfect.

But all Aimee's plans come crashing down when the private jet that's taking her from the U.S. to the ranch—where her fiancé awaits her—defects mid-flight and the pilot is forced to perform an emergency landing in the heart of the Amazon rainforest.

With no way to reach civilization, being rescued is Aimee and Tristan's—the pilot—only hope. A slim one that slowly withers away, desperation taking its place. Because death wanders in the jungle under many forms: starvation, diseases. Beasts.

As Aimee and Tristan fight to find ways to survive, they grow closer. Together they discover that facing old, inner agonies carved by painful pasts takes just as much courage, if not even more, than facing the rainforest.

Despite her devotion to her fiancé, Aimee can't hide her feelings for Tristan—the man for whom she's slowly becoming everything. You can hide many things in the rainforest. But not lies. Or love.

Withering Hope is the story of a man who desperately needs forgiveness and the woman who brings him hope. It is a story in which hope births wings and blooms into a love that is as beautiful and intense as it is forbidden.

AVAILABLE ON ALL RETAILERS.

***

Anything For You

Published by Layla Hagen

Published: Layla Hagen 2018
Cover: Uplifting Designs

***

Acknowledgements

Publishing a book takes a village! A big THANK YOU to everyone accompanying me on this journey. To my family, thank you for supporting me, believing in me, and being there for me every single day. I could not have done this without you.

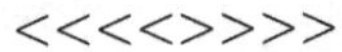

CPSIA information can be obtained
at www.ICGtesting.com
Printed in the USA
BVHW04s1616170718
521851BV00001B/1/P